PRODIGIUM

Twelve Tomes, Book One

By

CHRISTOPHER S.G.

Fort Worth
Roguely Publishing
2025

Contents

For Adaria, keeper of my heart

The World of Lidaesea

"For we are the ones who shall be written in the tomes of the gods and carved into the mountainous annals of our world."

-*Echrenam Frie, second Tomekeeper of Zhonitas.*

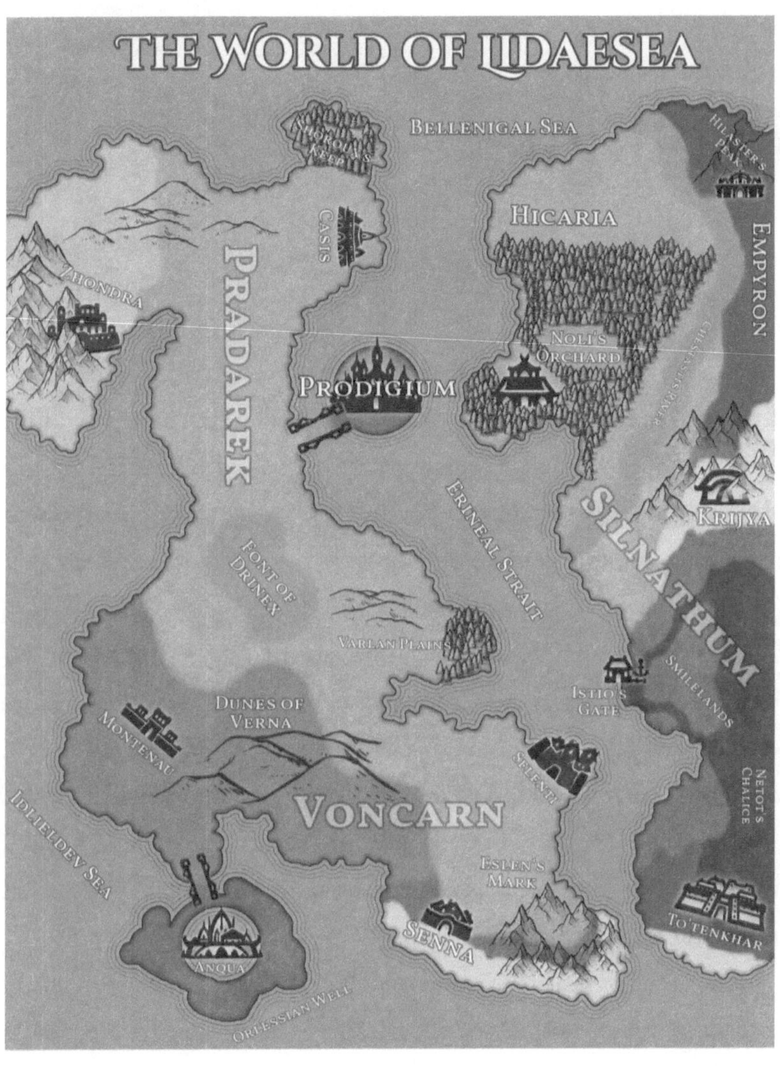

THE WORLD OF LIIDAESEA
BELLENIGAL SEA
HICARIA
HILASTER'S PEAK
EMPYRON
MOROIN'S KEEP
CASIS
PRADAREK
ZHONDRA
NOLI'S ORCHARD
PRODIGIUM
SILNATHUM
KRIJYA
FONT OF DRINEX
ERINEAL STRAIT
VARLAN PLAINS
SMILELANDS
ISTIO'S GATE
DUNES OF VERNA
NETOI'S CHALICE
MONTENAU
SELENTI
VONCARN
IDLIELDEV SEA
ESTEN'S MARK
TO'TENKHAR
ANQUA
SENNA
ORLESSIAN WELL

Prologue

At the turn of the seventh century, the gods of creation assembled within the celestial walls of Prodigium for the last time. Held aloft by their combined magic, Prodigium had long served as a neutral ground where the gods could plan and execute their greatest work. As the bells rang sweetly and the sky parted to the stars, the world of Lidaesea was at peace.

It was the calm before the cataclysmic storm.

Ghantei, goddess of light, sat upon her throne in the great hall. A celestial glow filled the room. Six chairs of gold, silver, and red resided on each side of the rectangular table placed in the middle of the space. Ghantei ruffled the pair of pure white wings that rested behind her and swept her silver hair to one side. She gazed at the eleven other gods seated at the table with piercing yellow eyes.

None of the gods dared to eat the bountiful feast laid out before them. Instead, they glared silently at one another. The tension amongst them was palpable.

One of them was a traitor.

Ghantei needed to know who.

"I will give whoever is guilty one last chance to confess," Ghantei said, her voice calm and sweet despite the events of the night. "Killing a god is an atrocious offense, and judgment must be made."

"The only god truly worthy to judge is Eslen," shouted Wogiwoj, god of the storm. His bushy red beard bounced on his belly as he spoke. "But what if he's the traitor?"

Eslen, god of judgment, stood up at the other end of the table. His face warped with anger and frustration. He pointed a finger at the rest of his peers and pushed his shaggy black hair from in front of his eyes.

"I demand you speak now!" he cried. "Speak, murderer, so I may cut you down in the name of justice. I will not let my name continue to be tarnished!"

There was silence once more. The baseless accusations and flared tempers had gotten them nowhere. Ghantei needed to devise a fresh approach. As she moved deeper into her thoughts, a silver ball rolled out from under the table. It was no bigger than her palm, and the scratching of its smooth surface against the marbled floors drew everyone's attention.

Ghantei shuddered.

A blast of pressurized magical heat swirled into purple flames that erupted across every exposed surface of the hall. Ghantei felt the flames run across her body before her mind could process the pain that they caused. She was flung backwards into the wall, her fellow gods and goddess scattered across the room, and was met with a wave of black.

Prodigium fell from the sky, its magical aura disrupted by the amethyst fires that consumed its body. Chunks of wood, stone, and iron rained from above as it crumbled into pieces and crashed into the earth. The resulting shockwaves of dirt and wind blew across the surrounding area.

Ghantei woke among the cinders and ashes of her once majestic home. Her pearlescent throne laid shattered at her feet, and smoke created a thick haze across her vision. Her wings were broken in multiple places. Magical symbols from the enchanted fire were burned deep into her skin.

"Haelfire," Ghantei thought aloud. It was the only thing that could damage their corporeal forms. The traitor had tried to kill the rest of them in one move. The goddess of light fought back tears. "How could you?"

Ghantei felt the light leave her body, replaced by a horrid chill. The sensation started in her legs, then crept up through her chest. Her breathing rattled as the small white particles of her magic blew away. Suffocating fear gripped her as she faced mortality for the first time. There was only one thing she could do.

The goddess of light forced herself onto her stomach and crawled through the smoldering wreckage. She called out to the others to no response. Her arm quivered, and every pull took more out of her. She needed to hurry.

"*Ghasfuoyarek*," Ghantei choked out before she collapsed on the marble flooring.

The last of Ghantei's light pooled into her core and left an empty feeling in its wake. The light melded into an orb that rose through her throat and out of her mouth. She observed what remained of her life essence as it floated above her body and rendered her a hollow shell.

Eleven more uniquely colored orbs joined hers as they lifted into the air. They blended with one another to form a spinning wheel of magical energy that crackled and popped, each rotation more rapid and violent than the last.

The visage of a tome materialized. Then three. Then twelve.

The wheel dissipated into snaps and bolts of leftover magic, and the tomes dropped onto the ground. Each bore the color and symbol of its respective god. Their leather covers were pristine, and all were filled with golden-edged pages the color of buttermilk.

Ghantei rolled onto her back and developed a tired smile. The tomes allowed the gods and goddesses to find new lives with their nations and the citizens within. In a sense, they could survive. There was still much to be done, and so much to create.

A wave of exhaustion washed across every inch of her. She had done what she could. Ghantei let out her final breath. Once bright eyes turned gray and her body dissolved into golden dust scattered by the winds.

Thus began the centennial cycle.

Commencement

A loud knock at the iron door pulled Yonni Sxem from her slumber. She stretched her arms high above her head and rotated her shoulders with a small pop. The seaweed gown that clung to her warm sepia skin stretched with her diaphragm. Long turquoise locks flowed in the water that encompassed her. She ran her hands through her hair to smooth it out, then turned to face the clamshell mirror across from her bed. Sparkling emerald eyes reflected back at her. The mirror itself was adorned with a handful of the kingdom's most exquisite pearls and glass made from the sands of the Silent Grotto. While it remained one of the best gifts her mother had ever given her, she missed the period it represented.

The knock repeated, each hit louder. Yonni swished her fin, dark blue with vibrant pink edges, and swam to the door. She could hear the shuffle of the queen's chosen in the hall, their tridents and javelins scraping the floor.

"Princess Yonni," a deep voice called from the other side of the door. "We're here to escort you to the main procession."

Yonni slid the door open and was greeted by the scarred, tan visage of General Gandreke. A trimmed white mustache covered the bottom portion of the mark that ran diagonally across his weathered face. Despite his crossed arms, he showed no signs of anger. In fact, Gandreke always treated the royal family with the utmost respect. As if in response to her thoughts, he bowed.

"Your Highness, I see you've just awoken," Gandreke noted. His steel blue eyes examined her while the rest of the chosen floated at attention behind him. "We can wait for you to prepare, but please, try to be swift. You don't want to miss your brother's homecoming."

"I'll be just a moment, general," Yonni replied and pressed the door closed. She swam to her wardrobe and pulled out the vibrant coral top that her mother had selected for her. Laid at the front of the mirror were two matching ribbons she laced around her arms. As she changed, she felt a tinge of excitement build within her. She wondered what it would be like to see Enerill again.

Yonni threw the door back open and gave Gandreke a silent nod. He swiveled around to the chosen, raised his golden trident in the air, and ran his gaze across each of them.

"We transport treasure today!"

"By the grace of Monalei!" they responded in unison.

Yonni moved closer to Gandreke as the group made their way through the castle's coral covered interior. The prince's arrival had everyone in the kingdom bustling, especially the royal staff. She overheard chatter from the cooks and the sea striders as they made their way past them toward the great hall. The smell of baked goods tickled her nose.

The kingdom of Anqua had been hidden deep within the Orlessian Well on the outskirts of Lidaesea since its establishment centuries prior. It was place that was often untouched by the land of elves, humans, and the angelic Wingsong that lived above the waters. The politics were straightforward. King Zariel, and Yonni by relation, had come from a long lineage of rule. There had never been any wars, any coups, or any other attempts at taking control. Even when the king passed, rule simply passed over to his beloved. That, in part, was what made Enerill's arrival so energetic. There had never been the return of a future king before.

"Are you excited, princess?" Gandreke asked, his eyes locked forward.

Yonni smiled at the general's attempt at casual conversation. His usual dour expression had melted away. They approached the pearlescent doors of the great hall and stopped outside.

"I just hope my brother remembers who I am amongst this newfound attention he'll be receiving," Yonni joked. "It makes me wonder how much of a fanfare I'll get when I return from my marriage arrangements."

"I'm sure your mother will do everything in her power to make you feel just as special," Gandreke replied. Ornate navy medals decorated the left side of his silver chest plate. He pressed his hand against them. "Just a bit of unsolicited advice from an old soldier, though. Don't be like Pema or Covalie. They married for money and fame. Always be true to your heart, arrangement or not."

Yonni placed her hand on his pauldron in acknowledgement. He ruffled her hair a bit in return. She tried to maintain a royal air, but the smile that fought to adorn her face made it difficult. His favoritism of her among her siblings had been apparent, despite his best attempts to hide it.

The doors to the great hall swung open and Gandreke ushered her inside. Yonni glanced toward the top of the staircase, far past the gathered tables and endless amounts of puffer fish balloons and algae candles. Her mother sat atop a throne of gold and jade, wrapped in a white top made from the finest seaworm silk. Her skin, the same tone as Yonni's, had shimmering green scales that rippled from her shoulders to her forearms. Her fin matched. Bright blue braids ran the length of her back. Queen Monalei was graceful, yet imposing, an embodiment of great leadership at the helm of the kingdom. She was everything Yonni herself strived to be.

"Good morning, princess," the queen said in a warm and welcoming tone. "Nice of you to join the festivities. We'll be traveling to the Raftworks as soon as the carriage is ready."

"Good morning, Your Majesty. I anxiously await our departure," Yonni bowed and swished her tail. Thoughts of the bustling center of shops, taverns, and artistry excited her. She could only imagine what it looked like for the celebration. The day was off to an incredible start.

Four sea striders pulled the carriage through Khalani's Current with ease, navigating every wild twist and turn it threw at them. Yonni watched from the carriage window as the wallu, enormous creatures that resembled a cross between dolphin and seahorse, made a low grumble and tugged against the reins.

Yonni thought about her two personal wallu, Cyntri and Evesa, and how much she yearned to return to them. The thrill of wallu racing was like no other, especially within the currents. She recalled her younger days of watching from the carriage as it trailed alongside the races. It was the best view of Anqua's most prestigious sport. It was also a great opportunity for the queen to select more riders for her personal fold.

Yonni listened to the rumble of the aquaways. The sound of the roaring waterfalls and rapids always enveloped her and brought her to a calmer state of mind. The song of the Idlieldev Sea, as she called it. She caught her mother staring at her.

"You're tense," Monalei noted. "Is there something wrong?"

"What if Enerill is... different?" Yonni answered after a moment of thought.

"I'm not sure I understand what you mean?"

"We used to be best friends before he left," Yonni clarified. "I was his second-in-command and followed him everywhere. He used to scare off my suitors to make sure that I was learning the proper ways of princess life."

Queen Monalei chuckled, her smile as bright as the finest pearls. "That he did. Often, if I recall."

"It's just... What if he doesn't want me around anymore?" Yonni mumbled as she looked toward her fin. "What if he thinks I'll embarrass him in front of his new military friends?"

The carriage slowed to a stop. The bang of Gandreke's fist against the carriage's roof interrupted the conversation. Yonni's nerves built steadily.

"Your majesty, we've arrived," Gandreke's voice stated from outside.

Queen Monalei reached over and gently tilted Yonni's head back up. Her dazzling emerald eyes met Yonni's own.

"You're my youngest, but you are by far my most mature," the queen said. "I never had to push you like your sisters or send you away entirely like your brother. You have always had a strong heart and stronger spirit, just like your father. Remember that.

"Let no one—family, or friend, or stranger—convince you that you are not enough. Your brother may very well follow in the king's footsteps, but you have yet to forge your own path. Now come, let us greet the masses."

Yonni said nothing in response, but placed both hands around her mother's instead. The queen's words settled in her mind as she reflected on them. She wanted to embark on a path that would bring pride to her family name.

General Gandreke opened the door to the carriage and extended a hand to Queen Monalei, then to Yonni. As the latter made her way out of the vessel, the crowd around them erupted into a loud cheer.

Merfolk filled every inch of the Raftworks, extending as far as Yonni could see. Magnificent colorful banners streaked across the rooftops and candles of green, yellow, and blue blazed wildly in the windows of the Raftwork's many establishments. The crowds pushed and swayed as everyone tried to garner a glimpse of the royals.

The queen waved to the masses in return. Shyness overcame Yonni, and she clung to her mother. Her hand lifted in an attempt at a light wave to a few of the closest individuals.

Horns bellowed from above and drowned out the noise of the crowd. Yonni jerked her head up in surprise and saw the cluster of brineback whales descend upon them. Forked tails paddled their massive cerulean bodies. Atop each were several scalite soldiers and a hefty, kelp-colored boat. Flakes of salt from the whales' crusted backs, a delicacy amongst the the Anquan people, drifted into the Raftworks like snow. The crowd grew even more wild.

Yonni watched as the brinebacks swam toward the edge of the Raftworks and came to a halt near their carriage. The scalites disembarked and slid the transport doors open. Dozens of academy graduates within exited to thunderous applause. They waved and cheered as the light of the surface world reflected off of their polished armors. The horns bellowed once more in a song of triumph.

Prince Enerill, last out of the transport, received the biggest reaction of all. His indigo hair was tied into a tight bun and the right side of his chest plate was embedded with dozens of ribbons, which Yonni knew were no doubt won through four years of military exercises. A long saber accompanied the left side of his cerulean fin, secured by a stylish bronze holster. It was easy to see he was not the same Enerill that left for the academy. Yonni observed a sense of accomplishment and pride emanate behind his peaceful demeanor.

Enerill made his way to his mother and sister, who both hugged him deeply. Happiness welled inside of Yonni as he squeezed them closer in return. Enerill let out a laugh.

"I'm glad to know I was missed," he said. His voice had noticeably deepened, but his energy remained unchanged. The tawny beige of his skin stood out next to his mother and sister.

"We're happy to have the heir to the throne return safely, my son," Queen Monalei responded. She swiveled to the crowd and raised his arm in triumph. More cheers and whistles reverberated through the water.

Yonni watched her brother and mother laugh and address the crowd with joy. Gandreke stood at attention nearby and kept a watchful eye on the scene. He sensed Yonni's gaze and turned his head to acknowledge her, but surprise spread swiftly across his face. Yonni blinked and felt her stomach drop. A deep burning pain shot through her head and a pressure swelled behind her eyes. They stung as she wiped them with the back of her palm. The surrounding water boiled.

Gandreke launched towards her, and the action caught Enerill's attention.

"Sis, are you okay?" Enerill asked in concern as he rushed in.

Yonni felt sharp stabs through various parts of her body and her breathing became more shallow. The world around her blurred and her vision doubled. A suffocating sensation built up inside of her, as if a giant puffer fish had inflated in her chest. She screamed in pain, but the voice she heard wasn't her own. The scream was low and metallic.

Gandreke put his hands on Yonni's shoulder and said something, but the sudden ringing in her ears drowned the words out. The ringing intensified until she couldn't bear it anymore. She reached up and covered her ears to no avail. The pitch grew higher, then suddenly, there was silence.

Yonni Sxem, princess of the Anquali, the metallic voice that had replaced hers boomed within her mind. ***You have been chosen as my champion. Take the power that I offer and use it to the fullest extent. Gather your tome and complete your task.***

The sound rushed back into Yonni's ears. She glanced around at the mass of queen's chosen and scalites that encircled her. The crowd had grown silent. Gandreke shook her and called her name while Enerill held their mother back. She felt the pressure in her head dissipate, replaced by a burning sensation on her skin.

"Princess Yonni, are you alright?" General Gandreke shouted. "Please respo-"

A sudden burst of frosted magical energy exploded from Yonni's body and knocked the entire group back. It shot across the crowd and froze the salt flakes mid-drift. Ice coated the edges of the banners. Instant relief washed over her, as if a massive weight had been lifted from her body, before she blacked out.

Yonni gradually regained consciousness and her vision pulled together bit by bit. Low candlelight enveloped her, and she barely could make out the purple walls of a cave. She took a shuddering breath. Frost magic held in her throat.

"Thank Drinex, she's alive," a worried voice expressed from the other side of the room. Yonni turned her head and saw the faint outline of her mother. "Sweetheart, please speak to us if you can."

Yonni let out a low groan and flipped onto her side. Her fin felt numb. As she took in her surroundings, she realized it wasn't just her mother. Enerill and Gandreke floated behind her.

"Where am I?" Yonni forced out.

Monalei moved forward and clasped her daughter's hand. She squeezed it hard, like she would never let it go again. The queen took a breath.

"We thought we lost you," Monalei whispered. Her voice cracked. "You scared us, Yonni."

Yonni remained confused at her situation. Her mother's noticeable discomfort only made her worry increase. She repeated her question.

"We've brought you to the Silent Grotto. It's the only place you can be safe," the queen answered.

Yonni studied the cave and thought back to her mirror. She had known of the grotto for years, but could never visit. It was a very sacred place, reserved only for the kings and queens of Anqua.

"Why are we here?" Yonni pieced together. She struggled to produce the words. Her mother exchanged glances with Enerill and Gandreke.

Gandreke scratched the back of his head. He looked hesitant.

"We brought you here to heal, Princess. Away from prying eyes," he said.

"Heal from what?" Yonni pressed. The lack of answers frustrated her. "You three know something that you're not sharing. What is it?"

"At the procession, you... changed," Queen Monalei explained. "Your eyes glowed, and you thrashed about. We thought there was an attack at first, but then you released an immense cloud of frost magic. Gandreke and I know magic of that nature can only mean one thing."

Monalei took another deep breath. "Yonni, my dear. Drinex has chosen you." Her hand squeezed tighter. "Do you remember the stories I used to tell you, all those years ago? Once every century, the gods select one of us from every nation to do their bidding.

"We've had skilled warriors, powerful politicians, and the best riders in the sea chosen in the past. I thought your brother was going to be the one he chose this time, but it was you, my sweet. You are the Tomekeeper of Anqua. You are the Spear of Drinex."

Yonni's breath stopped for a moment. According to her mother, the Tomekeepers of Lidaesea had long been some of the world's most respected leaders. Stories of their exploits had been passed down since the first cycle. Being selected as a Tomekeeper should have been praised as the highest of accomplishments, yet the atmosphere was off. Fear radiated in Monalei's eyes, while Enerill and Gandreke remained silent.

"Why are you worried? Isn't that a good thing?" Yonni questioned. Her voice dripped with panic, and her thoughts took a turn for the worse. "Is it going to hurt me? Am I going to die?"

Monalei placed both hands on her daughter and let out a low shush. "A Tomekeeper is a powerful position, but it comes with heavy consequences. Everything will be explained, Yonni, but not by us. We need to get you to Prodigium as promptly as possible." Monalei tilted her head to the right. "Gandreke, please gather the queen's chosen. We leave at once."

Gandreke left without a word. Enerill moved to his mother's side and put his hand on Yonni's forehead. The latter looked up at her brother's face and guilt took control.

"Probably not the homecoming you were expecting," Yonni lamented. "I'm sorry."

Enerill shook his head and gave her a half-smile. "Mom's right. Our priority right now is getting you to Prodigium, and soon."

Yonni looked at her mother, then back to Enerill. She still didn't understand. Prodigium was the capital of Pradarek and the kingdom of the Wingsong. It was far from the place that any Anquan would go, especially one that had never been to the surface. Exhaustion settled into her bones.

"Why Prodigium?"

"Because if you've been chosen," Monalei answered, "that means the other Tomekeepers have as well."

Tome/keeper/s

The dead, gray earth stretched far into the horizon before it dropped into the sharp, twisted trenches that gave the Smilelands its name. Ink-black slush spewed through the indentions, a river of death straight from the necrotic cesspool known as Netot's Chalice.

Netot, god of darkness, was not known for his mercy. Everything that faced the frigid embrace of death was welcomed into Netot's arms, but that made him apathetic. Netot never stepped in to do the dirty work himself. That honor fell to Istio, the goddess of war, and those who followed in her hunger for carnage and thirst for blood. Everyone feared the idea of death, but Istio's harbingers made it a reality.

Verina Hinlon, self-proclaimed harbinger, stared at the follower of Netot as he hobbled across the gray. Her beady hazel eyes tracked the movement of his black tunic from the ashen hillside like a vulture stalking its prey. The follower, unsure of where she was, tried his best to move in a sporadic pattern. She adjusted the hood of her jade cloak and clutched the worn, padded grip of her bow tightly. The first arrow she embedded into his right leg had been for the fun of making him suffer. The next would pin him to the ground and allow her to slither up. All the while, she'd relish in his screams.

Verina took aim, pulled the arrow back, and listened to the creak of the bow's string as the pressure stretched it. It was a melodic sound. She released her grip and watched the arrow fly towards its target. The flared metal tip glinted briefly in the sun before it struck the back of the follower's left leg with perfect precision. He howled in pain as he tumbled to the ground and cursed her from afar. She took her time as she stepped down the hillside and made her way toward him. More curses sprayed from his mouth when he saw her.

Verina leapt at the Noctide man like a rabid animal and planted a black boot into his chest. He wheezed and coughed as she pressed him into the ground, his face red from the blow. She moved her foot over and stomped on his left arm, then did the same to his right to hold him in place.

What a sad, sniveling waste of life, she thought.

Verina crouched low and studied her trophy. He was pale, more than most of the Noctide she had seen in her time, and his scruffy black hair was layered with grease. Multiple piercings, common amongst the children of Netot, dotted every stretch of free space across his gaunt face. She pulled her dagger from the holster hidden within her cloak and teasingly ran it from the nape of his neck to his stomach.

"What do you want from me, haelspawn?" he cried. His arms fought against her legs to no avail.

"I'm doing your god a favor in honor of mine," Verina stated, her voice monotone.

She raised her dagger high and caught a reflection of her carefully painted face in the terror of his widened irises. Large, dark circles encompassed each eye, and small red diamonds chained together across her honeyed skin from her cheek to her nose. Green droplets, a tribute to the symbol of Istio, dotted her forehead. Her lips were as black as the shadows that she lurked in. It was all skeletal, haunting, beautiful. It was the last face he would ever see, and she wanted to make sure it left an impression.

Verina plunged her dagger into the Noctide and reveled in his shrieks. They were sweet and true, the most natural and exposed sound a person could make in her opinion. When the shrieks gurgled out, she withdrew her blade and wiped it clean against the palm of her leather glove. She stared at the red fluid of life with a deep longing and looked around in shame to make sure no one else was nearby. The urge to taste the copper on her tongue grew stronger by the moment, and she fought it with every ounce of her being.

No one's around, she argued with herself. *What's the harm in just a single lick?*

Verina pulled her hand to her face in defeat when a sharp, burning pain suddenly stabbed her in the center of her palm. She dropped the dagger as it spread outward toward the tips of her fingers and across her wrist. Her skin sizzled as the pain permeated deeper into her body. Green magical energy seeped outward through her clothes and coalesced into a glowing ball that consumed her.

Verina Hinlon, slayer in my name, an airy voice hissed through her thoughts. ***You have sworn loyalty to me and now your commitment has made you my perfect champion. Use my power, seek your vengeance, and gather your tome. Your task awaits.***

The ball absorbed into Verina's body with searing agony. She gritted her teeth and felt it seep into her soul, then let out a cackle. She had done everything she could to gain Istio's favor, and she had been rewarded in turn. Her cackle turned into an endless fit of psychotic laughter as she rolled around on the ground and stared into the sky. Tears of joy formed in the corners of her eyes.

Verina's fun had just begun.

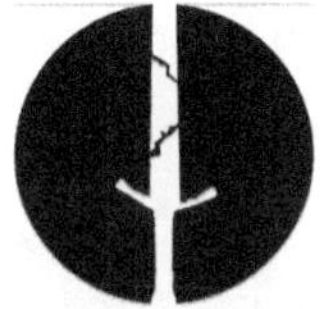

Tuvhe Vull pushed past the blistering winds and biting chill of Eslen's Mark as he made his way up to the Soule Flame on the mountain's edge. Eslen's Mark cracked apart the ground, two large slashes in the shape of a V that stretched from the base to the valley below. The caverns left behind were rumored to be bottomless. Tuvhe placed his hand in front of his amber eyes as the blizzard obscured his view. He didn't want to lose his footing and find out if the rumors were true.

His metal boots crunched into the knee deep snow. The white compounded with every step, and dryness taunted his eyes and tongue. Flecks of snow stuck to his long, black hair and blended with the ivory of his face. Still, he knew he had to press forward. Tomhaus Deriden and his brother Yarcon had left to tend to the Soule Flame days ago, as was tradition for the young adults of the Devement, yet they never returned. The village of Senna became abuzz with fantastic stories of what happened to them— witches, monsters, and traveling Noctide or Terrolaffs —to the point that Tuvhe took it upon himself to find out. No one else would have.

Tuvhe looked ahead and squinted his eyes. He could barely make out the shape of the outpost aptly labeled "Judgment's Edge." If the Deriden brothers were headed to the Soule Flame, it was the only place they could have rested. If the carceras soldiers and their adjudicarum leader had no note of their visit, then the Deridens had already been buried six feet under the snow.

Tuvhe rubbed his shoulders and his plated armor clinked. Up ahead, he saw the small embers of a fire drift into the storm. His eyes went wide.

Not just one fire. The entire outpost was ablaze, hidden behind a cloak of thick snow. Tuvhe ran towards the gate with his hands raised high.

"Hello?" he shouted as loud as he could. "Is anyone here? Are you injured?"

Silence.

"Please, if you need help, I'm here! I've traveled from Senna to check on the Flame."

There was still no answer.

A rustle echoed from behind the outpost's main cabin. Tuvhe place his hand on his sword and steadied himself for potential battle. His senses screamed that something was afoot. As he rounded the corner, a harsh shriek echoed from above.

Tuvhe's head shot up and he saw the giant beast drop towards him, claws outstretched. He pulled his sword out in a slashing motion to catch the frostwolf across the cream-colored fur of its chest, then stepped back as the creature tumbled into the snow. A low grumble arose.

Tuvhe stepped closer to the flames that engulfed the main cabin and used the heat to stay warm. A small white creature with fanged teeth and pointed ears popped out from under the frostwolf's body. It stared at him from afar, eyes like bright blue marbles, and let out a deafening shriek.

Ravilors, Tuvhe thought. *The little goblin freaks must have raided the camp.*

Tuvhe pressed against the door of the cabin and pushed it open against his better judgment. He knew what morbid site awaited him. The flames failed to hide the mangled look of the fresh corpses and the expressions of pained terror permanently affixed to their faces. He counted the bodies.

Only five, Tuvhe noted. *That means the Deridens either passed through, or didn't make it here at all.*

Tuvhe placed both hands on the hilt of his sword and tightened his grip. The thuds of more Ravilors jumping across the rooftops gave way to a swarm that assembled in front of him. Tuvhe counted at least thirty. He tried to stay steadfast in the increasingly futile odds. If he was going to die, he was going to take out as many of them as he could.

A sharp pain speared through the front of Tuvhe's head and into his mind. He staggered, but continued to hold his blade steady. His stomach churned.

Tuvhe Vull, seeker and protector, a low, pompous voice called to him. ***Your commitment has deemed you worthy of being my successor. Take my sword, serve as my right hand, and claim your tome. Do not fail.***

White light emanated from Tuvhe's hands and spread into his sword. It bended and shaped it into a new form. The pain struck again and he was forced to close his eyes. He let out a guttural scream, then the world went silent.

Tuvhe opened his eyes. His body laid on the frosted ground, untouched. What was once harsh snow had fizzled into soft powder that fell lightly from the sky. Smoke wafted from the cabin, now reduced to ash and charcoal. Daylight peaked over the horizon.

Tuvhe glanced at the sword in his hands. It was the same one he always carried with him. He examined it, but there was nothing of note to be found.

"Was it all a dream?" he asked aloud.

Tuvhe went to stand and slipped on a patch of ice. He lifted his head and caught sight of the scene ahead. Trails of crimson streaked the snow. The bodies of the ravilors and their frostwolf companions were strewn across the grounds, slaughtered through skilled slices. There was an eerie air of efficiency to it all.

Tuvhe sheathed his sword and inspected his armor. Red splashed across the chains and stained the white fur lining. He took a deep breath. To be chosen as a Tomekeeper was one thing, but to be the Tomekeeper of the Betrayer was another.

I'el Rivini felt the heat of the sun caress her warm beige skin through the holes in the foliage above her. The air smelled of the strawberries and honeydew that grew in the lower fields of Noli's Orchard.

It was another pleasant day among the Phreeton Elves of Farnen's Grove. The trees of the Hicarian Forest were vibrant and full, the bounties of the orchard had been plentiful, and the sound of frolicking children drifted alongside the breeze.

Children? I'el thought, eyes still shut. *That's odd. The children should be with their instructor for the day.*

Her body snapped upward.

"By the Protector, I'm teaching the kids today!" she yelled as she pulled herself up and scrambled to look presentable.

As much as I'el loved to nap in the sun, the twigs and leaves wreaked havoc on her bright orange locks. She dusted off what she could, then opted to tie the rest into a bun. No one would question her change of hairstyle in the middle of hunting season. She glanced over her chestnut-colored leather pants and olive green tunic to make sure she looked presentable.

Last chance, I'el, she told herself. *The elders can't find out you've been slacking again. Even worse, Friston can't see you look so unkempt!*

I'el smoothed out her clothes and tightened her fingerless gloves as Friston Slil and the children that accompanied him crested the hilltop. There were six, four boys and two girls, each with their handmade bow in hand. She would have normally thought it was the cutest sight ever, but Friston drew all her attention away. He offered her a wave and one of his usual beaming smiles. I'el melted.

The vest of leaves he wore hugged his chest, and the breeze tempted her with the slightest peek of the muscles underneath. His bright ponytailed blonde hair lit up even more in the sunlight, complimented by his crystalline blue eyes and the lone sapphire earring pierced through the sharpened tip of his left ear. He was the picture of Phreeton grace in her eyes.

I'el's face grew hot as he walked over to her.

"Beautiful day, isn't it, I'el?" Friston asked. His silvery voice was just as perfect as he was. He pointed a finger toward the edge of her right shoulder. "You, um, have something there."

I'el panicked internally and swiped the object from her shoulder. She looked and saw it was just a small twig, thankfully not enough to give away her secret nap.

"Thank you, Friston," I'el replied in the most honeyed voice she could muster. She offered a bright smile of her own and returned his gaze with violet doe eyes.

The children chased and whacked each other with their bows beside them. Friston let out a small laugh and turned to the mischief. I'el studied his body intently.

"Okay, younglings," Friston called to them in an attempt to establish order. "Line up for Miss Rivini."

The children followed his command and formed a crooked row, bows readied. I'el walked past each of them and studied their form while Friston watched them from the side. She adjusted their postures and grip until the entire group had the same stance.

"The most important aspect of hunting is having the right posture when firing your bow," I'el instructed with a raised finger. "You can be the best tracker in Lidaesea, but you won't bring home anything if you can't hit it." The children replied with stifled laughter. "I know!" I'el continued. "You wouldn't believe how many times I missed the most magnificent game because I didn't make the effort to learn the basics."

The children laughed again, more hectic than before. Friston stepped forward.

"You all need to listen to Miss Rivini. She's the best hunter we have in the grove."

"But she's funny!" one child, a young girl with curly brown hair, responded. "She keeps playing with the vine!"

I'el looked toward her own raised hand in confusion. The twig that she had plucked from her shoulder had now sprouted into a thick, green vine. The vine expanded more, weight increasing in her hand, then wrapped around her arm and snaked its way toward her body.

"I'el, what are you doing?" Friston asked as he stepped in front of the children.

"It's not me," I'el stuttered in response. "I don't know what's going on!"

The sound of her voice echoed into the recesses of her own mind. Friston and the children behind him blurred and melted into a multicolored field. I'el felt lightheaded at first, then a hard force slammed against the back of her skull.

I'el Rivini, my blossoming flower, a sweet, melodic voice sang through her pointed ears and into her thoughts. ***You have always been one with nature and the people around you, tending to the seeds of the grove. I have selected you as my champion. Go forth, find your tome, and grow into the empowered leader I know you will be.***

As her vision returned to normal, I'el felt the vine wrap around her whole body. It spread across her as it formed into a sturdy cocoon. The cocoon expanded and the vines forced her into a small central chamber. She looked out of the slit between the vine's many entwined branches, a prisoner to nature.

"I'el, are you alright?" Friston inquired as he ran his hands along the cocoon, looking for a way to break her free. The children stood frozen in awe behind him.

"I think we need to go to the elders," I'el answered. Fear and uncertainty clung to her voice. "Once I'm able to get out, that is."

The Chosen Path

Yonni took a deep breath and steeled herself for the journey ahead. The role of the Tomekeeper was the greatest honor an Anqualai could have beyond the crowns themselves. They were the wardens of peace and voice of the gods, revered across every nation in Lidaesea. There would be training and meetings, as well as political delegation and military assessment. Her mind reeled at the thought.

Thankfully, as far as her research had shown, the Tomekeepers were never forced to go to war on their people's behalf. The gods did not endorse it. Most spats had been settled before violence was a factor. Even the northern nations in Silnathum—those of the Terrolaffs, Noctide, Pyrolites, and Wojlidoj—managed to stay their blades.

A Tomekeeper, Yonni repeated in her mind, still in disbelief. *Quite the exclusive club.*

She felt the nerves build and her back tense as the carriage came around the corner of the courtyard, drawn by a quartet of sea striders and flanked in the front and back by two units of the queen's chosen. It was overkill from a protection standpoint, but Yonni understood it was her mother's way of ensuring her safety.

Enerill patted her on the upper back and pointed toward the carriage. The sly grin on his face made Yonni feel he must have thought the same thing. "All this time away and I see she's still the same," he laughed. It was pleasant to see he was still capable of doing so.

Queen Monalei wrapped up her conversation with Gandreke and swam over to the siblings.

"Best of luck on your journey!" Gandreke called to them. He bowed and disappeared back inside the castle walls.

"Is he not coming with us?" Yonni asked her mother in confusion.

"Not this time," the queen answered. "I need him to stay behind and tend to a few matters on my behalf. Once the other kingdoms discover you've been selected by Drinex, he'll have to deal with the diplomats and other unsavory parties that come our way."

Yonni nodded. Gandreke made the most sense to rule in her absence, even though Enerill was next in the line of command. In the day that had passed since her selection, her brother's rigid schedule and militaristic behavior hadn't transitioned well into palace life. She leaned forward and saw Enerill in deep thought.

"Maybe I should stay behind too," Enerill voiced, as if reading her thoughts again. "That allows me the chance to learn from Gandreke and put my schooling to use."

The queen tilted her head toward Enerill in surprise. "Are you sure? It's not like you to miss out on an adventure."

Enerill let out a hearty laugh.

"I'm not the same silly boy, Your Majesty," he responded. "My days of escaping the castle walls are well behind me. I'm afraid I've settled into the lifestyle of an old widow."

The queen's eyes snapped toward Enerill and her face twisted into a look of displeasure. Yonni fought the powerful urge to not tease him further and add fuel to the flame. Enerill realized his poor choice of wording and turned toward the queen.

"My apologies, mother," he said with his head bowed. "I was merely joking. I shall take my leave."

"Yes, you shall," Monalei confirmed coldly.

The teal wallu let out light trills as the carriage pulled up to Yonni and her mother. One of the sea striders opened the door. The two women took their seats, the light in the land above fading away. Yonni swiveled to say goodbye to Enerill, but found he was already gone.

"Night's coming, Yonni," Monalei observed. "That means we should arrive at the Font of Drinex by dawn."

"And from there, Your Majesty?" Yonni inquired.

"Smooth sailing all the way to Prodigium."

Verina crossed the ashen wastes of the Smilelands and climbed back up the hill until she came to a jagged black rock that was half of her height. She wrapped her hands around the side and pressed the sharpened edges into her palms, wincing as they broke skin. The rock rumbled and turned clockwise to reveal a small hatchway.

Verina opened the hatch and dropped into the darkness below. An incline broke her fall and she slid towards its bottom, spit out into a tunnel covered with glowing green fungi. She crouched and made her way through the narrow tunnel until she reached a large, open cavern.

A sprawling, wooden city spread across the lagoon that encompassed the cavern's floor. Bridges crossed in every direction, and the small circle of light from the cavern's opening bounced off the water to cut through the grim darkness. Istio's Gate—or simply "The Gate" as most Terrolaffs called it—was a city that many had heard of, but few had seen. Or, more precisely, seen and lived to tell the tale of.

Verina clambered down a ladder and onto the nearest bridge. it creaked under her every step, and her boots squeaked from the water that covered her soles. As she made her way to the other side of The Gate, she peered out into the rows of simple shacks that lined the lagoon's edge. The tide flowed against the stilts that supported them.

The sound of terrified screams caught Verina's attention. Her gaze shifted to the fishing stall on the bridge's opposite end where the owner slashed a crooked blade at his emaciated victim.

Ugh, tourists never learn, Verina groaned internally.

She stepped off the bridge and walked up to the shack she called home, the fifth in a row of twelve. The door buckled against the hinges and smacked into the wall as she flung it open. Verina pulled her hood off and shook the moisture from her hair. Her short bob, cut roughly by her own dagger, was a light silver that created a ghostly halo. She pulled her dagger from its holster and threw it into a nearby table with a solid thunk.

"You've been gone long enough," the scratchy, drunken voice of her father floated from around the corner. She heard the scuff of furniture and his fumbling footsteps across the wood. He popped into the doorway and sneered. The wisps of what remained of his hair angled in different directions, and the weight from years of uninhibited drinking gave him a rounded belly beneath his fisherman's garb. He grinned, teeth yellow and cracked, and rubbed the sweat from his greasy red forehead. Beady brown eyes narrowed to slits. "Best have brought some coin, now."

Verina took a small russet sack, half the size of her hand, and threw it at her father. He snatched it from the air and dumped the contents onto the floor. Verina watched as he struggled to count.

"Only eight merrillans?" he huffed. Verina shrugged. "I told your worthless self to not come back with less than thirty! Eight'll barely get me a pint of the weak stuff," her father fumed. He kicked the coins across the floor with a loud clatter.

"I've been hunting all day," Verina argued. "What have you done except look at the back end of an empty bottle?"

Her father stumbled forward with intense fury, hand raised at her defiant comment. Verina stepped to the side and shook her head as he passed. She refused to be struck, and he was never fast enough to catch her. Verina pictured her mother and the torment she went through in her stead. Torment she was no longer around to bear. Infuriated, she reached out and grappled her father's wrist.

"Listen, you drunken old swine, because it will be the last thing that you hear," Verina spat. "Istio herself has chosen me. I am marked for greatness, and I will see it through. You no longer rule my life."

Say it, Istio hissed. ***Look in your heart. You know the words.***

Verina closed her eyes.

"*Jeha.*"

As she spoke, the burning sensation crept up in her hand again, then spread to her arm. Green magic flowed out of her cloak and crossed onto her father. He grunted and yelped as the acid swept over him. He yanked his arm against hers, but couldn't break free. The hold she had was unusually strong. Verina stared at him with a wicked smile burned into her face. Her grip tightened, the reflection of magic like dancing green fireflies in her irises.

Verina's father fell to his knees and begged for mercy. The magic inched up his body to his neck. Verina twisted his arm to the ground and put her face close. His hot breath made her nose crinkle.

"Goodbye," she whispered. "And good riddance."

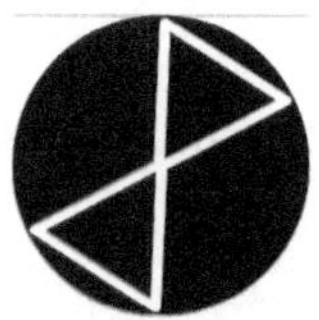

Utic Delj raced through the desert city of Montenau, desperate to reach its outer wall. The smell of potent spices and fruit swirled together in the air as he dashed through the market square. Utic slid under a passing merchant cart and elicited a curse from its owner. He turned toward the skiff bay and pushed himself to run faster. An ominous brown cloud, as big as the horizon, inched closer every second.

Utic cursed his older siblings under his wheezes. Nine older siblings, and not a single one could be bothered to watch Uvet. He wiped the sweat from the cool bronze of his forehead with the sleeve of his cream-colored tunic. Uvet, the youngest of the family, should not have gone to the bay alone. That was an issue by itself. The others should have stopped him, though, or warned him of the incoming storm. That was another.

As always, it was up to Utic to clean up after their mistakes. Utic, the caretaker. Utic, the fixer of messes. Utic, the invisible. His lungs stung from the extra dust that swept through the air.

As he reached the city gate, Utic heard a loud shout from the side. He looked towards its origin and saw a guard in heavy armor, a groundshifter, signaling him. The groundshifter pointed his palm toward Utic.

"You can't go out that way!" the groundshifter shouted as the wind whipped around them. "The storm is coming in. If you go, you'll be caught in the middle of it all!"

Utic moved closer, but only enough for the guard to hear him. His gray eyes burned in the wind. "I need to go! My brother is caught out there!"

The guard shook his head and glanced upwards. Dirt blotted out the normally blazing sun. The rumble of the storm increased.

"You have five minutes," the groundshifter relented and emphasized the time with his hand. "After that, the gate is locked!"

Utic waved in thanks and pulled the door of the wooden gate open. A wave of sand splashed across his face like small razors. He pushed against the ever-mounting wind and pulled the hood and mask of his tunic over his face. Each step he took with his open leather sandals sank into the endless body of tan and copper sand as he made his way toward the bay just to the right of the gate's entry. Utic saw the wood planks of the bay's dock ahead.

Uvet sat behind a nailed down bench that wobbled against the pressure of the wind. His legs and arms were balled up to protect him from the storm. Utic pressed onward, then called out his brother's name. Uvet perked up and waved at his rescuer. His ten-year-old frame shook in the midst of the storm's gusts.

"Why didn't you leave when you saw the storm coming?" Utic reprimanded his brother when he neared the bench. "You know you can't survive the brute force of these things!"

Uvet's lip quivered, and he looked away in shame. "I wanted to ride the skiffs like you do. I didn't think about it."

Guilt wriggled into Utic's mind. He knew his younger brother loved to watch the sand surfers ride their skiffs across the dunes. Utic had even promised to show him the basics before he was bogged down by everyone else's chores. He didn't blame Uvet, only himself.

"Come on, little brother," Utic sighed with a gesture to move closer. "I promise I'll bring you back out, but we need to get back through the gate."

Utic estimated around three minutes had passed, which meant they had less than two to get through the gate before it locked. Utic pulled his brother up and turned around to guide him. The gusts increased in speed and smashed into Utic's body like a wall of bricks. He tripped and stumbled, yet refused to give up. It wasn't just his life on the line.

The frame of the door came into view and Utic felt relief replace the heavy weight on his body. The deafening crack of wood sent a shockwave of fear through him immediately afterward. Utic faced the sound and saw the mast of a sand skiff break in half behind them. Another gust of wind toppled it.

"Get down!" Utic yelled at his brother as he jumped in front of the mast. The rounded side smashed into the middle of his chest and ripped the breath out of his lungs. Utic fell to the ground and pulled down his mask. He gasped for air that the sand-filled sky could not provide him. Uvet leapt to help, but Utic gripped his arm in response.

"No," he uttered in choked words. "Can't go. Make the gate. Leave. Now!"

"I can't leave you, Utic," Uvet cried. Tears streamed across his face. "You'll die!"

"Now!"

Uvet stood with a shuddering breath and ran toward the gate door. He banged on it incessantly until the groundshifter opened. Uvet tried to point to his brother and demand help, but the guard ignored his pleas. Utic witnessed the guard yank his brother back inside the city walls and slam the door closed.

Utic tried to stand, but his legs wouldn't allow it. The sandstorm's might exhausted the little energy he had left from his cross-city trek. The blow to the chest was just the signature on his death sentence. His hands grasped at the sand as it sifted through his fingers. More covered the lower half of his body. The crunchy, earthen taste filled his mouth. He closed his eyes and waited for the eventual suffocation.

Utic Delj, compassionate yet unnoticed, a stern female voice called to him from the sands. ***Do not fear, for I have noted your deed. Rise from the sand, my chosen. Make your name and collect your tome.***

Utic felt the sand shift around him, ebbing and flowing like water around his body. He was weightless in that moment, as if the responsibilities of the world and his impending death were no longer a concern. It was pleasant, warm even. His lungs swelled with fresh air and strength returned to his body. Utic closed his eyes and let the sensation swallow him whole.

The ground opened, and sand lifted him until he rested against the desert dunes once more. Night had fallen. The stars twinkled, beautiful jewels in the blackened sea above and accented by Lidaesea's triplet moons. What was once blistering heat had shifted into frigid temperatures that chilled him to the bone.

Utic rubbed his hands along the sides of his arms to warm up and examined the surrounding landscape. The city of Montenau was nowhere to be found. Not a single sight of its high slate walls arose in the distance, either.

A lone ball of shimmering amber light served as a beacon where sand met sky. Utic examined it closely. The ball moved toward him at impeccable speed until the shape of a barge came into view, the amber light from a series of lanterns at its front. Utic waved madly as the barge, bulking and rusted, whirred to a stop nearby. He ran towards it, hands raised as a sign of peace.

A single, elderly man with a fur jacket and a long, scruffy white beard that ran to his stomach walked toward the barge's edge. Sun-bleached goggles covered his eyes.

"You lost, boy?" the man asked in a gruff tone.

"I'm from Montenau, sir," Utic answered. "But I need to get to Prodigium."

The man stroked his beard and gazed at the stars, then turned back and kicked the ladder next to him. It hit the sand with a small puff of dust.

"Today's your lucky day then, boy," the old man answered. "I'm heading toward the Varlan Plains to drop off my cargo. I suppose I can make a detour towards the Font. That's the closest I can get, then the rest is up to you."

Utic gave the man multiple thanks and made a vow to himself as he ascended the ladder. No matter what came his way, he would complete the journey to Prodigium and become somebody that made Verna, and his family, proud. He had finally been seen.

No, even better.

He had been chosen.

Demons and Dragons

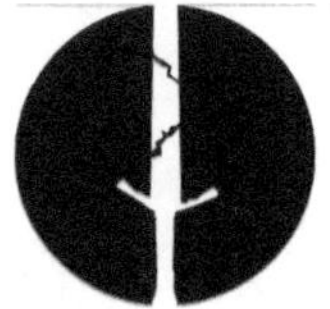

Tuvhe dug the metal fingers of his gauntlet deep into the snowy earth and hoisted himself up onto the last rock. As he clawed his way over the edge, he let out a sigh of relief. The entry to the temple of the Soule Flame was in sight, only a few paces down a worn flagstone path. He rolled onto his back, snow stuck to his hair, and fought the desire to take a much deserved nap.

"You can rest at the Flame," he encouraged himself aloud. "At least there, it will be warm."

Tuvhe forced himself up and walked along the path, careful to avoid the patches of ice that glazed over the stone's surface. The silver capped roof of the temple poked above the dead limbs of the trees. Sharpened branches snapped against his armor as he pushed through and into the courtyard outside of the temple doorway.

The courtyard, once a sight to behold for all Lidaeseans, was now a ghost of its former self. Broken stones littered the corners, and dead vines wormed through every crack and hole time had dealt. The flower beds, empty for centuries, were nothing but frozen chunks of dark brown soil. The door itself was a heavily patinated mess, the once awe-inspiring etchings of Eslen's accomplishments now weathered to barely visible scratches.

Metal scraped against stone with every step Tuvhe took toward the door. The stifled sound of laughter from inside the temple caught his ear. He pushed the door open and peeked his head inside.

"Tomhaus? Yarcon? Are you two there?" he called in a hushed tone. The rush of outside air kicked up a cloud of dust. Laughter continued to echo through empty halls that felt more tomb than temple. Tuvhe stepped forward and quietly closed the door behind him. He examined the bronze-laced interior of the entryway, but nothing looked off. The laughter beckoned him further toward the temple's main chamber. "Hello?"

Tuvhe walked through the open archway of the chamber and halted in surprise. Tomhaus Deriden was face down in a pool of deep red that spilled into the grooves of the temple's floor. Yarcon hovered over him, dagger in hand and a mad grin stretched from ear to ear. Behind him, the roaring inferno of the Soule Flame, housed atop a granite goblet, cast a scarlet glow across his body.

Yarcon's head rose to meet Tuvhe's glare, and his blue eyes radiated madness. "Vull, you madman. You made it past the ravilors?"

Tomekeeper, the pompous voice in Tuvhe's head called out. Another sharp pain developed in his mind as it spoke. ***Be wary. This one carries a darkness unseen since I ascended.***

Tuvhe stepped forward, his hand inches from his sword. The temple of the Soule Flame was a sacred place, one that the act of the maddened Deriden had defiled. A deep desire to find the truth ignited inside him.

"Tell me what happened here, Yarcon," Tuvhe suggested calmly. His left foot stepped into the red beneath. "Why did you kill Tomhaus?"

Yarcon responded with an open-mouthed guffaw and a point of the dagger in Tuvhe's direction. "You just jump straight to the hard questions, don't you?" he responded.

His irises blackened, then twitched. The auburn of his short, coarse hair took on a browner tone. Tuvhe gently slid his hand closer to his sheath. Yarcon didn't notice.

"You see, it's a miracle," Yarcon continued. "The Soule Flame talked to me! It showed me the things I was too blind to see."

"What does that even mean, Yarcon?" Tuvhe pressed. None of the legends regarding the flame ever spoke of an ability to speak, much less show visions.

Yarcon stepped up to meet Tuvhe, who braced for an attack in return. The latter's breathing slowed. Yarcon slapped his knee and doubled over in more hideous cackling.

"You really think I want to kill you, Vull?" Yarcon got out between bouts. "I'd squish you if I did. Besides, you're not my enemy, right? No, not like ol' Tomhaus over here, dead as doornails. You want to know a secret?"

Yarcon leaned in and beckoned Tuvhe forward with a flick of the dagger. Tuvhe didn't budge. Yarcon's voice lowered to a whisper. "The Flame said we'll be dead before the third decade. All of Lidaesea will be wiped from existence. It also warned me Tomhaus was going to push me into the Mark on the way home. Dirty sod was going to steal my girl. And you know what the worst thing is?"

Tuvhe tugged on the hilt of his sword to loosen it.

"It told me she was going to be happy. Happier than she ever was with me." Yarcon's eyes watered, yet his smile never faded. It seemed eternally plastered to his face. As the tears streaked down his cheeks, a thin trail of black slime formed in their wake.

Tomekeeper, the voice returned. *Your Yarcon is no more. Whatever is left is unmitigated evil.*

Tuvhe stared at Yarcon and studied his eyes. He shuddered. Yarcon's irises wriggled and split into three. Tuvhe drew his sword and held the point against Yarcon's throat.

The Deriden brother laughed again.

"You weren't supposed to see that," he said. "You shouldn't even be here. The ravilors were instructed to kill everyone. Everything. This husk was all I needed to remain. His nectarine pain sustains me."

"And what is your true name, demon?" Tuvhe questioned.

Yarcon licked his chapped lips. "Ask your friend Eslen. He knows."

Listen to me, Tomekeeper, Eslen replied. *You cannot let him escape. Strike him down. Finish this before one becomes many.*

"We are already many," Yarcon said.

Tuvhe stumbled back. "How can you hear him? He's in my head."

Yarcon tilted his head to an inhuman degree. "You won't be alive long enough for me to bother answering."

Yarcon let out a screech and jumped forward, his dagger aimed for Tuvhe's heart. A singular word crept up into the Tomekeeper's mind. He drew his sword and swatted away the dagger with a counter-clockwise motion, then kicked Yarcon in the chest. The young man stumbled back and fell over his brother's body.

"*Dahfuolenitehn!*" Tuvhe shouted as he raised his sword. It shifted back into the familiar shape he had seen once before: an elegant falchion made of silver and hued in a white glow. The guard jutted out and downward into a sharp, diagonal point, and the hilt was encrusted with ice. A carnelian red outline ran along the edge of the blade, composed from the crushed bits of a jewel Tuvhe had never seen.

Judgment has been passed, Eslen declared.

Tuvhe's arm suddenly raised against his will, ready to deliver a fatal blow. He was an observer in his own body. Despite his attempt to regain control, his arm remained raised.

"I'll be seeing you again, Vull," Yarcon grinned.

Tuvhe's arm swung down, and the demon ceased to exist.

I'el steeled herself at the foot of the staircase that led up toward the synthesis chamber, the meeting place of the Phreeton elders. The chamber and the staircase that connected were directly carved out of the trunk of the Obsidian Oak, an astounding three-hundred foot tree that the goddess Noli herself had grown. Its vibrant green leaves clashed against the deep black of the tree's bark, giving them a floating appearance once the sun set.

Atop the staircase stood two sentreenals, hulking humanoid creatures of bark and vine with burning yellow orbs for eyes. They made no noise and only ever silently watched. I'el had never seen them in battle, and hoped she'd never have to. She swiped pollen off of herself and tried to walk through her story.

Friston had sliced her out of her cocoon of horticultural doom with a serrated knife he carried around. The task alone took most of the day, but she was thankful for her freedom. Friston told her he would run ahead to prevent the elders from adjourning their council and give her time to prepare.

Do I give them a speech? she pondered. *Or should I just show them my powers outright?*

I'el looked at the piece of vine clasped in her hand. She held out her palm and furrowed her brow, then her thoughts focused entirely on making it move. The vine didn't react, but she garnered the attention of the sentreenals. One elbowed the other, who just shook its head. I'el didn't need to hear any harsh words to understand she was being mocked. A fierce, heated gust blew her hair back.

Among the branches that laced the top of the Obsidian Oak, a frightening cyan dragon with translucent purple wings landed and stretched. Four curved tusks adorned its rectangular face, two around its bottom jaw and two under its piercing golden eyes. Spikes trailed from the back of its head all the way to its forked tail. It tilted its head up and released a bellow that reverberated through the forest and every part of I'el's body.

Qenolev, my poor friend. He's lonely, the melodic voice in I'el's head rang.

I'el looked around in surprise, but couldn't track where the voice was coming from.

Calm, keeper. I am guiding you from the mental space, Noli explained. ***Only you can hear me. Do not call attention, and act as you normally would.***

"That's much easier said than done. I have a goddess talking to me," I'el rebutted aloud. The sentreenals looked at one another again in confusion.

By Ghantei's grace, I've chosen an imbecile, Noli sighed. ***You don't have to speak aloud, keeper. I can hear your mind.***

I understand! I'el thought with an energetic nod.

Please continue. The sooner you embark, the sooner we can connect with the tome.

I'el walked up the steps and gave a small wave to the sentreenals as she passed. The doors embedded within the Obsidian Oak opened with a heavy creak, and the scent of lilac and sage welcomed I'el in. The circular chamber was a warm mahogany color, with swirling rings engraved into the walls, lit by orange-hued lanterns and a pulsating emerald crystal that hung overhead. Seated in the middle of the chamber, across seven seats at a singular table, was the council of elders.

Lord Valwell Slil and Lady Bresha, Friston's parents and leaders of the Phreeton people, rested comfortably in the center. Friston stood against the wall behind them with his arms crossed behind his back. He offered a small, and noticeably more reserved, smile.

"I'el Rivini, our troublemaker turned Tomekeeper apparent!" Lord Valwell exclaimed with a raised goblet. "Please, come tell us how you persuaded our great goddess into blessing you with her power."

I'el chuckled nervously and shuffled toward the council. Each of the members studied her. She could hear their thoughts churning.

"I'm not sure how to answer, My Lord. I did nothing but wake from a nap."

A light rumble of uncomfortable laughter arose from the council.

Masrak Tawn, general of the Phreeton army, drummed his fingers on the table. His flowing silver hair accented the sharpened features of his face.

"Surely Noli, mother of our gardens and provider of our homes, has some grand plan for one such as yourself, as she does for us all," he droned. "With that said, I have a hard time believing someone with your past would be chosen to begin with. Please, share with us anything that can prove you have been blessed with the powers of the vine."

I'el glanced at the vine in her hand again. She wanted to do something with it—make it grow, move, or maybe even form another cocoon—but if she failed, the elders could call her treasonous. Or worse. It was too much of a gamble. Instead, she needed something simple that no one could argue against.

"Qenolev!" I'el spouted with a raised finger. The council glanced at one another with raised eyebrows. She stepped forward. "The dew dragon above us is Qenolev. He seeks more of his kind."

"Young lady, if I may," Tawn responded with a raised hand. "The dew dragon that lives with us in the Orchard has been around for centuries. So long, in fact, that all records of his name have been erased from time. You could spout any name and claim it to be true. As for your statement that he's lonely, well, that isn't hard to decipher."

"No, she's right," the powerful voice of Lady Bresha echoed across the chamber. Her moss-colored robe rippled as she stood. Ice blue eyes stared down at the other members of the table. "My great-grandfather was the dew dragon's caretaker. Only those in my family lineage have been allowed to know his name, for it holds great power. The only way I'el would have learned is if the dead spoke to her. Or a goddess."

I'el let out a barely noticeable sigh of relief. She fidgeted with the vine in her hand.

Good thinking, Noli complimented.

Lady Bresha turned to I'el and extended out her hands. "I'el, my sweet huntress, you have been given a wonderful gift. Of all those that call Hicaria their home—from the Orchard to the Grove to the Falls—you were selected to wield a beautiful power. Do not waste it. You will need to make your way to Prodigium."

Lord Valwell stood up and moved next to his wife. He was a head shorter, but had a solid stature and broad shoulders. His free hand pressed against her lower back.

Friston was the perfect blend of the two. The young elf mimicked a silent clap for her from behind them. She had gained the approval of Friston and his parents, and that alone was worth being chosen.

"We shall send word to the boats at Silver Falls to prepare for your arrival," Lord Valwell announced. He took a swig from his goblet. "Once there, they'll take you across the Erineal Strait to the mercantile city of Selenti. We can arrange a carriage for you to take after that. Then, I'el, it will be up to you. Make us proud."

I'el felt an odd surge of emotion inside her. It was warm and comforting, but also energetic. The council relied on her, and she couldn't deny that it was a powerful feeling. Lord Valwell called for a toast that most of the council joined. I'el beamed at Friston and soaked up the attention.

Kliev Rorn did a running slide into a bundle of speckleberry bushes and laid flat against the ground. His tan rabbit ears tilted toward the earth and listened for the footsteps of his pursuers. He caught the patter of footsteps from a mile away, rapidly approaching. He held his breath.

Kliev's pursuers stomped past the bushes and continued into the distance. Kliev allowed himself the smallest of breaths and tried to determine where exactly things had taken a turn for the worst. He parsed through his memories.

First, he had stood in the middle of Krijya's grand hall with a flagon of ale in one hand and a roasted leg of mutton in the other. Chief Vintar's eldest daughter had asked about his plans for the evening when it felt like a war hammer had smashed into the top of his skull. Kliev remembered his ears twitching, a thunderous voice telling him something about a book, and a bolt of lightning shooting through the ceiling of the grand hall. It struck him where he stood. There was white light, followed by a deafening ringing in his ears and the feeling of hundreds of electric volts coursing through his veins. The bolt's energy left a sprawling arrangement of branches inked into his back like the tattoos that covered his chest and right arm.

The ale marred Kliev's memory a bit, but he was sure that the resulting fire had caused Vintar's daughter to get burned. That, he figured, was the reason the chief sent a squadron of warriors after him. Or, it could have been because the great hall had been reduced to a pile of ash, waiting to be scattered amongst the winds. Regardless, Kliev was in trouble. There was no way he could make his way back to Krijya until Vintar cooled his head.

Kliev ran a hand along his honey blonde hair, shaved on the sides and pulled back into a topknot. The voice had told him to go to Prodigium and, ever the adventurer, Kliev believed a journey halfway across Lidaesea might be just what he needed. He jumped to the top of the limber pine tree next to him and scanned the horizon. The sparkling turquoise of the Chestastis river flowed at the base of the Krijyan mountains to separate the lands of the Wojlidoj from the country of Hicaria and the forests of the Phreeton. A little past that, across the thickets, was the edge of the Berrenigal Sea.

"A river, a forest, and a sea," Kliev thought aloud. "Quite the journey indeed."

I'll say! boomed the voice in his head. ***When do we eat?***

Kliev jolted sideways, surprised by the voice, and placed his weight on a smaller branch. It snapped clean and sent him tumbling down twenty-five feet of pine toward the rocky tundra below.

In Death, Silent

Verina studied the rippling waters of the lagoon, transfixed by the calming sound of the tide as it splashed against the pillars of the dock. She breathed in the musk of the cave air and reminisced about all the times her father had threatened her.

That wouldn't happen anymore.

He had been reduced to a puddle by the magic that coursed through her veins. Finally, he had been converted into his true spineless and slimy form. She snickered.

That was quite the showcase, Tomekeeper, the woman's voice whispered in compliment. ***I'm impressed.***

Verina snapped her head up and looked around with a glowing smile. "My goddess? You grace me again with your presence?"

Yes, Istio confirmed. ***Let's not call attention to it. Information provided to others is a weakness they can take advantage of. Always keep things close to your chest. Use your thoughts. I'll allow it.***

Do we have enemies, my goddess? Verina thought. *We are safe among your worshippers.*

From this point onward, Tomekeeper, everyone is either an enemy, pawn, or prey, Istio asserted. ***Understood?***

Verina nodded just enough to acknowledge Istio and turned her attention back to the ships that now entered the docks. There were four in total, the first three worn down by the tides of time itself. The last, however, stood out among the group.

It was a stunning black carrack with rectangular, rich blue sails on the front and middle masts. Two triangular white sails, smaller and placed to the sides, helped complete the lumbering frame of the ship and add a splash of brightness. Verina imagined in the pure dark of the night sea, they appeared like a pair of ghastly eyes dashing across the water.

She clutched her satchel, full of what little belongings she had, and made her way down the ramps and toward the bay the carrack was floating into. A ship as regal as the carrack had to be coming from—and heading back to—Prodigium. All Verina needed to do was sneak on, make her way down to the hull, and hide until it docked once again.

Fwen Inati pulled back the strand of olive green hair that dangled in front of her pallid face and tucked it into her bun. Wisps of dark magic absorbed into her skin. As she stood, she smoothed out the wrinkles on her plum-colored dress and turned toward her parents.

Duke Venhal and Duchess Carth sat on iron thrones at the end of the gothic banquet hall. Venhal had a look of displeasure on his face, while Carth seemed deep in thought. Fwen stepped forward and adjusted back into her pristine posture.

"So, my daughter has been blessed by Netot today," Duke Venhal exhaled. His glassy gray eyes narrowed. "Quite a way to get out of attending To'tenkhar Academy."

"Silence, husband," Duchess Carth commanded. She tossed him a look of disgust. "Do you not comprehend the magnitude of this? The power we could wield? The knees we could bend in and outside of the Noctide?"

Fwen placed her hands behind her back, fingers interlocked, and continued to let her parents squabble as usual. Once again, she had no say in the matter. She pressed the tip of her right canine into her lip and retreated into her thoughts. A lifetime spent learning the ins and outs of politics, of making a name for herself amongst the members of the court, only to be propositioned to To'tenkhar Academy like a prized horse for the sake of more familial influence.

Fwen turned her attention to the purple crystals that emitted a soft glow from above. The onyx wings that had erupted from her back were now merged into a heavy cloak. Her shoulder blades ached.

Pain for power, I suppose, she thought. *And chosen by the god of death himself? What power, indeed.*

"Are you listening, child?" Carth berated. The bangs of her raven-black hair fell in front of her face and gave her an unhinged look. "I commanded you to show us the powers of Netot. Once we know what you're fully capable of, we can put you to good use."

Fwen scoffed and motioned with her hands. "Barely chosen and you already want me to perform for you, mother? I don't know how to use these powers yet. I can't even shift the wings back from this accursed cloak."

Carth sneered, tilted her nose up, and turned to her husband. "She's as useless as you are. Send for transportation so that this wretched pup can be on her way to Prodigium."

Duke Venhal pursed his lip and shifted his attention to Fwen. He made a shooing motion with his hands. Message received, Fwen curtsied and rotated on the ball of her left foot to face the doors. Her red eyes blazed with a renewed sense of purpose. She would be back, but she needed an army first.

Yonni observed Queen Monalei as she slept silently on her end of the carriage. Even at rest, the queen was as perfect as could be. Yonni yawned. She understood why her mother was fast asleep—she rarely got a moment to breathe—but Yonni couldn't bring herself to keep her eyes closed. She was too excited, and perhaps too nervous, about the situation at hand. The land above was a tantalizing, yet terrifying, place. There was only the smallest sense of ease within her because she knew that her mother would show her around.

Yonni peered out of the window at the current passing by. Streams of water and bubbles from the aquaway splashed across the glass. She had never taken the aquaways out of the kingdom, only the ones that led from district to district as needed, but she marveled at the vast network the Anqualai had created.

Maybe one day I can travel to the depths, she thought. There were places, and things, rumored to be hidden deep beneath the kingdom of Anqua at the base of the Orlessian Well that Yonni yearned to discover.

Some things are better left alone, Drinex's metallic voice grated in her mind. **Be wary of the siren's call to the unknown.**

Yonni wasn't sure how to respond to the god that occupied her mind or his often intimidating—and unsolicited—advice. She pressed her hand up against the cold window and felt the vibrations of the current on the other end.

Simple acknowledgement is enough, Tomekeeper, Drinex stated. **I'm not fond of wasted breath and empty answers, but I also expect a modicum of respect.**

Are all of you this full of yourselves? Yonni questioned.

Most, Drinex responded promptly.

Yonni rolled her eyes and let out a small sigh. She tried to focus on the terrain outside, searching for a landmark to determine their position. Her tail flicked impatiently.

A small rock smacked into the window and flew back into the current, startling the mermaid princess. As she leaned in to investigate, another one, slightly bigger, impacted the same spot and cracked the window. The crack webbed out swiftly with the tinkling of compacting glass. The cries of distressed wallu picked up outside.

"Mother?" Yonni squeaked. She reached over and tapped the queen's arm. The latter stirred. "Mother, something is-"

Brace! Drinex commanded in an ethereal shout that overwhelmed Yonni's senses.

The carriage flipped with the sound of crunching wood and coral. The cracked window exploded, and shards of glass joined the chaos as Yonni and Queen Monalei tumbled inside. Loud thuds barraged the carriage from the outside, mixed with screams of terror, confusion, and pain from the guards. Yonni felt a heavy pull as the pressure in the carriage shifted and the suction of the aquaway threatened to claim her. The queen clasped the side of the carriage's seat and grabbed Yonni's hand.

Another force impacted the carriage and loosened the queen's grip. Yonni flew back against the window before being sucked out completely by the pull of the current. She tumbled around in the flow, her sense of direction thrown off entirely. Slabs of coral and metal from the other carriages slammed into her. No matter how hard she tried to swim against the current, it was too much. Yonni felt herself drift further away from her mother and the rest of the guard, forced to watch as boulders and jagged rocks tore through what remained of the caravan. Yonni screamed out for her mother.

Drinex, what's going on? Yonni panicked.

It's a cave in from the tunnels. It must have slipped into the aquaway. Princess, you need to protect yourself or you won't survive, Drinex warned. ***Repeat after me.***

"*Nasfuocarin,*" Yonni recited as Drinex placed the word in her mind. Bubbles from the current zipped to her body, wrapping around and combining into a singular form. She bounced along the current in her bubble of protection, sliding around in the slick interior. The bubble sped up and shot upward into a smaller, darker tunnel.

Shadows enveloped Yonni for a moment before light from the land above reappeared. She could feel the state of her body changing as she rose. Her stomach and lungs grew heavier, and an odd tingling rippled down the length of her neck. Suddenly, a shimmer caught her eye. She glanced towards it and saw a layer of golden light grow. The normally shadowed water around her brightened.

Yonni's bubble launched from the tunnel with a pop and rocketed toward the light, making its way across a magnificent trench full of fluorescent creatures and plants. It was like walking into a dream—a flashing rainbow world hidden from those too far above and those too far below. Stone pillars ran up the side, creating what Yonni thought looked like a stone bowl.

We've arrived, Drinex announced. ***The Font is my special sanctum that only keepers of the past have seen.***

The bubble popped and Yonni spun, tail flicking as she tried to regain her balance. She shook her head, hair flowing in the water, and looked up toward the golden light once more.

"We need to get back, Drinex," she said aloud, thoughts of her mother's safety at the forefront of her mind. "I need to make sure they're okay."

The current only flows one direction, Tomekeeper, Drinex responded. ***Not only that, but you were taken through a different tunnel. Even if you could go back, the chances of finding the rest of your people are slim. The only way to truly return is to cross the land back toward the Anquan Circle. That, or continue forth toward Prodigium, claim your tome, and we can have better control over the seas themselves.***

Yonni reflected on Drinex's words and, despite fearing for her mother's safety, agreed that there wasn't anything she could do in the moment. She had been raised to keep pressing forward in the wake of disaster. It was the royal way, after all. Regardless, she felt gross inside for willingly leaving her mother behind. She tried to tell herself that it was what the Queen would have wanted, and that ensuring her arrival in Prodigium was the most important thing, but it did little to assuage her emotions.

Yonni swam to the light and reached out with her hand. As she pressed her fingers against the skim of the water's surface, it rippled outward. There was a whole new set of experiences for her waiting on the other side. Countries and kingdoms she had never seen, and types of people she had never met. There were foods to try, sights to see, and smells to breathe. Yet she was destined to face it all alone. There was no other way.

You're not alone, keeper, Drinex put forth, having invaded her thoughts.

"Thank you, great voice in my mind," Yonni responded with a bit more bite than she had intended. "I do have a question, however. How am I supposed to cross the land above without legs?"

Kliev's legs burned fiercely, yet he willed himself to keep going. Vintar's men had managed to find him in the aftermath of his treetop tumble, and there was no way he was going back to face any sort of punishment from the overzealous Chief. Unfortunately, the jagged and crooked mountainside seemed to be working against him every step of the way. Whether it was the sharp, stabbing pains from stepping on loose rocks or the even sharper, even more stabbing pains of stepping on broken branches, Kliev was exhausted and in more pain than he ever thought possible. His rabbit ears twitched as he heard a high-pitched whistle from somewhere behind him.

Kliev studied the area for a surefire way to escape his pursuers. He snapped his fingers in excitement. A small ledge caught his attention and led to a relatively steep drop just to the east of his location. While a drop that deep would hurt a normal human, the Wojlidoj and their absorbent skeletal structure laughed in the face of danger. He scrambled toward the ledge and leapt down.

Yet again, Kliev's knack for doing before thinking got the best of him. The drop was even further down than he had anticipated, and the shock of landing put a strain on his bones that the rest of him wasn't expecting. He let out a yelp as his body froze and he tumbled down the side, smacking into trees and rocks on the way down to the mountain's base. The sloped ground dropped off again into the turquoise river he had seen from up high, its choppy waters dragging him along to its depths.

Kliev spat out a mouthful of water as he floated to the top. The chill of the Chestastis seeped into his core and wrapped around his lungs. He coughed and tried to take a deep breath, then reached out and grabbed a tangled knot of roots from the river's side.

Kliev held tightly as more frigid water splashed against his face. He tugged the roots to ensure they were secure, then hoisted himself out quickly and rolled onto his back across the forest soil. Birds sang among the branches.

I'm not going to lie, keeper, Wogiwoj howled in laughter from the inner depths of Kliev's mind. ***That was pretty great!***

Kliev gurgled and coughed out the last of the water that burned in his lungs. He stood, exhausted, and waved his fists in the air. "Aren't you supposed to protect me?"

I could, Wogiwoj answered, ***but that makes things way less fun.***

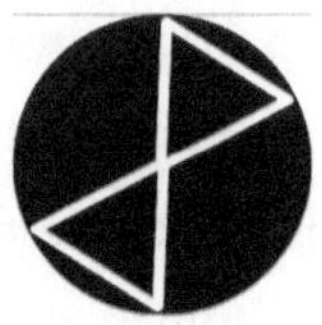

"Verna, protect us," Utic pleaded under his breath. The barge shuddered and the rusted metal groaned as another tentacle whacked it in the side. Utic felt his footing slip and he rolled into a pile of crates. Splinters stabbed him in the back.

"Man the harpoon, boy!" Orghov, owner and captain of the barge, yelled over the roar of the ducoleo. The creature, a gelatinous pink squid slightly bigger than the barge, swam through the sand around them. It crept closer, then leapt above the barge and crashed into the dunes on the other side. It let out a small squawk before it burrowed back into the ground. Orghov pulled his goggles tighter.

"That infernal beast will be coming back for us any moment now," he explained. "Make sure you're ready."

Orghov pulled a lever next to his captain's wheel and the barge lurched forward with a loud bang and a blast of flames from behind. Utic slid across the floor and to the side, where he was able to latch onto one of the barge's side railings. He lifted himself up, legs shaking, and made his way to the harpoon launcher soldered to the barge's front. As the barge picked up speed, the sand beneath them began to swirl.

"I think that thing is keeping up with us!" Utic shouted at Orghov. The latter nodded in response and rolled the wheel to the left. The barge shifted, crossing over a small hill before dipping back down. The ducoleo jumped out again from where the barge had just moved. Orghov let out a loud curse.

"It's coming back around. It's now or never!" he shouted at Utic.

Utic hopped on to the launcher and rotated it around to face the ducoleo's direction. Large sprays of sand shot out from the ground as it borrowed through. Utic felt his hands tremble against the grip of the launcher. He had only learned to use one in case of an emergency attack on Montenau, but that moment never came. Shooting a moving sand beast was an entirely different situation, one he was woefully underprepared for.

Calm, Tomekeeper, Verna instructed sternly. ***I would be made a fool if my chosen were to die before even gathering his true power.***

I'm just a bit frightened by the giant creature trying to eat me, Utic responded. His racing thoughts made it harder to talk in his head.

Most things will. They eat, maim, or kill. Such is life. The sun does not grow colder because you find the heat to be too much. We adapt.

Yes, Verna. Utic replied. Despite his inner doubt, he wasn't about to argue with a goddess.

The ducoleo breached the sand once more and zoomed closer to the barge. Its eye was like a green marble drenched in black oil. The stare bore right into Utic's soul. He steadied his grip, focused his vision down the launcher's sight, and fired the iron harpoon at the monster.

It missed.

Utic reached down and frantically tried to grab another one. Behind him, Orghov yelled something incomprehensible. His hand wrapped around the harpoon and lifted it into the firing chamber. He pressed it forward until it clicked, then replaced the spent ignition crystal in front of the hammer. The ducoleo rushed forward and swerved around to face the barge head on. Utic knew he'd only get one more shot in.

Stop the sand, keeper, Verna chimed in. ***Trust your heart. You know the words.***

Utic nodded, then waited for the ducoleo to get closer, hands steady. It squawked again and leapt from the sand toward the barge.

"Matcahver!" Utic shouted. The sand around the creature suddenly solidified into a dense chunk of sandstone. It let out a cry of pain as the back half of its tentacles got caught and the force slammed it back into the ground. Utic fired again. The iron harpoon whizzed through the air and into the ducoleo's eye with a squelch. The impact sent it back just enough for Orghov to maneuver the barge around it.

"How the hael did you do that?" Orghov shouted from the wheel. "You didn't tell me you were one of those so-called Tomekeepers."

Utic loosened his grip on the launcher and stood. His palms throbbed with pain. He made his way to the back of the barge as Orghov pushed the lever for the throttle back up. The barge drifted across the sand before coming to a stop.

"I don't know what happened," Utic told him. "I just knew what to say. It's like a whole language just unlocked itself inside my head."

Orghov chuckled. "Well whatever it was, it sure saved us. Think you can conjure up some more of those magic words and get us to the Font faster?"

Fwen boarded her family's boat, the *Midnight Lily*, her boots thudding against the sanded wood with every step. The small chest of personals she carried behind her scraped against the ground. She looked around at the crew, a well-organized gang of the best sailors in To'tenkhar, and perhaps even all of Silnathum. As she stepped further onto the deck, a middle-aged man with a ponytail and a ruffled uniform walked up to greet her.

"Madame Inati," he said with a bow. "It's a pleasure to have you on board."

Fwen gave only a single nod in response. She preferred silence when possible. One couldn't calculate and be aware of every acute detail if they were busy running their mouth.

"I'm Captain Halnaur," the man continued, unphased. "You parents have tasked me with bringing you safely across the Erineal to Selenti. I've had your quarters below prepared already. You may do as you wish."

Fwen took the captain's words as an invitation to leave, and did just that. As she stepped down toward her room in the ship's hull, the smell of salt started to tickle her nose.

She despised sailing. The tides churned her stomach and the food was pitiful at best. It was, however, better than being stuck with her parents. She pressed open the door to her cabin and slid the chest into the corner. Fwen closed the door, removed her boots, and laid along the thin, feather stuffed bed she would call her own for the next four days. Her eyes drifted closed. The creak of her wardrobe opening occurred not long after.

Fwen waited patiently, eyes still closed, for the right moment to strike. Too soon would give her attacker a chance to fight back. Too late would mean her death. She reached out and grabbed her assailant's wrist. Her eyes opened to the painted face of a female Terrolaff hidden within a green cloak, dagger pointed toward Fwen's heart.

Of course it's one of those killer clowns, she groaned to herself.

"What are you doing here, you murderous miscreant?" Fwen fumed aloud.

"Sending you back to your cherished Netot," the woman snarked. She placed her free hand against the bottom of her dagger and pressed it toward Fwen's shoulder.

The right side of Fwen's cloak slithered up and knocked the dagger from the woman's hand. It clattered across the floor and came to a rest at the door. The left side of the cloak broke off, becoming a shadowed tendril that wrapped itself around the woman's neck. It lifted her up with ease and constricted her throat.

"You don't have to worry about that," Fwen imparted. "He's already with me."

Fwen felt a slight burning sensation coming from the tendrils. Despite not being a part of her physical body, she could still feel and move them like any other limb. The burning increased until it became a sizzling pain that ate away at her magic.

This one isn't as she seems, Tomekeeper, rang the ice cold voice of death itself. ***I sense magic. Stay your hand.***

Fwen dropped the woman to the floor and stepped back. Her tendrils retreated back to her side. The woman stood, her body radiating hues of noxious green energy.

"You're a Tomekeeper too?" Fwen inquired.

"I follow the whims of my goddess, just as you follow yours. I would do anything to please her," the woman answered. She paused and looked off to the side, then turned her attention back to Fwen. "Istio says I don't have to stain my blade with your blood. Yet."

Fwen shot a tendril toward the dagger and picked it up. She pulled it back toward her, then used the tendril to press the blade into her index finger. She felt the prick of pierced skin and rubbed scarlet along the tip. The tendril tossed the dagger back toward the Terrolaff.

"Consider your blade stained as a sign of goodwill," Fwen asserted. "What do I call you?"

"Verina," the Terrolaff responded. "Verina Hinlon."

"Well met, Verina. I am Fwen of the Inati Family, To'tenkhar's current rulers. If you would like to hear me out, I believe I have a plan that can appease both of us."

Fwen cracked a devilish smile. After all, an army was only as strong as its best general, and there was no better candidate than one hellbent on pleasing the goddess of war herself.

Against the Grain

I'el tracked the rustling bushes, her left eye closed and her right focused on the movement. She nocked her arrow, pulled back, and held it tightly for a moment. The smoothed wood felt natural between her fingers. She let out a slow, steady breath then loosened the grip of her fingers and let her arrow fly.

The bowstring popped in her ear and the arrow disappeared into the bushes where she heard a savage howl respond. A grimphom, one of the horrifying humanoid lizards that lived under the Phreeton ruins outside of Silver Falls, ripped through the bushes with its muddied claws. It let out another howl as it snapped the arrow that pierced through its thigh and then sniffed the air for I'el's scent.

Grimphom weren't smart, but they were deadly for the unprepared. I'el knew from the second she left Farnen's Grove that the creatures had her in their sights, but they didn't know she had her fair share of experience hunting their brethren. It didn't take much for her to coax one into position and sneak behind it.

Two more appeared from the neighboring trees and dropped down to check on their injured companion. It barked some sort of order at them instead. The three grimphom split up and crept across the forest to I'el's position.

She slipped up against a tree and placed her arms across its trunk. The mud that coated her and her bow blended in with its dark brown bark. One of the grimphom passed in front of her, its eye swiveling across every inch of the tree. The amber ring of its iris shrank against its black sclera. It blinked and kept moving. I'el moved deftly behind it, placed her bow around its head and kicked it in the back as she simultaneously pulled the grip forward into its neck. There was a snap followed by silence as the grimphom's body fell into I'el's arms. She gently lowered it to the ground. One down, two more to go.

I'el crouched down into the grass and pulled her hunting knife from the sheathe at her hip. She flipped it around, blade downward, and plunged it into the back of the wounded grimphom as it limped around the tree. She uppercutted into its rectangular jaw before it could make any noise and delivered three more fatal blows. Two down.

I'm impressed, Noli commended. ***I apologize for the imbecile comment earlier.***

I'el furrowed her brow. *I may not be the quickest to learn, or the best at conversation, but I'm very good at what I do.*

The third grimphom stopped and lifted its head into the air as she approached. It seemed calmer than the other two and slightly more aware. I'el watched its nostrils flare and realized it was picking up a scent.

It can't be mine, she thought. *I covered myself up.*

Her eyes glanced down toward the mint-colored blood that adorned her hands and knife. She tilted her head in uncertainty. The grimphom clicked its teeth and turned back toward I'el's direction. I'el laid flat against the ground.

It's going to find me if I don't do something quick, she determined.

Try to talk to the forest, Noli offered. **There is life all around you that can help. Use my knowledge and speak.**

I'el ran through the words that Noli deposited in her head and came across one that she thought was the best for her predicament. She pressed her palms into the cool earth of the forest. The sound of the grimphom walking closer melded with the songs of the birds and the buzzing of the insects. She could hear the water coursing through the roots of every plant around her.

"*Nolavohpe,*" I'el whispered. A mix of roots and vines burst out of the ground around the grimphom and wrapped around its legs and arms to hold it in place. I'el stood and lifted her hands in triumph.

"Ha!" she shouted. "Try to work your way out of that!"

The creature's eyes swiveled around rapidly in what I'el felt was an attempt to determine an escape. It huffed and then flicked both eyes in her direction. The grimphom opened its mouth, saliva dripping between its sharp teeth, and let out a stuttering squawk that resounded through the forest. I'el's smarmy grin dropped when she heard the sound repeated several times. The grimphom had called for help. She chucked the knife between its eyes and silenced it, but it was already too late.

Tuvhe stared down at his metal boots as he felt the eyes of nearly everyone in the village drilling into him. He didn't blame them. If one of the other adjudicarum had shown up covered in blood spatter, he would be curious too. He made his way down the main street of Senna's lower district and into Yegori's Forum, where Marshal Cavner and the rest of his judgen and adjudicarum gathered for their day's work. Snow dusted the rooftops and gave the city a soft white glow. Tuvhe knocked at the spiked metal gate of the Forum and waited for one of the jurinite guards to open it.

Be cautious of what you tell them, Eslen warned. **We both know I'm somewhat of a black sheep among the gods.**

Tuvhe let out a tired chuckle. *That's one way of putting it, Eslen.*

The bronze-armored jurinite opened the gate and let Tuvhe through. The latter walked up the cobbled steps of the Forum's main building and entered. The adjudicarum were assembled in eight rows of ten, each clad in the same silver armor that Tuvhe wore. Ahead of them, the seven judgen stood in a singular row, their golden chest plates and gauntlets sparkling in the rays of sunlight that managed to break through the building's stained glass windows and cracked roof. Marshal Cavner, an older man of imposing stature and the only one to be dressed entirely in gold, stood on a platform at the back. His fluffy white mustache bristled as he spoke to the assembly of soldiers in front of him.

"That is why it's of the utmost importance that we patrol the perimeter. We cannot risk anything going wrong during the festival of the frozen flame. Am I understood?"

A resounding "yes, marshal!" rang through the chamber. Tuvhe was about to step forward and make his way into the group, but someone behind the marshal cleared their throat loudly. Tuvhe leaned to the side to get a better view and let out a sigh of frustration when he saw the maroon robes of Duke Walry, leader of the city of Senna.

Do you have an issue with that man? Eslen inquired.

No, not him specifically, Tuvhe answered. *The duke is... fine. It's more so his-*

"Tuvhe Vull!" an icy voice shouted from across the room. "Are you going to hide in the shadows, or will you make your presence known?"

Tuvhe straightened his back and stepped forward as everyone turned to look at him. A young woman with striking features, a long black ponytail that reached down to the small of her back, and crystal blue eyes that put the brightest of diamonds to shame rounded the Duke. She crossed her arms against her ivory dress and gave him a look that would freeze even the hottest suns.

Oh, Eslen remarked. *I think I understand what happened here. Hael hath no fury.*

"Will you continue to stand there with that vapid expression or are you going to explain to us why you look like the rear end of a horse?" the woman demanded.

"The blood isn't mi-"

"I wasn't talking about the blood, Vull."

Tuvhe heard snickering from various parts of the assembly. He stepped toward the middle of the rows, not wanting to give Rialev the satisfaction of knocking him down a peg in front of everyone else. She was the grand magistrate, the daughter of the duke, and he may have deserved it—if he was being fair to her—but the situation at the Soule Flame was far too important to be swept aside for a lovers quarrel.

"I've returned from the Soule Flame and uncovered dark magic at play," he informed the room. "There seems to be something stirring up forces outside of the Mark."

"What proof do you have of these claims?" Rialev retorted.

The duke stepped in front of Rialev and placed his arm up, as if making a barrier. The creases in his forehead deepened as he chewed his lip. He ran a finger across the tip of his nose and cleared his throat before speaking.

"Tuvhe, what you're suggesting is quite a predicament. Especially this close to the festival. Do you have anything physical that can help us? Whose blood is on you?"

"Judgment's Edge has been destroyed. It was burned down by a horde of ravilors that killed everyone inside. I tracked the Deridens to the Flame and found Tomhaus dead, killed by Yarcon's own hand. He was possessed by some malevolent entity with three irises."

A look of familiarity flashed across Duke Walry's face before shifting into a falsified expression of doubt. He pressed a fist to his mouth and coughed.

"What did you do to Yarcon? If he murdered his brother in cold blood, why is he not here to face punishment as the Sennan laws state?"

Tuvhe hesitated.

Your duke is hiding something, Eslen murmured. ***I can sense it wafting from him. He's trying to draw attention away.***

"Yarcon could not endure sentencing because he was too far gone by the time I met him," Tuvhe answered for all to hear. "It was him or me, and I couldn't risk him coming back to Senna and causing more harm."

"Your concern for our people is commendable, but you know the laws," Marshal Cavner responded. "Only judgens or myself are allowed to carry out on-site execution. That is not a decision an adjudicarum can make, especially for a task that was, if I recall correctly, taken on entirely by yourself and without the permission of your command."

Tuvhe tried to argue but the marshal held his hand up and continued. "We will send out a small group to investigate Judgment's Edge and the Flame, then we shall reconvene for further discussions. Until then, I'm afraid you'll have to be placed in a holding cell."

Tuvhe shook his head at the thought. "I can't be placed in a cell for doing what's right. You don't understand the severity of the situation. Something was coming this way and only I could stop it in the moment."

Marshal Cavner drew his sword from the sheath and stabbed it into the platform. His rounded face reddened with anger. The room grew still.

"You would dare question my command? What gives you the right to tell me what you can and cannot do for breaking our laws and striking down our citizens?"

"**I do!**" Tuvhe yelled in a voice that wasn't his own. His normally brown eyes burned with white heat and his body bent back in an unnatural way. "**I was prepared to stand by and listen to you speak, but it's clear that you have no sense of true justice anywhere in your being. You claim power in the name of being powerful, not in the name of making things right. I will not let someone as incompetent as you stop me from completing my journey.**"

Tuvhe fell to the floor in a clatter of metal and regained control of his body. He heard Rialev gasp and whisper his name. Marshal Cavner stood in frightened silence, as did those around him. Duke Walry cleared his throat once more.

"You've been chosen as the Tomekeeper of the Betrayer," the duke huffed, getting more heated with each word. "There is no greater shame. We cannot take anything you say at face value, nor can we remove you from this plane of existence, you conniving waste! I, Duke of Senna, do not wish to see you in this fair land any longer. You will not bring your plagues and your dishonor to my great people. You, exile of exiles, are to leave immediately!"

The adjudicarum around Tuvhe snapped to attention and withdrew their swords, pointing them at the disheartened Tomekeeper. He raised his hands and got up without a fight. As he stepped backward from the assembly, he locked eyes with Rialev and, instead of the rage or disappointment he was expecting, saw sadness.

That hurt even more.

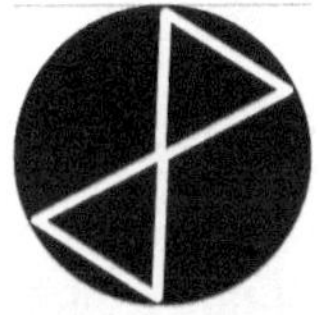

Utic looked up at the twinkling jewels of the night sky and wondered when he would be able to see his family again. For all they knew, or cared, he died in the storm the day before. Regardless, he pictured the joy he hoped they would have if he opened the door and told them of his great adventure and even greater power.

Your admiration for your family is sweet, Verna said. ***Do not let that cloud your mind or affect your decisions, though.***

Utic heard a scrape from behind him and turned to watch Orghov struggle with the tossed crates. He grumbled something beneath his breath before planting a foot through one in anger. Utic stood up and walked over to help the elderly man.

"Well if it isn't the mighty Tomekeeper," Orghov teased. "Come to bless an old crow with those powers? They move crates?"

"No, I don't think so," Utic laughed in response. He kneeled down to grab one. "I'm pretty used to helping out with tasks like this anyway."

Orghov studied him as he stacked the crates back in pairs. "Why you?"

"I'm sorry?" Utic responded in confusion.

"Why choose you?" Orghov clarified. "I grew up hearing stories of the mighty Tomekeepers and all the influential things they've done for Lidaesea. Always imagined them as the picture perfect mixture of intelligence, strength, and beauty. You're just some gangly boy from Montenau."

"Thanks," Utic sneered. "This gangly boy just finished all your work for you."

"And a fine job you did, boy!" Orghov said. "I don't mean to be rude. It's more so out of curiosity. What did Verna see in you that made her think you'd be worthy of wielding such powerful magic? What makes any of us worthy?"

It's a fool's quest to try and find hidden meaning in our actions, Verna chimed in.

Utic smiled in response.

"See! You wonder what I wonder!" Orghov exclaimed. Utic realized he must have mistook the smile to be towards his own comment. He shrugged and let the man continue his train of thought. "What makes fate come down and say 'Today I'm going to change your life. You'll be a beggar no more. No, today you'll be the fairest knight in the land. Maybe a prosperous king, or the most dashing pirate in all the sands!' What I wouldn't give to have just a piece of that glory."

Utic watched as Orghov stepped to the railing of the barge and leaned over to soak in the sight of the desert extending past the horizon. It was a sea of sand, each dune a wave and every rock that dotted it a bubble from its depths. He seemed to be deep in solemn thought. Utic contemplated going over to console the man, but was at a loss for words. Instead, Orghov's voice drifted back to him.

"What was that word you used earlier, boy? The one that made the sand solidify."

Utic joined the old man at the railing. "Matcahver. It means 'stop the sand'."

Orghov threw out his hands and yelled the word at the top of his lungs. The evening breeze tousled the desert particles but nothing else happened. He nodded in understanding.

"It seems like words alone don't do anything. You need the power of the gods themselves. It was worth a try. Say, boy, can you do me a favor?"

"Only if you stop calling me boy and call me Utic instead," the Tomekeeper bargained.

"Alright, Utic," Orghov agreed with an unnecessary inflection on the name. "Will you spin the sands for me? My old lass and I used to sit on this barge and watch the pits of Hourglass Cove whirl around every night before she passed. I haven't been back since. Not the same, you know?"

Utic gave Orghov a tender smile and went through the Lidaesean lexicon in his mind.

"*Qasilvera.*"

The sand in front of the barge began to slide and shake before it turned into a swirling funnel. The soft rattling of the grains of sand passing over one another filled the air. Orghov placed the tips of his fingers on an ornate sapphire pin that adorned the upper right side of his jacket. Utic realized upon closer inspection that it wasn't actually a pin, but rather two sapphire earrings melded together to look like one. The old man seemed adrift in his own memories at first, then muttered words that Utic could barely hear.

"Thank you, Tomekeeper."

Irada Holst was halfway through harvesting the cornfields when he came across the body of an unconscious man. The unknown male was roughly the same age, give or take a year or two, and was wrapped in a large orange cloak. Underneath the cloak was a pair of loose-fitting brown pants and a long sleeved shirt the color of an eggshell, but it was the sharpened spikes sticking out from the soles of his leather boots that caught Irada's attention. He was clearly an Asceniate, one of the people that lived in the mountain nation of Zhondra. How he managed to make it halfway across Lidaesea and into Varlan was a mystery Irada couldn't wait to solve. Irada tapped the man's boot with the blunt end of his sickle and braced for a jump, but nothing happened.

Maybe you need to splash him with some water, a high-pitched and syrupy voice advised him.

Irada looked around nervously to make sure no one else was nearby. "Do I have that power, Heivara?" he whispered.

Water is Drinex's thing, the goddess of the hearth answered back. ***I'm afraid you'll need to find some. Oh! You can use the wagon to take him back!***

Irada looked at the decrepit wagon full of the corn he had worked all day to gather. He knew what the right thing to do was, but that didn't make the idea of leaving behind half of his hard earned bounty any better. His speckled mare whinnied as rain drizzled from the clouds. Irada clicked his tongue, dusted his grimy hands against his ripped brown tunic, and grabbed a shallow iron bucket from the wagon. He placed the bucket on his head, sliding the handle under his chin, and proceeded to drag the man toward the wagon. Irada was used to lifting heavy loads, but the deadweight of the unconscious man felt like sandbags had been tied around his feet. The man's pants and boots carved into the mud as Irada pulled him up to the wagon's side.

Irada hopped into the back of the wagon and started to throw as much of the corn as he could to the side. Every piece pained him that much more. Once the wagon was half empty, he slid his arms under the man's and used every ounce of his strength to hoist him up.

The rain picked up from a drizzle to a thunderous storm. Lightning flashed against the dark clouds swelling in the sky and a crack of thunder boomed through Irada's core. He turned and hopped over the wagon's edge, then onto his mare. He took a moment to tuck the wavy chocolate hair that went halfway down his back into the bucket.

"Hey, Heivara," Irada said as he lightly poked the mare's side. "I just realized that you said we needed water to wake this guy up, and now it's raining. I guess that didn't work."

Yeah, you're right, Heivara replied. ***Whatever happened really knocked him out. Maybe we can try smelling salts next?***

Fwen awoke with a start as the hull of the *Midnight Lily* rumbled violently. Verina, asleep on a makeshift bed at the foot of Fwen's, snored loudly. Fwen jumped up and cracked her neck. She didn't remember falling asleep. In fact, the idea of falling asleep and letting the psychotic harlequin stab her mid-dream had been more than enough to stave away the exhaustion.

Verina had kept her blade hidden away, but Fwen didn't know how long that would last. At some point, however, Verina had nodded off and, as a result, Fwen figured she must have as well. The ship rumbled again.

"Verina!" Fwen yelled at the dozing Terrolaff. "Something is wrong."

Verina rolled onto her other side with a mumble and snored again. Fwen scratched the top of her head in frustration. She turned to grab her rapier, a gift from To'tenkhar Academy for her acceptance, and rotated back around to stop mere inches from Verina's face. She flinched in surprise.

"You woke me up," Verina droned. She wiped her eyes and smudged the black circles that surrounded them.

"Yes, I did," Fwen stated. "Something is happening up top."

Fwen extended out a hand and let Verina exit the cabin first, not intent on letting her new partner slip behind her. The rest of the ship's cabins and hold were eerily empty, yet Fwen could hear voices shouting from the main deck. As the duo ascended the staircase, Verina pushed open the hatch and was met with a sudden blast of heat. She waved the air away and raced through the hatch. Fwen followed quickly behind.

Up above, flames whipped and fanned against the navy sails. The crew of the *Lily* ran around in hysteria as cannon fire crashed across the deck and the starboard flank. Another ship, beige in color with bright red sails, was hooked into the *Lily's* side and pulling closer.

"Are those pirates?" Verina wondered aloud.

"Yes," Fwen confirmed. She could feel her fury swelling as the wood of the *Lily* chipped and cracked around her. "And they just picked the wrong damn ship to board."

Yonni despised the phrase "fish out of water". It was insensitive and mocking, but the words perfectly encapsulated her situation. The air above was much thicker than she had anticipated. Each breath felt like she was swallowing a large ball and shoving it down into her lungs. Her hair had frizzed from the lack of moisture, and her skin burned slightly every time the thing called "wind" decided to blow by. Worst of all, though, was the transformation from fin to legs.

Drinex had promised her that it would be relatively quick and painless. He said that like every Anqualai, her body would naturally adapt to the change in environment and know what to do. It was nothing but lies.

Instead, Yonni had to endure what felt like an eternity of painful evolution.

First, her fin had to dry out and she suffered through the horrible itching of her scales shedding. Then, once she had shed enough, her fin popped into two oozing halves that made her instantly nauseous. The color changed to better match her skin tone, and the last of her scales retreated into her skin. Each felt like tiny needles being pressed into her body and left colorful flecks that dotted her legs. Afterwards, she was forced to gather enough seaweed to craft a skirt long enough to spare her dignity. Night had fallen once more by the time she completed her transformation.

After legs was walking. Learning to walk was a whole other endeavor, one that she desperately wanted to give up on.

I promise you it gets better, and goes faster too, Drinex tried to comfort her.

Yonni ran her hand through the tangles in her curly hair and let out a frustrated yell. She stood, falling immediately back to the sanded shore of the Font. She stood again, took two steps, and faced another tumble. Yonni pounded her fists against the shore and cursed the earth.

"Lady, are you okay?" she heard a child's voice ask in quiet concern.

Yonni looked up to see two children, a boy and girl she guessed to be around ten and eight, staring back down at her. The girl had two red ponytails, a yellow dress, and a shiny blue pearl tucked onto her arms. The boy, dressed in a sleeveless white shirt and red pants, scratched his leg and repeated his question.

"Isn't it a little late for you children to be out playing by the shore?" Yonni inquired with a sincere tone. "Where are your parents?"

"Our mom works at night up at the textile store," the boy answered. He pointed toward the top of the curved shoreline. "It's not as busy, so she lets us come pick out shells for her, long as we're careful."

"Your legs are scary," the girl chimed in. "Why do they look like that?"

Yonni thought about the best way to respond. She didn't want to lie to the children, but she also didn't want to say anything that went over their heads. She pointed toward her legs. "I'm a mermaid who just got my legs. I don't really know how to walk. Can you help me?"

The kids looked at each other in surprise.

"A mermaid? Wow!" the girl shouted. She jumped up and down enthusiastically. "This is the best day ever!"

"We can help," the boy added. "But you have to carry some shells for us. Oh, and I want to learn to speak wallu!"

Kliev pushed through bushes and branches as he made his way through the moonlit forest of Hicaria. His senses were heightened by the dark and he felt his back tense up at the slightest noises. He sniffed the air for some semblance of civilization, but was only met with the stench of moss and pine. Kliev wrinkled his nose and bent his ears in. While the long ears were great to keep him warm in the snowy mountainside of Krijya, they kept smacking into every tree or stick to the mucky surface of the vines he passed.

Where's your sense of adventure, keeper? Wogiwoj boomed. *This whole journey is about getting out of your comfort zone, and I can definitely tell you're uncomfortable!*

Kliev's stomach gurgled loudly. He tried to remember the last time he had eaten.

I could go for a snack too, Wogiwoj agreed. *A big leg of mutton, some pitchers of honeyed mead, and a couple of pies.*

"If that's a snack, I worry about what a meal for you is," Kliev responded. "Come to think of it, I'm not feeding you, am I? You're not sucking out my life juice?"

That's disgusting, Wogiwoj expressed. *I just live through your experiences. At least for now.*

Kliev stopped. "Wait, what do you mean for now?"

Before Kliev could get an answer, a scream echoed through the forest. His ears twitched and twisted to find the direction. He tracked the scream and the sounds of a tussle to the south of his location. Kliev rushed toward the sound. As he ran, large stone columns steadily appeared.

Ruins, maybe? he thought as he hopped on top of a crumbled gray slab.

Looks like it, Wogiwoj confirmed. ***Probably from those old elves.***

Kliev hopped over to another pillar, then a second slab. He dropped flat to his stomach and watched as five odd lizard-like creatures chased someone across the ruins. Kliev squinted his eyes to try and make out who it was.

That's a Phreeton woman! Wogiwoj informed him.

"And a real stunner at that," Kliev added. It was time to save the damsel in distress. He dropped down, smoothed back his hair, and took off as fast as he could. Up ahead, the woman shot two of the lizard creatures squarely in the chest with arrows, and a third in the face. They fell to the ground in just enough time for Kliev to jump over their bodies. Another arrow soared, this time to the fourth lizard's knee. It squawked and stood still, claws gripped around the arrow's shaft. Kliev took the chance to smash his own knee into the back of its head.

The final lizard leapt onto the woman's back and pressed her face first into the forest soil. Despite her struggles, she couldn't shake it off. It croaked at her and pulled its claws back for one last slice. Kliev grabbed the throwing ax off of his pack and launched it into the back of the lizard's head with a sickening thwack. It made a screeching noise and stumbled away from the woman. She flipped over and delivered a kick into its stomach.

Kliev leapt through the air and landed in front of the woman. He threw his hand up at her and cleared his throat.

"Don't worry, madam. I'll take care of you from here."

He gave her a wink and turned to face the still-screeching creature. He clapped his hands together and pointed toward the sky.

"*Carinogi*!"

A singular bolt of lightning flashed from the sky and struck the ax in the creature's head, serving as a conduit and exploding the lizard into a mint cloud that covered Kliev and the elven woman. He turned to her with a look of sheer excitement, his chest heaving from the adrenaline.

"What the hael is wrong with you?" the woman cried out, desperately wiping the mint green spatter off of her face and clothes. Chunks clung to her orange hair. "Why would you explode it?"

Kliev gave her a look of confusion. She should have been grateful, not frustrated. He didn't understand what went wrong.

Odd way of saying thanks, Wogiwoj noted. ***But I like her!***

Pillars of Fire

The sound of steel clashing against steel rang out over the open sea. Cannon fire volleyed between the *Midnight Lily* and its attacker, shredded wood and shrapnel erupting from the tops and sides. The crew of the *Lily* fought boldly as the attacking pirates, covered in bright red and yellow tattered clothes, overwhelmed them all. Verina didn't care about the lives of the crew or the wellbeing of the ship. She simply wanted something to stab.

From the moment Fwen had awoken her and she smelled the sweet scent of smoky disaster above them, Verina's heart was pounding. The Noctide royal had let her guard down to sleep, and it took Verina all the self-control she had to not make it a permanent rest instead. Istio had commanded that she wait and see how things turned out. The goddess of war even told her that Fwen could prove to be a useful pawn in the long game. Verina had no choice but to obey.

Now, nothing would keep her from doing what she did best. She was a beast let loose from her cage, a rabid animal ready to rip apart anyone in her way. Her hand reached up and grabbed a rope hanging from one of the masts. She ran and jumped, using the motion to swing across the gap between the two ships. She drew her dagger mid-flight and landed on one of the pirates at the ship's edge. A couple of quick stabs and a roll led her to her next target, then the next. She laughed giddily at their screams.

Verina looked back toward the *Lily* and caught sight of Fwen being surrounded by a group of scoundrels. She thought about throwing one or two or her blades over to help, but held off.

Let her have her fun too, she decided.

"Noklintei!" Fwen shouted from the middle of the crowd.

The words carried a dark magical aura across the air that ran a slight chill down Verina's spine. Shadowed tentacles whipped out of Fwen's back and wrapped themselves around various parts of the pirates' bodies. A few moments of snapping and crunching later, Fwen stepped over the bodies of her victims and made her way across the deck. Verina was impressed.

She'll definitely be a good asset, Istio hissed. ***Just make sure you stay in control, and don't let her gain the upper hand.***

Verina stabbed the pirate sneaking up behind her in the gut without even looking his way.

Yes, Istio. I'll play along as you commanded.

A loud thunk drew her attention towards the center of the deck. An inhumanly tall man with a blazing red coat, long wavy blonde hair, and the body of a barrel stepped towards her. His wooden left leg thunked heavily against the ship's deck with every step. Verina guessed the middle-aged man was the captain of the pirate's crew, and an intimidating one at that.

"You think you can hop aboard my ship and stab all my crew down with that little toothpick of yours?" the captain growled, his jaundiced eyes drawing her attention. He tugged at the oversized cutlass by his side.

"That's what you call a crew?" Verina mocked. She crouched down and angled her dagger outward. "They all seemed like sorry excuses for men to me. Even died with tiny whimpers."

She hit a nerve in the captain and he let out a guttural roar. He charged forward and swung his sword down toward the space where Verina was standing. She leapt back, spun her dagger, and jumped to the captain's side. She stabbed him once in the ribs and then in the right thigh before he smacked her away. Verina tumbled into a roll and thrusted her dagger into the wood to stop her momentum. The captain followed closely behind with a boot to her chest. It knocked her onto her back and filled her lungs with fire.

"All that talk for two good hits?" he said as he stood at her feet and pressed his sword against her neck.

"Where's the fun in killing you outright when I can make you suffer first?" the Tomekeeper responded smugly.

Verina kicked the Captain in his right kneecap and made him buckle. She took advantage of the moment and scrambled around him to grab her dagger and jump on his back. She tried her best to wrap her legs around his torso, squeezing with all of her might as she started to stab and slice with no plan in mind. After the first twenty, she stopped counting. Her vision tunneled and she lost control of herself entirely. All the anger she had welled up in herself over the years leaked outward into her blade. She felt possessed, yet oddly at peace.

Slice and stab.

Stab and slice.

"-u to stop, Verina!" Fwen's voice broke through her haze.

A sludgy tentacle wrapped around Verina's hand and kept it in place. She looked up at the young Noctide woman in a dulled stupor. Fwen's pallid face looked even more drained in the rising sun.

"It's over," Fwen stated. "I won't tell you to stop again."

Verina looked down at the ghastly acidic mess that was under her. Her breathing had become strained and heavy at some point, and the muscles across her entire chest felt like they were pulled in every direction. Her right arm was numb. The darkness receded.

Verina turned her attention to Fwen. "Did I do this?"

Fwen gave her an odd look in return and extended a hand. "Are you okay? I mean beyond the obvious 'killing to please your goddess' bit."

Time seemed to slow as Verina fell deep into her thoughts. She stared at Fwen's hand, elegant and surprisingly dainty, and wondered if she should accept. There had only been one person who truly cared about her, and while there was a strong chance Fwen was just feigning so in an attempt to win her trust, something about the gesture seemed genuine.

Verina took Fwen's hand and stood with her help. Her legs wobbled from hours of squeezing a corpse. As the sun rose from the ocean's depths, she looked out toward the *Midnight Lily*. Its sails had been shredded down to a bare minimum, masts were cracked in half and hardly holding, and holes from cannon fire dotted the deck and side. Charred marks ran along most of the edge and up the pillar of the central mast. The crew of the *Lily*, a fourth of what it once was, tossed the bodies of the pirates into the choppy waters below.

"Captain Halnaur informed me we should still be able to make it to Selenti, but barely," Fwen told Verina. "Our lack of sails will cost us a day's travel, but our ignition crystals could provide us a necessary boost, should we need one. That means, unfortunately, that we will be unable to fire the cannons should we get attacked again."

Verina locked eyes with Fwen, raging fire against glittering gold and green.

"Then we take them on ourselves. Anyone and everyone foolish enough to come at us. What better pair than death..."

She paused for emphasis, pointed at Fwen, then pointed back at herself.

"and war."

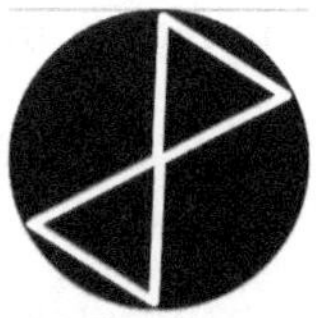

Utic braced himself as the sand barge skidded against the harder rock of the Font and came to a steady crawl. The back engines hissed and blew out a puff of saffron-tinged smoke. Orghov guided the barge in carefully, anxious to avoid scratching the side against the wood of the dock. There was a shudder of metal, then a stop.

"Another clean landing," Orghov said triumphantly. He shook the sand off of his beard and coat.

Utic peered down the docks. The fishing village of Konasus was the arrival point for any travelers anxious to see the Font. A multitude of shacks and huts lined a number of sprawling dirt roads that stretched back to the edge of the hillside. In front of him was the market with stalls squished tightly together, each selling various types and colors of aquatic wildlife that could only be found in their backyard. The area had a strong smell to it that threatened to cling to his clothes.

Further down the hillside, just barely in view, was the cusp of the Font itself. It was a massive stone bowl that was said to produce a rainbow of glowing colors at night. Travelers to Montenau talked often about the purple squids that would gather during their mating season and splash geysers of water into the air. Utic shivered at the thought. He had dealt with one too many squids already.

"Enough daydreaming," Orghov uttered with a hard pat to Utic's back. "You go on ahead and try to find someone to take you the rest of the way to Prodigium. I'm going to find some buyers for my wares."

He guided Utic toward the barge's railing and kicked the ladder down. As the Tomekeeper descended, he gave a small wave and a few parting words. "Reconvene by sunset. I don't want you by yourself come nightfall."

Utic nodded and dropped off the stairs and onto the dock with a thud. He made his way down the path and into the market. Crowds of people bumped and shoved him as he tried to make his way through. Panic quickly set in. While the crowds in Montenau were bad, there was plenty of space for people to spread out within the market's main square. In Konasus, the same number of people were shoved onto roads a quarter of the size. He could feel his chest getting tight. Utic pressed against the swarm of people around him and forced himself out of the mass with a stumble and a gasp.

Utic didn't know where to begin looking for travel in the overcrowded market, so he opted to go down one of the side roads instead. It curved and rolled down to the edge of the village and closer towards the Font.

Are you okay? Verna asked. ***I can feel the stress on your body.***

Yes, Verna, Utic responded quickly. *I'm just trying to find an alternative. Don't worry.*

I trust your actions, keeper. Besides, it's nice to gaze upon the Font again.

Were you there when it was created? Utic inquired. He quickly realized it was a horrible question to ask. Surely the gods knew of each other's feats.

Do not assume, Tomekeeper, Verna remarked. He forgot that she could hear his thoughts. **I was not present when Drinex created his Font. In fact, I didn't know until he surprised me with it.**

Utic stopped outside the door to a shack covered in gleaming shells. *Wait, what do you mean? Were you two together?*

Before Utic could get an answer, the door swung open and whacked him in the face. He felt his nose squish in and cried out as he was thrown onto his back. He placed his hands over his face as a pounding pain started to develop behind his eyes and forehead.

"Oh no! I'm sorry!" a high-pitched, animated voice yelled out. "Please forgive me. Oh, by the grace of the queen, I really am sorry."

Utic removed his hands and blinked. The sunlight flared against his newly sensitive vision. As his eyes adjusted, he could make out the blurry shape of a younger woman kneeling in front of him. He blinked again and his vision cleared. The densely packed curls of the woman's turquoise hair and her shining emerald eyes were unlike anything he had ever seen, complemented beautifully by the sepia of her skin. He was at a loss for words.

"Are you alright?" the woman asked as she pressed her hand against his cheek and looked him over.

Utic blushed and scrambled to his feet. "That was my fault. I should have been paying more attention to where I was walking."

The woman looked down in embarrassment. "Um, do you mind helping me up? I'm having a hard time standing."

Utic obliged and held out a hand. She took it and stood, shaking the entire time. He placed his arms under hers to help provide support.

"I know you asked me, but, are you okay yourself?" he questioned. "You can barely stand. Maybe you're a little dehydrated?"

The woman let out a snort and covered her face immediately in shame. "That's one way to put it, yes. I'm from Anqua, actually. This whole land thing is very new to me."

Utic's eyes went wide. "Anqua? You mean to tell me you've traveled all this way? Why?"

She's a Tomekeeper, Verna interrupted. ***I can sense it. I'm not sure why Drinex chose a young woman this time, though.***

"A Tomekeeper?" Utic accidently said aloud.

The woman froze.

"You're Drinex's Tomekeeper?"

Her eyes widened. "How did you know that?"

"Well, you see... Um," Utic stuttered. "Verna says hello."

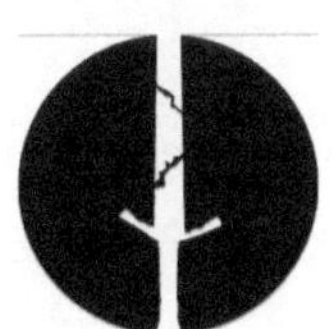

Tuvhe watched the snow drift down across the graves as he sat under the cemetery's lone tree. The gnarled branches above him creaked under the building weight of the snow, but never broke. It reminded him of his own spirit, in a sense. He removed his gauntlet and slowly ran his hand over the rough edges of the six markers in front of him.

"I'm sorry I failed you all," he uttered quietly. "I promise I'll make things right. I'm heading home."

Tuvhe shimmied his gauntlet back over his hand and kneeled down. The snow crunched softly under him.

"I don't know if I'll ever be able to come back. I've been cast out. If I return, I'll come here right away and share all my adventures. I'll tell you how much Prodigium has changed since we left. And if I can't return, well... I'll always carry you all in my heart."

The snap of a twig behind the tree drew his attention. The flit of a white dress and crystalline eyes disappeared behind the trunk. Tuvhe looked back towards the graves of his younger siblings and gave a bow of respect.

"I could sense you watching," Tuvhe said aloud to no one in particular. He was met with silence. "I just want to say before I leave that I'm sorry. I know it might not mean much, and you might not ever forgive me, but I'm sorry for hurting you. I was hoping to make things up some way, somehow, but I'm sure you know better than anyone that my hands are tied."

A snowball impacted the back of his head and burst into a cloud of white powder.

"I should have expected that," he continued. "If this is the last time I see you, just know that while I don't deserve you in any capacity, I do love you. Dearly."

Tuvhe stood and wiped the snow from his hair. He paused for a response, then made his way down the hill toward the cemetery gate. Steps away from the gate, another snowball splashed against his armor. Tuvhe swiveled to face Rialev as she stood on the hilltop. Her dress billowed in the breeze.

"Tuvhe Vull, you are an idiot and a coward," Rialev asserted. She wrapped her arms around herself and looked off to the side. "You're right. You don't deserve me. So when you come back—when, not if—I want you to ensure you've become a man that does."

Tuvhe placed his hand on his heart in response. No more words needed to be shared. He opened the gate and walked down the cobblestone path toward the city's main archway.

Do you trust her? Despite the fact that her father is clearly hiding something? Eslen asked. He had been silent since his outburst in Yegori's Forum. Tuvhe didn't know if it was from shame, or simply because he had nothing else to say.

"I trust her more than I trust you after what you did," Tuvhe stated boldly. There was no point in hiding his secret any longer. Word of his newfound partnership had spread quickly.

I only stepped in because I saw that something was wrong, Eslen explained. ***This place is sick. It has a dark presence festering beneath its surface that needs to be cleansed. The duke has something to do with it, but I don't know what yet. Help me obtain my justice, and I'll see to it that you get yours as well.***

The chant of low incantations reverberated off of the glassy surface of the obsidian fight pit as Zall Destus entered. Lava bubbled around the pit's perimeter and gave off a scorching heat that would have cooked most people alive. Such was the blessing that Hilaster, god of fire, gave to his people. To Zall, and the other Pyrolites of Empyron, the heat of the volcanic Hilaster's Peak was nothing unusual.

Zall stepped up to the ivory totem shaped like their sacred animal, the hilvundata, and dipped his fingers in the bowl of thick tar that sat atop it. He smeared it across his face and arms in the style of the Pyrolite's spiritual symbols and was careful to avoid the spiraling black tattoos that covered his arms and chest. They were a work of art dedicated to Hilaster himself, a sign of pure devotion to the Betrayed that took years to develop. Every spiral was a battle fought, and every spike that ended them a kill taken. Zall was among the most decorated of the Pyrolites, and Hilaster chose him for that exact reason. The Tomekeeper walked to the opposite end of the pit and faced its entry.

"Bring in the next combatant!' Empress Bahn yelled from her extravagant wicker throne at the top of the pit. Her jewelry, composed of platinum, hilvundata fangs, and red diamonds, jangled as she waved her arm toward the entry. The chanting below her increased in volume.

Zall studied the Empress diligently. She was only slightly older than he was, and her flowing white hair—dyed from a mixture containing the volcano's ashes—stood out among the jet black of everyone else. Her skin was a dark olive compared to Zall's light brown, but their chestnut eyes were the same.

Zall hated her with every fiber of his being.

Bahn had taken everything from him. All that he scratched and clawed for was stripped away in a singular moment on her behalf. She caught him staring and gave a wicked smirk that made his blood boil.

Thunderous footsteps drew his attention back toward the entry where a blaishand, a muscular mammoth of a soldier clad only in black leather straps, made his way in. The blaishand pushed the totem over and roared.

So the empress wants a challenge? the raucous voice of Hilaster noted. ***We'll make this quick, then. Show them who you are. Show them that everything burns.***

Zall scratched the side of his shaved head, then took three steps forward and snapped his fingers.

"*Behfuohil.*"

A ball of flame launched from his hand and onto the ground where it erupted into a full column of fire. The column shot forward and engulfed the blaishand. As his screams filled the arena, Zall summoned another column. The second column swerved around the burning man and hit the spilled grease of the totem, igniting it instantly. The pool of flames flickered furiously.

Zall watched as the blaishand dropped to his knees, screams silenced. His blood began to boil again.

"That's all you have for me?" he snarled at Bahn. The small knot of hair at the back of his head bounced. "This weakling that couldn't even withstand a slight singe?"

Bahn stood, furious, and clapped her hands together. Five more blaishands quickly made their way out into the arena.

"That's better!" Zall hollered. His body shook with excitement. "Now watch them burn!"

That's right, Hilaster egged him on. ***Make them suffer. Make her pay for ever doubting you.***

"*Hilasev!*"

Balls of white fire rained down onto the blaishands and against the obsidian floor. Zall basked in the heat of it all, and for the first time in years, he laughed.

Irada held the smelling salts under the mystery man's nose and hoped for the best. He had grown sore from carrying his weight around the farm and opted to finally put the man in a bed of hay in the barn. It was a simple solution, but it would have to do until Irada could wake him. The man's nostrils flared at the smell of the salts and he bounced up with a gasp.

I told you! Heivara cheered.

The man scooted off the hay and fell to the barn's muddy ground. Irada quickly dropped down to help him back up.

"Are you alright, mister?"

The man waved Irada away and winced in pain as he tried to walk. He gave up after a few steps and crumpled to the floor. Irada watched from behind, unsure of how to proceed.

"I got it," the man groaned with a mouthful of what Irada hoped was just mud. "I just have to get my legs to respond."

He rolled over and tugged at the laced V-neck of his shirt. His hands trembled slightly. Irada reached over and grabbed a flagon of water.

"You should drink up," Irada told him. He offered the flagon. "I'm not sure how long you've been out, but that should help."

"What do you mean?" the man questioned in a brash voice. He ran his hand through his short taupe hair. "Where am I?"

"I found you out in the fields on my rounds," Irada recounted. "I was gathering corn when I saw your body. I carried you to my wagon, came home, and now you're here. I'm Irada, by the way."

"Yeah, yeah," the man said impatiently. He pointed his thumb at himself. "Qio. Qio Lod. That still doesn't answer my question, though. Where is 'here'?"

"Varlan," Irada answered. "We're outside the village of Dwelar, in the plains, to be specific. Tiny place of about eighty people."

"The Varlan Plains?" Qio repeated irately. "No, No, No. I need to get to Prodigium as soon as possible!"

Irada stepped back and thought about the odd situation he found himself in. If Qio was in such a hurry to get to Prodigium, and given his unusual arrival, that meant that he was a Tomekeeper as well.

Correct, Heivara confirmed. ***I can sense it.***

Is there any way to mask that, Heivara? I don't know about this guy. I don't want him to learn about us just yet.

We're only detectable to one another once our magic is used, Heivara informed him. ***Think of it like a big smoke signal. The more magic, the bigger the signal. Since you haven't used any yet, you're hidden for now.***

Irada pulled himself out of his mental retreat and saw that Qio was already outside of the barn. Irada followed and called out to him. Qio whipped around in frustration.

"What do you want?" he snapped. "I need to go. Now."

"First, I need you to breathe," Irada responded. "I can tell you're still having a hard time walking. You're stumbling like a newborn foal. Dwelar is right between Selenti and Prodigium. I can grab the wagon and we can head out, but you'll have to let me take care of a few things first."

"And if I refuse?"

"Then you'll be walking your way to Prodigium, because no one will want to deal with that sore attitude."

Irada didn't want to call Qio on his rudeness, but he had no choice. He wanted answers about the Tomekeepers, how Qio ended up in his fields, and so much more. There was no way that he could let Qio walk away. Irada held his breath and hoped that his reasoning worked.

Qio let out a deep sigh and stuck his hand out. "Yeah, sorry. I don't mean to be harsh, I've just had a bit of a rough journey so far."

"Well, tell you what, Qio. You can tell me all about it while we wrap up my duties," Irada proposed and shook his hand.

I'el desperately wanted to throttle Kliev, and they had only been together for half a day. Something about the way he spoke, like he was the smartest and mightiest man in Lidaesea, rubbed her entirely the wrong way. He refused to apologize for covering her in grimphom gunk and kept spouting something about saving her, then immediately tried to flirt with her after. It was maddening. She thought back to her sweet Friston and how he could never be so crass.

Strength in numbers, Noli had told her, as if that would have smoothed things over. I'el looked back at Kliev as he curiously approached a white ball burrowed into the ground.

"No, don't touch that!"

It was too late. I'el jumped forward and tackled Kliev to the ground as the puffpom whistled and rose into the sky. It vibrated with a shrill whine and shot its thorns into the ground around it. I'el felt one stab through the wool of her pants into the back of her calf.

"Thanks for the save, beautiful," Kliev said with yet another wink. "Want to make sure I didn't get hit by one of those nasty needles?"

I'el plucked the one from her calf and stabbed it into Kliev's shoulder. He cursed from the pain.

"Oh look. I found one," she fumed.

I'el picked herself up and checked for more thorns. The tangles of her hair fell in her face. It still reeked of grimphom. She shook them back into place and glanced down the path. They just needed to cross the creek and make it around the bend to Silver Falls. Kliev stepped up behind her.

"What's the plan?" he inquired.

"We go a bit further down. There's some rocks that we can hop across and from there, nice and easy."

Kliev pressed up against a hefty log and crossed his arms. "Nothing's going to try and eat me, right?"

"Nothing except that beareetle you're leaning on," I'el answered. She knew it was harmless, but Kliev didn't need to find out so soon.

The log shuffled and shook as the beetle's head poked out of the log's open end. The white bony casing around it gave it the appearance of a bear's skull. The beareetle screeched and Kliev hopped back in response. His ears quivered lightly.

"You're fine, bunny boy," I'el teased. "He only eats plants."

Kliev adjusted his vest and posture. "Yeah, I totally knew that. I was just playing along with your joke. You know, letting you have a laugh."

I'el raised an eyebrow at him and nodded slowly. She turned and started walking to the river.

Noli popped back into her head. ***You don't have to be so mean to him,*** she said. ***He's just trying to impress you.***

I'm not a fan of the tough guy act, I'el responded. *I like the soft, sweet nature of a man like Friston. You know, someone who will sing me songs while we lay in a field and stare up at the moons. Someone who checks in to see how I'm doing and wants to be half of a team with me.*

I find that sometimes plants grow stronger when they are planted into unknown soils, Noli remarked.

The soft trickle of water signaled that the duo had reached their destination. I'el looked across the gently flowing creek to the path on the other side. There were a handful of large rocks interspersed throughout, just wide enough to jump on.

"Last one to the other side has to sleep in the buff tonight!" Kliev announced as he sprinted ahead of her.

I'el felt her cheeks get hot when she realized what Kliev had said and rushed to get across the rocks herself. Her jump was further than a human's, which meant she could cross two or three rocks at a time, but it was no match for the fantastic leaping ability of a Wojlidoj. For every three she passed, Kliev passed five.

You're going to let him win? Noli asked in surprise.

"No way!" I'el shouted. *"Nolavohpe!"*

Vines sprouted from the water and wrapped around Kliev's ankle. They tugged him into the creek with a splash. I'el laughed as she got ahead of the soaked, and sulking, womanizer. She landed awkwardly on the next rock and slipped into the water face first. The rush of cold made her whole body tingle and shake.

I'el dragged herself out and spat out the water in her mouth. The taste of soiled fish lingered on her tongue. Kliev followed behind her as she wrung out the excess from her clothes.

"Let's call it a tie, yeah? No one loses," he muttered in defeat.

I'el agreed and pushed through the trees, then around the small hill to the breathtaking view of Silver Falls straight ahead. The log cabin of the trading post rested on a floating platform in the middle of a lake, connected to the mainland by a rickety bridge. Towering behind it was the titular waterfall, its rapids like cascading currents of liquid mercury. I'el loved everything about it.

"What is that?" Kliev quaked and pointed. I'el turned to investigate the shadow that eclipsed them and the chirps that accompanied it.

"Oh, that?" I'el breathed a sigh of relief. A ship attached to two canvas balloons and drawn by swarms of thistlewisps, human-sized birds covered in flowers that grew from the moss on their feathers, emerged from the clouds. "That's our ride!"

My, those have gotten bigger, Noli noted.

"I thought you said we were getting on a boat?' Kliev questioned in disbelief. His voice and expression dripped with fear.

I'el gave him a bright, goofy smile.

"Uh, yeah! That is a boat, silly. An air boat. How else would we get to Selenti?"

Yonni clung tightly to Utic's back, her new legs supported by his arms as they ran through the marketplace. At that moment, she was thankful the woman in the textile shop had been nice enough to gift her a soft white pair of what people on the land above called "pants", even if she didn't seem to fully believe Yonni's story. Even better, her detour had put her on a collision course with another Tomekeeper.

Things are looking up from here, Drinex added. ***We can get to Prodigium that much quicker, and you have someone to travel with to keep you out of trouble. Though I'm not certain why Verna chose a young man this time.***

What is the story between you two, anyway? Yonni pried. Drinex's personality seemed to become more pleasant now that Utic and Verna had arrived.

One for another time, Drinex stated succinctly.

Utic slowed as they arrived at a rusted barge, his breath shallow.

"Just have to climb the ladder," he wheezed.

Yonni didn't respond. She stared out across the sand and rock as the sun set. Streaks of orange, yellow, and red melted together with splotches of blue and purple to blanket the horizon in one of the most eye-catching sights she had ever seen.

"You get to see this every day?" she said in awe.

Utic took a break from climbing to gaze in the same direction as Yonni.

"The sunset? It's great isn't it? In Montenau, there are these square balconies that you can go up to and watch as it sinks behind the dunes. Maybe I can show you sometime."

"I'd like that," Yonni replied enthusiastically. "It sounds like a great time!"

Yonni was happy that Utic was so friendly, even if he came across as a bit unsure of himself. He seemed like a good-natured person, and a great guide to show her around the land above. Thoughts of the other Tomekeepers entered her mind. She wondered if they would all be just as warm and welcoming.

Utic clasped the barge's railing and pulled them both over the edge. He crawled to the center of the deck, Yonni still tightly attached.

"Orghov!" he called out. "I'm back!"

A hatch on the floor of the barge was thrown open and an old man with a white beard and goggles popped out from inside. He sniffed and rubbed his beard.

"What's this, Utic?" the man asked playfully. "Making friends?"

Utic helped Yonni off of his back and walked over to meet him.

"You won't believe it, Orghov. She's a Tomekeeper! For Drinex, in fact. She came all the way from Anqua, and now we can head to Prodigium together. Isn't that great?"

"That's amazing!" Orghov exclaimed, arms outraised. "I'm glad I sent you into the village then. Were you able to find transportation?"

Yonni watched as Utic silently cursed to himself.

"No, I forgot in my excitement, then saw the sun was setting and came right back."

"No matter," Orghov replied. "I worked out a deal and think I can get everything settled."

The old man turned to Yonni and pulled his goggles down. Dark tattooed lines spiraled out into sharp points from around his eyes. It was a symbol Yonni had seen before, but couldn't recall from where.

"Two Tomekeepers. My, have I been blessed tonight."

Yonni felt a hard object whack her against the back of her head and send her to the floor of the barge. Utic yelled something she couldn't make out before he was silenced by a whack of his own. She heard the thud of his body hit the barge and Drinex's voice call to her, but it was lands away. The old man's croaking laughter settled into her ears before she succumbed to the black blanket of unconsciousness.

Of Mountains and Molehills

Qio Lod studied the ramshackle village with a hint of disdain. Irada had been right when he mentioned that Dwelar was a small village of eighty people. In fact, Qio could argue it was even less. The shacks were barely held together from the mud that coated the crevices in place of clay, and a single wide path divided the village into equal halves. The Asceniates didn't have much back in the Zhondran mountains, but they were able to do a lot more—and a lot better—than the poor excuses for homes and clothing that the villagers of the Varlan Plains did. It was all such a pitiful sight.

Judge, and you too will be judged, the mellowed voice of Zhonitas imparted.

Look who finally decided to show back up, Qio complained. *It would have been nice to have some guidance after you blasted me halfway across Lidaesea.*

To adventure is to begin anew. Only through the bonds of our companions and the growth of our self through trial can we truly understand our path in life, Zhonitas told him.

That's a whole lot of empty words from someone who lived out his days on top of a cliff, Qio criticized. *How about you do me a favor and just go back to being silent?*

Qio felt a piece of his soul grow cold, then disappear entirely.

"Huh. Well, I guess that worked," he mumbled under his breath.

"Did you say something?" Irada said from beside him. He pulled back the horse's reins and slowed the wagon to a stop outside of a shack even smaller than the rest. Irada took off his straw sunhat.

"Wait here for just a second," he told Qio, then jumped off the side and moved to the back. Irada rustled through some of the bags and pulled out two dulled twine sacks. They were stuffed to the brim with fresh produce straight from Irada's farm.

"Why does this house get two when the others only received one?" Qio asked.

Irada didn't answer. Instead, he walked up the stairs and knocked at the crooked door of the shack. After a moment, an exhausted young woman and four small children opened. The children threw up their hands in joy.

"Mr. Holst is here!" one of the children exclaimed.

"I hope you brought carrots!" yelled another.

Irada handed the woman both sacks and waved to the kids.

"As promised," he said. "I'll be back again soon, okay?"

The woman nodded and shooed the kids back inside. She turned and quietly thanked Irada, then closed the door. Irada made his way back and hopped up onto the wagon.

"You didn't answer my question," Qio nagged. "Why two sacks?"

"She's got four little ones and a fifth on the way," Irada answered as he snapped the reins. The wagon jostled forward. "She has to have extra to help the baby develop."

"Isn't it her husband's job to provide for her since he's the one that decided to give her that many kids?" Qio snarked.

Irada put his hat back on and tilted it down over his eyes. "Her husband just passed, Qio. She's a widow."

Qio fell silent and bit his cheek. He didn't mean to sound so crass, but honestly, there was no way he could have known. At least the excuse of it gave him comfort. He tightened the strings of his shirt.

"Since you're so keen on asking questions, mind if I ask a few of my own?" Irada said to break the silence. "That was the last delivery, and there's a whole lot of nothing to keep us entertained between here and Prodigium."

"By all means," Qio responded with a wave of his hand. He leaned his head back against the seat of the wagon and closed his eyes. "How long until we get there anyway? You said we're close, right?"

"Yeah," he heard Irada answer. There was a brief pause. "I mean, close is a relative term, but it seemed close on the map. I'd say at our current speed and the distance... nightfall?"

"Oh," Qio remarked. "That's not too bad."

"Of tomorrow, that is. Nightfall tomorrow."

Qio bit his cheek once again. It kept him from saying the things he really wanted to. He couldn't afford to lose his ride to the capital, after all. A small sigh escaped his lips and he scratched his head. The country dirt caked in his hair started to irritate his scalp.

"What do you want to know?"

"Well, for starters," Irada answered, "how did you end up all the way over here?"

Qio chuckled. He figured that would be the question of the day. His hands slipped behind his head and he basked in the warm sunlight of the plains.

"Alright, farm boy," Qio began, eyes still closed. "I'm what you call a Tomekeeper. I don't know if you've heard about us out here in Dwelar, but we're a pretty big deal. Every century, twelve of us are hand select-ed by the gods themselves to serve as their ambassadors. We gather in Prodigium, get some incredible abilities and a standing ovation, then we get to rule our individual nations. Or advise them. Or something. I can't quite remember what it is, but it's important. In fact, traveling with me is probably the most exciting and life-changing thing that will ever happen to you!"

Irada gave a hefty laugh. "That does sound pretty impressive."

"You know what's crazy about it all?" Qio ignored Irada and contin-ued. "I was on top of the world already with the Asceniates. I'm talking about a great home, people constantly wanting my attention, and the most mesmerizing sights. Then I get this voice in my head, right? He's talking to me and telling me he's Zhonitas, then I feel this incredible gust of wind. It was bigger than anything I've experienced. It made every storm I've ever witnessed pale in comparison. It swept me up and I just took off. Have you ever imagined what Lidaesea looks like from above, Irada? Like the view that the gods get to see every day?"

"I can't say I have," Irada managed to squeeze in.

"That's because you don't dream big. You're content where you are, on your farm shucking corn. Me? I'm always thinking on a grand scale. When I was looking down on this world, it felt like I was in control. I really did feel like one of them."

"So what caused you to crash here in the plains?"

Qio opened his eyes and stared up at the clouds. He could have told Irada what really happened, but there was no need to. Once he reached Prodigium, he would never have to see or deal with the farm boy again. Instead, he had an image to uphold.

"Zhonitas sent me back to earth," Qio answered coolly. "He wanted to remind me that, at the end of the day, I was just a mere mortal."

Silban Awn ran down the hallowed halls of Prodigium, wings tucked tightly against the back of his golden armor. The staccato of his boots across the marbled floors echoed down the chambers as he passed. He had to hurry. It wasn't every day that the monarch himself sent a request for a personal meeting. As he approached the doors to the great hall, Silban skidded to a stop. He dusted off his armor and ruffled his slate-colored feathers.

Silban pushed the door to the hall open and stepped inside, posture straightened and movements swift. He traveled along a sprawling red carpet past the monarch's personal dining table to the opposite end. Despite being a member of the monarch's carefully selected personal guard, Silban had never seen the ornate decorations and intricate paintings of the great hall himself. It was beyond awe-inspiring.

Monarch Cason Mivano sat on Ghantei's rebuilt throne, wings as white as the pearls that were embedded in his armor sprawled out across the armrests. He was an imposing, yet almost perfect, individual. Despite being in his later years, the monarch looked no older than thirty. His white hair and beard were cut short and with impeccable precision. The gaze of his vermilion eyes was unbreakable. There was no better person to serve as the face and leader of Prodigium, and Lidaesea, as a whole.

Silban stood at the foot of the stairs and placed his arms behind his back, then bowed.

"My apologies for the tardiness, Your Excellency. I moved as quickly as I could."

"There is no need for apologies, Awn. You and your brothers have always been the best among my guards," Monarch Mivano told him in a strong, booming voice. "In fact, that is why I have summoned you today."

"I live to serve, as have all the members of my family before me," Silban said. His eyes held onto the legs of Ghantei's throne. He didn't want to show the monarch any disrespect by looking down or away, yet he felt he wasn't worthy enough to converse with the ruler eye-to-eye.

"Silban, I have a great task for you. One that I know only you can accomplish correctly," Mivano stated. "I've gained word from the kingdom of Anqua that their Tomekeeper has been chosen."

The news came as a shock to Silban's ears. The new century had just started. There should have been at least a decade or so before the talk of new Tomekeepers occurred. He listened intently as the monarch continued.

"The daughter of Queen Monalei Sxem, Princess Yonni, has been confirmed as the first of many. I received word from General Gandreke of the Anquan armies that Monalei and her daughter should be arriving at the Font of Drinex soon. From there, they will make the trip to our magnificent kingdom."

A buzz coursed through Silban's veins. The talk of Tomekeepers was an exciting prospect. They were known to change nations and sometimes the entirety of Lidaesea itself. To be gifted by the gods, and especially by the grace of Ghantei herself, was life's ultimate honor.

"I've heard rumblings from the other nations that their Tomekeepers have been selected as well. Only a few are unsure of where, or who, they may be. As such, I've sent out squadrons of your fellow celenians to go and investigate. They have been writing back and keeping me informed. We believe that we know of five of the twelve Tomekeepers: The chosen of Drinex, Noli, Netot, Shoroux, and Hilaster. I am currently investigating rumors regarding the Tomekeepers of Zhonitas and Eslen, the Betrayer."

Silban held back a sneer. Just hearing the name of the Betrayer was enough to make him sick. To believe that a god could turn against his peers and still be offered a chance to carry out his whims was a horrible injustice. The irony of the Betrayer being Eslen, god of judgment itself, was even more bitter. He turned his attention back to the monarch.

"That means, Silban, that there are five more still unaccounted for: Istio, Heivara, Verna, Wogiwoj and, of course, our most beloved lightbearer, Ghantei. The other four will show their faces soon. That is to be expected, after all. Part of being a Tomekeeper is collecting a tome to keep. My first task for you, as such, is to prepare a welcoming celebration for them in our name. This occurs but once a century so, please, spare no expense."

Warmth wrapped around Silban and he had to catch himself from grinning too widely. The monarch had just entrusted him with the Banquet of Tomes, one of the most important and often talked about traditions of the Great Selection. That he could leave his own mark on history gave Silban an overwhelming sense of elation. Concepts fluttered throughout his mind.

"Not only that, but in regards to our own potential Tomekeeper, I've gone back to look at those who have guided us in the past. Naveah, Temlenson, Ostoiray, and more. All were widely regarded to be the best in their time. That means, if the pattern holds, the most likely candidate to serve as Ghantei's chosen is your eldest brother, Reveticus."

Silban nodded in affirmation. Reveticus was known amongst all in the kingdom of Prodigium as the "Hero of Kephram's Keep" after saving the titular village that stood outside of the city's walls from being overrun by a horde of shadowreeves. It was a sight to behold for sure, and one that was going to be talked about for centuries to come.

In Silban's thoughts, there was no better choice for Ghantei's Tomekeeper.

Yonni's vision blurred as she slipped back into consciousness. The smell of fish was the first thing that she noticed. It was different outside of the safety of the water. Something about it smelled old and rotten. She wrinkled her nose and looked at the darkness around her. Yonni tugged at her arms and felt the pull of cold metal around her wrists. She figured the old traitor must have chained her while she was blacked out.

Yonni searched around in the darkness for Utic, what little light she had more than enough for someone who spent years in the ocean's depths. Destroyed crates and shredded scrolls littered the floor of the barge's hull. Utic was laid up against the wall across from her, still unconscious.

"*Drinoev,*" Yonni whispered and outstretched her hand. Water poured down from the cracks of the hull and amassed into a ball in her hand. She lightly tossed it at Utic and splashed it across his face. He sputtered and shook from the sudden wetness.

"Where are we?" he asked groggily.

"I think we're in the hull of the barge you brought me on," Yonni answered. "Is there a way out of here?"

"The only time I've been down here was for a brief moment to look for a chest," Utic informed her. "I didn't get much of a chance to explore. The only way out I know of is up the ladder and through the hatch."

Yonni peered over at the rusted rungs of the ladder in the center of the hull. She couldn't climb the last one, so that seemed like a no-go. The princess sighed. The hatch door above them creaked and opened in response. A singular ray of light shot across the floor and illuminated the inside.

Orghov hopped down every other rung until his boots smacked against the hull floor. He glanced over the two captives as they squinted their eyes from the burning sunlight.

"Well, looks like the pups are up," he crowed. "How was your sleep? Peaceful, I hope?"

Utic lurched forward to attack but the chains yanked him back to the floor.

"How could you?" he cried. "I trusted you!"

"You trusted a man you've never met with your life, and that's a pretty admirable thing," Orghov responded. "But I would argue there's too many sick and hateful people in the world. You honestly can't trust anyone. Look where it gets you! Stabbed in the back and shackled to the floor."

Orghov looked over to Yonni. She felt a sick, slimy feeling in her stomach. He inched closer and she recoiled back.

"It's not every day I get to see an Anqualai in person," he mused as he looked her over. He broke out into a yellow-toothed smile. "I'm surprised you managed to make it as far into Konasus as you did. Good thing too, or you never would have joined our little excursion."

"Where are we?" Utic yelled from behind him. "Where did you take us?"

"Me and my lovely crew of four decided to make our way up toward Senna. There's a lovely buyer looking for fresh fodder for some sort of experiments or the like. It's all beyond me. I just deliver. I don't ask."

"A crew?" Utic questioned. "Where were they the whole time?"

Orghov spread his arms and spun. "Taking a break in Konasus, of course!"

"And what about your wife? Was that a lie too?"

Orghov's smile flipped and his eyes lost their fire. "No, Utic. She wasn't. But I want you to remember one thing, above all else: losing the ones you love leads you down some dark, twisted paths."

Orghov sniffled and then turned around. He grabbed the rung and made his way back up to the deck. "I'll return for you soon. In the meantime, enjoy the quiet."

The hatch slammed shut and the hull was dark once again. Yonni let out a shudder. She tugged at her chains once more and waved at Utic.

"Are you alright?"

"Not really, no," he answered quietly.

"Can I cheer you up with some good news, then?"

Utic let out a despaired half-laugh. "What could possibly lift my spirits?"

Yonni crafted another ball of water and splashed it against the links of her chains. "*Repadrino.*"

The water froze instantly and Yonni shattered her chains with another light tug.

"The good news, Utic, is that we can leave."

The Aether Engine

Zall was accompanied through a doorway full of hanging scarlet beads that signified the entrance to Empress Bahn's chambers. The circular room was as cold and stony as Bahn's demeanor, its walls a mixture of obsidian and gabbro drenched in warm orange embers. Bahn's wicker throne had been moved to the center of the room, across from a pond of flowing lava. She gave Zall an icy glare as he entered.

"That little show of yours was unappreciated," Bahn bristled. She leaned forward in her throne and waited for a bow. The tension in the air was palpable. Zall stood at the edge of the pond and basked in the fiery warmth instead, stance spread and arms behind his back.

"The others seemed to enjoy it," Zall uttered belligerently. He turned his nose up at her for extra emphasis.

"You think you can come into my chambers and disrespect me, your empress? The one chosen by our people to lead?"

"When I've been chosen by our very god himself, yes," Zall replied.

Bahn stood in anger and her throne flew back from the force. A handful of her cinderion guards rushed into the room, lances drawn. She held her hand up to stop them. Zall was unphased.

"You think your toys can stop me?" Zall threatened. Embers and ashes gathered from the lava pond and coalesced in his hand. "You took away my life, Bahn. Give me a reason why I shouldn't do the same to you right now."

"I wasn't responsible for the things that happened to you or your family. That was entirely on your father," Bahn replied. Zall could sense that there was something different in her tone. Fear, perhaps.

"I'll give you a reason," a nasally voice interrupted from behind Zall. He rotated around and the cinderions moved in closer. Imperator Asmedeus Cole, Bahn's right hand man, walked up to Zall. His lanky figure was hidden under his bright red robes, but the wrinkles on his skin and his bony arms still gave him the appearance of a desiccated corpse. He outstretched a long skeletal hand in Zall's direction.

"You have been given great power, but if you truly think that you can run things around here, you are sorely mistaken. I will cut you down where you stand, even at the sacrifice of my greatest troops. I would rather lose a Tomekeeper than be held under the thumb of one."

Cole inched closer, his breath rancid in Zall's nostrils.

"Do you honestly believe that you can kill the entire Pyrolite army before they slice you down to ribbons?"

"I can damn well try," Zall growled.

Cole leaned into Zall's left side.

"Yes," he whispered. "But then you wouldn't be able to find out what happened to your family's kithronk."

Zall let the flames in his hands dissipate. The kithronk was the last remnant of his family and its legacy, a literal spirit totem carried through the centuries that contained detailed records of his bloodline. To lose it or have it destroyed was the biggest dishonor a Pyrolite could face. Zall refused to let his family's name be besmirched.

Cole's sunken eyes narrowed. "As I thought."

So that's how they've kept the muzzle on you, yeah? Hilaster echoed. *Don't worry, we'll play their game for now. But after we get to Prodigium and get that tome, let's destroy it all. I'm talking about a full-forced scorched kingdom moment.*

Zall mentally agreed. He relished the thought of watching everything crumble. A scraping noise caught his attention from the beaded doorway. Two Wingsong celenians, personal knights to the monarch of Prodigium, forced their way past Bahn's guards outside. Their wings, fluffy and vibrant white, took up an unnecessarily large amount of space.

"Empress Bahn of the Pyrolites, we apologize for the interruption," one of the celenians, an older man with shaggy gray hair and a bushy beard, stated with a bow in Bahn's direction. "We've been sent on behalf of Monarch Mivano to investigate the truth behind rumors of your Tomekeeper."

"I'm right here," Zall grumbled. He raised his hand and summoned a wave of fire around it as proof. "Consider the rumors true. You want to assess my combat ability too?"

"That won't be necessary," said the other celenian, a younger woman with a brunette knotted braid. She seemed overly stern for someone her age. Bred and born a soldier, if Zall had to guess.

What's going on with you, keeper? Hilaster asked. *I can sense your nerves building.*

There are too many people crowded into a small space, Zall answered. *I don't like it. Too much talking as well, and not enough of it with fists.*

Agreed, keeper. Why don't we go get some air?

Zall looked past the beads of Bahn's doorway and caught sight of the Wingsong's golden-trimmed chariot outside. It beckoned him, open and unguarded. He couldn't think of a better way to insult Bahn, anger Cole, and set off on his journey to the capital with a bang.

Hilaster, Zall called out mentally. *Are you thinking what I'm thinking?*

Kliev dry-heaved over the edge of the airship's railing. His breath was quick and shallow as his body and mind begged to be placed back on the ground. The sea sparkled under the airship like a thousand gemstones dancing in unison.

There was no escape.

Kliev felt the gaze of one of the horrid creatures locked on to him. He turned to face it, the thistlewisp's sharp and hungry eye declaring him its next meal. His ears twitched.

"Isn't this great?" I'el said, pressed against the railing next to him. She was staring off into the sky and soaking in the sunlight like an exquisite flower, lost in her own world. Kliev didn't know if she was aware of his panic and pain and chose to ignore it, or if she was just ignorant to it as a whole. Given what little he knew of I'el so far, though, her lackadaisical nature seemed to point to the latter. She was fierce when she wanted to be, sure, but outside of that she was relatively carefree. Unless, of course, Kliev said something about her beloved Fritton or Tristen or whatever the name of the elf boy back in her village was.

Aw, is someone feeling a bit jealous? Wogiwoj teased. **You have to man up, keeper! Take life by the horns of its helmet and bend it to your whims. Go get the girl!**

I'el? Kliev questioned. *You think I'm feeling some sort of way about her? Sure, she's stunning, and smart, and a great warrior, but she has no interest in me whatsoever. It's so unusual. I mean, I'm me. I'm Kliev Rorn, one of the best—and most dashing—fighters in all of Krijya. What's not to love? Plus, Wogi, don't you find the ears perturbing? They're not like ours, but not like a normal Human's. They're sharp, but long. It's so odd.*

I've known my fair share of love across the realms, my boy, Wogiwoj said with a mischievous chuckle. **You learn to appreciate all shapes and sizes.**

Of ears?

Hm? Oh. Yes, of course.

Kliev shrugged and put his back against the rail, then slid down next to I'el.

"How are you holding up?" she asked as she tucked her hair behind her ear. The three silver rings running up the side glinted. Kliev looked around for a moment.

Tomekeepers can't hear each other's thoughts, right, Wogi?

Not unless things have changed, keeper.

"Hello? Are you going to answer?" I'el inquired.

"I'm... I'm f-fine," Kliev stuttered. "I don't know what you mean."

"You've been awfully quiet since we left. And your ears keep twitching."

Kliev reached up and grabbed his ears. They betrayed his attempt to be cool and collected. "I just don't like those horrendous things pulling the airship."

"You mean the thistlewisps? They're just birds, Kliev."

"You don't seem to understand the nature between bird and bunny," Kliev asserted. "It wants to eat me."

A hiss of air escaped from the balloons above them interrupted I'el's response. The body of the ship swayed and descended toward the sea. Kliev popped his head up over the rail and caught sight of the approaching city. It was a sprawling metropolis of cream and crimson buildings that stretched from the edge of the ocean and up into the vast greenery of the Varlan Plains. Rich blue canals snaked through the city.

"It seems like we're landing," I'el said, unmoved.

"That's Selenti?" Kliev uttered. "It's such a far cry from the frosted wonders of Krijya, but what an incredible sight."

"Really?" I'el said in surprise. "I just think about all the trees that were cut down to make room for it."

"You've been before, then?"

"A handful of times. All the families in Farnen's Grove take turns delivering food from the Orchard to Selenti. It's all dispersed out from there."

"And you don't think it's a sight of wonder?"

"Maybe when I was younger," I'el shared. "I had a bad experience that changed my outlook."

Kliev nodded in understanding.

"How about this: at some point, when you're comfortable with sharing, you tell me about what happened in Selenti, and I'll tell you what happened to me as a kid and why I don't like birds. A share for a share, if you will."

I'el looked at Kliev and gave him a soft smile, then rolled her eyes as it turned into a bigger grin.

"Alright. How can I resist the temptation to learn more about the magnificent Kliev Rorn?"

"It's a deal, then."

The ship came to a soft landing against a stone pad on the edge of Selenti. The rest of the air in the balloons released and the brown canvases deflated. The thistlewisps cawed and chirped as their talons tapped against the stone, flower coated wings outstretched in the sun.

"Don't worry, Ms. Rivini," Kliev proclaimed as he stood and held out a hand. "You've got the Tomekeeper of the storms here to protect you. I have the best combat skills in all of Krijya."

I'el laughed and stood on her own.

"Thank you for the offer, Mr. Rorn. I feel much safer in your overwhelmingly masculine presence. Please, don't let me out of your sight."

"Alright, alright," Kliev said as he awkwardly retracted his hand. "I'm just saying that I'm here for support."

"That's better," I'el responded as she playfully tapped his nose and walked past him. Kliev felt his cheeks get hot. The wooden ramp of the airship dropped against the stone and the passengers aboard disembarked. He followed I'el's lead down the ramp and around the ship's side. Further down, a number of boats were docked along the pale cream sands of Selenti's beach. One in particular caught his attention.

"What do you think happened there?" he asked and pointed towards a black ship full of holes with burned navy sails. The carrack had definitely seen better days and barely held together. It was a shame such a work of art had been reduced to a terrible fate.

"Hey, look out!" I'el warned.

Kliev felt himself bump into the crowd entering the pier ahead. He took a step back and a cloak of jade in front of him whipped around. The owner scowled. Her face was painted over in the style of a decorated skull that sent fear straight through Kliev's whole body. The last thing he wanted to do was anger a Terrolaff. They were all a little too crazy.

"You'd better watch where you're walking, furball," the woman spat. In the blink of an eye, she had withdrawn a dagger and placed it against the side of Kliev's neck. He held his breath as the tip of the blade started to dig in. The woman looked at him with frigid, malevolent eyes. "Tell me why you shouldn't die right here, right now."

A hand grabbed the Terrolaff's arm and slowly pushed it down. "Not here."

Kliev let out a breath and his attention turned to the harlequin's side where another woman, with eyes that burned like fire in the dead of night, stared him down.

Fwen looked the Wojlidoj over. He was sturdily built, more so than most of his kind, and his posture was different as well. It was straight and refined instead of the usual hunch Wojlidoj tended to have. Something was off, but she couldn't gather what yet.

This one is a Tomekeeper as well, said the voice of death incarnate. ***Make that two.***

A young elven woman around Fwen and Verina's age ran up behind the man. "Kliev," she said, just loud enough to be heard. "I told you to look out."

Fwen squeezed Verina's arm and gave her a quick look. She nodded in affirmation. She could sense it too.

"He's perfectly fine," Fwen told the pair. "I would actually like to apologize on behalf of my friend here. We were attacked by pirates on the way and she's a bit jittery."

Verina shot Fwen a look of displeasure over the comment, but it didn't matter. There was an advantage to maintaining the element of surprise, and they ran the risk of revealing their identities the longer they stayed near the other two Tomekeepers.

They can't tell what we are yet, can they, Netot? Fwen double-checked.

No, Netot answered. ***You and Istio's pet have been scarce in your usage of the abilities we've bestowed. These two have been quite the opposite. I can smell the magic wafting off of them. At worst, they could sense there are Tomekeepers nearby, but not trace it back to you.***

Understood, Fwen responded. She cleared her throat and gestured at Verina.

"Come along, Nirave. We're running behind."

Verina thankfully played along and pointed her dagger at the other two Tomekeepers before sheathing it in her robe. Fwen adjusted her own cloak and led Verina back into the crowded pier without another word.

"Don't ever speak for me," Verina scowled. "I've had enough of that in my life."

"Duly noted," said Fwen. "But as long as we're working together, I will do whatever it takes to maintain our advantage. Reflect on that."

The pair traveled silently through the pier and over the bridge that connected it to the city proper. The oceanic vista faded into a maze of canals and silver-roofed villas that comprised Selenti's crowded blocks. Fwen slipped into an alley and Verina quickly followed. She made her way through to the other side and into an older square. A handful of stone buildings lined the square and a dried up fountain caked in grime stood in the center.

"If I may ask, where exactly are we going?" Verina inquired. A hint of exhaustion lingered in her voice.

"We're hiring our transport to Prodigium," Fwen stated.

"In a run-down district at the edge of Selenti?"

Fwen walked up to the door of the middle building and knocked seven times. It opened with a creak and the sound of music and joyous shouts drifted out. The stench of spilled alcohol drifted out.

"Don't judge a book by its cover, Verina. You should know that."

"Are you saying that because of the artistry across my face?" Verina let out a squeak of a laugh as the two entered. "Come now, Fwen. Must you always be so drab? You should try to inject some color into your life. Some shades of red would look great on you."

Why do you insist on making the pet yap? Netot sighed.

Fwen ignored them both and followed the music and shouts down the hall and into an open tavern. Cups clinked and flagons thudded on tables as the patrons inside cheered and jeered at one another. Fwen walked to a table in the far corner where a lone Noctide sat with his head against the wall. She pulled out the chair with a loud scrape and sat.

"To what do I owe the pleasure?" the Noctide grumbled. He rubbed his eyes with his thumb and index finger, clearly hungover.

"I need passage to Prodigium. Quickly and quietly," Fwen answered. Verina took a seat next to her.

The Noctide scooted away uncomfortably. His eyes narrowed.

"What is this?" he hollered and pointed at Verina. "You go and bring one of them in here? She'll kill us all!"

"The Terrolaff is working with me. Don't do anything dumb and she won't be forced to step in."

The Noctide spat on the floor and the black ring in his nostril twisted. "The agreement your parents sent was that you get to Prodigium. You. Alone. The extra will cost you."

"And if I refuse to pay? She's my bodyguard. Where I go, she goes." Fwen argued.

"Then best of luck getting across the plains and through Kephram's, even with your little powers," the Noctide sneered and slammed his hand against the table.

Verina stood, withdrew her dagger, spun it around and slammed it through his hand before Fwen could even process a response. The man screamed in pain and tried to grab the blade, but Verina slapped his hand away. The Terrolaff leaned in close.

"You're making this more difficult than it needs to be. You're going to take us, or it's your hand. Then your head." Verina threatened. She twisted the dagger a bit for extra emphasis. The man screeched accordingly.

"Yeah, alright!" he cried out. "Please, no more!"

Perhaps she has her uses after all, Netot commented.

Did you really need to be convinced of that? Fwen replied. *Verina may be out of her mind, but she has a code she adheres to. That alone is rare.*

Verina sat back in her chair and kicked her boots onto the table. Fwen was impressed, a feat not easily accomplished. Her hand reached across the table and tugged the blade out, then handed it to her companion. She leaned in to meet the Noctide man's watered eyes.

"I'm glad you've come to see things our way. Now walk us through your plan."

Fuchsia smoke erupted from Ramji Wrine's lab with a sizzling bang. She kicked open the door into the outer quarters to avoid the noxious smell of sulfur and petrol, coughing as the fumes filled the air. Her hands waved wildly to try and dissipate the smoke. Footsteps rushed down the hallway outside.

I told you that wouldn't work, an ethereal voice that was concurrently male and female said.

"Actually, you said that there was a high probability that it wouldn't work," Ramji corrected aloud. "Your words. Not mine."

She tousled her messy black bun and pulled the strings of hair that had fallen out of it behind her ears, then readjusted her circular glasses. They slipped slightly back down the bridge of her nose. She pulled out a small piece of parchment and charcoal stick from the overalls that clung to her thin frame and jotted a note.

"Three parts of archimehacy is too much for this particular recipe. Two parts may yield more satisfactory results."

Use of archimehacy at all will make the solution more volatile, Tomekeeper. It would be better to use galenilly or some parsed down form of woodryhme.

"Incorrect, Shoroux," Ramji stated. "Since your last venture on our side of the spiritual boundary, galenilly has become scarce and woodrhyme has been known to serve as a leading cause in esper poisoning."

My apologies then, Tomekeeper, Shoroux expressed. ***I was not aware of such advances in knowledge.***

"Apology accepted," Ramji replied.

The footsteps from the hall grew louder until they stopped outside of the door. She stepped back and it opened. Her father gasped for air in the doorway.

"My. Brilliant. Daughter," he huffed between breaths. The long, gray ponytail that ran down his back swung with each one. Chartreuse eyes that matched Ramji's own stared at her behind rectangular glasses. "What happened? What was that explosion?"

"I was adapting the recipe for our combustible fuel to make it more… well, combustible," Ramji explained. She placed one hand behind her back and shrugged. "I figured if I used three parts of archimehacy that it might give it the extra kick I was in need of. Alas."

Her father shook his head. "Where did you even get archimehacy? It's banned in most of the realms."

"From your personal inventory, of course."

"Great Ghantei," he sighed. "Please ask before you do such things. Archimehacy is an unstable compound. Even just the tiniest measurement over can, quite literally, explode in your face. If something happened to you, I…"

He trailed off and Ramji adjusted her glasses once more.

"I'll be careful, father. I promise."

Trescoise Wrine let out a heavy sigh and stroked his pointed goatee. Ramji figured he needed a moment to determine if the situation was worth doling out a mild punishment or if he should just let it slide. He beckoned her.

"Come along," Trescoise finally said. "I want to show you the newest development I found with the aether engine."

Ramji jumped for joy. The mysterious box hidden away deep within her father's lab had been the main topic of her mind for weeks since it was first uncovered. It was a remnant of lost times that held far too many secrets, and the sheer possibilities were too enticing to leave unexplored. She followed her father as he walked down the hall and led her around the corner into a rectangular room with tables and tools of every variety scattered across. Towers of yellowed books were placed haphazardly along the surfaces of his lab, many the lightest tap away from toppling. Scribbled notes of parchment covered in her father's handwriting were nailed into the walls.

In the room's center was a large cube with abstract etchings full of pulsating mercury. It emitted a dull hum that reminded her of an unending bottom C on a chromatic lyre. The sound always managed to calm Ramji's often chaotic mind, and hearing it in the background of her studies tended to help her focus as well. She walked over and ran her hands over it. The cube vibrated ever so slightly. It was emitting power but to what remained unknown. It was, for all intents and purposes, an "engine". They just needed to determine how it worked.

"I've found that the engine responds to ionized charges," Trescoise informed her. "I believe that it needs to be given a hefty and constant dose of ethereal energy in order to power. I've traced the etchings and have reason to believe they're not artistic in nature, they're-"

"Pieces," Ramji finished with a smile. "Pieces of a puzzle that need to be shifted into place."

Good deduction, Tomekeeper. You two are indeed correct, Shoroux confirmed. ***This "engine", as you call it, is a gate. One not intended for mere mortals to pass. I did not want to reveal its true nature until I was sure I could trust you, for within are many***

things that the rest of Lidaesea can not yet know about. I can tell you how to unlock it, but you need to promise me one thing.

"Anything," Ramji whispered.

Your father cannot enter.

Ramji's smile dropped and she turned back toward the man who raised her, lost in his notes. They had researched the engine together. Everything she knew in life and science, he had taught her or encouraged her to learn. To not include him in what was their biggest discovery felt like a betrayal.

Yet the temptation was too strong. Ramji needed to know what the engine could do. There was no way around it.

"Tell me," Ramji said.

Shoroux imparted the words and Ramji placed her hand on the middle of the cube's front side. She looked back at her father, who was still distracted, and took a breath.

"*Kantehnfuosho.*"

A pulse of energy reverberated from her hand into the aether engine. The cube rumbled and the hum it emitted escalated notes. It clicked, then popped apart and reshifted into an archway as each piece snapped together. The arch glowed brightly and pink light spilled across from the edges to meet in the middle. Ramji's father toppled over the books next to him in surprise.

"Great Ghantei!" he exclaimed. "It's absolutely astounding. How?"

Ramji swiveled around to face him. Her heart felt heavy at the sight of his unbridled excitement. She fidgeted with her hands. Her nerves had kept her from revealing Shoroux's existence to him. He was a man of hard science, and there was no place for magic in his mind. The claws of anxiety gripped her chest and her breathing quivered.

"It's magic, father," she admitted. "And so am I."

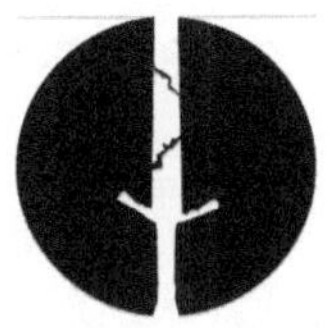

Tuvhe had been riding along the trail from Senna to the Font of Drinex for what seemed like days when he spotted the smoke drifting above the treetops. While not an unusual sight on its own, the fact that it was in the middle of the Crystalands—an expanse of dead vegetation and rock that connected Eslen's Mark with the Dunes of Verna and the Varlan Plains—made it more curious. Nothing could survive for more than a day out in the frigid abyss, and not even the local wildlife cared to call it home.

There's something over there that's pulling me in, Eslen informed him. ***Something familiar. I can't tell what it is for sure.***

Tuvhe climbed down from the wagon and withdrew his blade. His survival instincts screamed that he was walking into a trap yet, like Eslen, he felt a tug in the direction of the smoke for some unknown reason. He gripped his hilt tightly. It was better to be prepared either way.

Tuvhe walked through the dead trees and over the thin patches of clear ice that blanketed the ground. Spiked crystalline structures that gave the area its name jutted out in every direction. The heels of his boots cracked through the ice to give him some semblance of solid footing.

As he approached the source of the smoke, the ground rose into a hollowed out hillside. A rusted sand barge was tied down into the snow with a singular fire crackling atop it. Four older men laughed around the flame, drinks clasped in hand.

"Excuse me," Tuvhe called up to the men. "I was passing by and saw your fire. Can a traveling soul rest by the warmth for a moment?"

One of the men, tall and rotund, tilted his head toward Tuvhe and said something to another, much older and with a beard. Tuvhe could barely make out the spirals that encircled his eyes before he covered them with a pair of tattered goggles.

What's a Pyrolite doing out here so far from Hilaster's Peak? Tuvhe wondered.

Nothing good, Eslen muttered. **Those spirals were a symbol of death. There's also something magical within the hull. No, more than one. Other Tomekeepers, perhaps?**

Why don't we find out? Tuvhe suggested as the barge's ladder fell to the rock.

Zall held the side of the chariot as it flew up and over the craggly path down the volcano. It landed with a crack and the wheel's bounced against the frame, spinning wildly as the vehicle continued to pick up speed. Zall leaned his head back and let out an excited howl. Adrenaline coursed through every part of him. The sound of flapping wings followed behind.

"Tomekeeper, cease this absurdity at once!" the older celenian shouted at Zall. The duo had been close behind since he first took the chariot and zoomed away from Bahn's residence. The thrill of the chase had lit a metaphorical fire behind him. Zall pulled his arm back and felt the power flow to his palm.

"*Hilasev!*" Zall shouted as a flaming sphere manifested. He flung it toward his pursuers and made them split apart. He glanced in each direction at his potential targets before he decided on who he wanted to pester more. He called forth another fireball and launched it in the male celenian's direction. It curved and the celenian rolled to the side to avoid it, just as Zall had planned.

"*Behfuohil!*" he said as the fireball slipped under his pursuer. It stretched upward into its pillar form and ripped through the edge of the man's left wing. The soldier cried out and lost altitude, careening to the ground where he impacted and rolled.

Great job, keeper! Hilaster complimented.

"Coltiel!" the celenian woman yelled as she watched her companion crash. She faced forward and placed her arms at her side. Her wings arched in and she dived toward the chariot. Zall braced for an attack, but the woman flew past and further down the pathway.

"Giving up already?" Zall mocked her as they continued their descent. He flicked more fireballs at her for fun. "That's right. Run away!"

The woman suddenly opened her wings and caught the heated draft of the volcano. She launched backward toward Zall and the chariot, narrowly avoiding both as she flew above his head. She reached out, grabbed the back of his vest, and yanked him off of the cart. The two landed on the path and tumbled down violently. Zall felt the jagged edge of one rock stab into his side and a couple of smaller ones scraped against his hand and knee. His head smacked into the road and made his vision spin.

Zall landed on his back and slid across the path, feeling the burn of his leather vest against his skin as he skid. The woman landed next to him, her body wrapped in her wings. She forced herself up as she came to a halt and wasted no time stomping her way over to Zall.

"Listen well, Tomekeeper," the woman said as she planted a boot onto Zall's chest. A deep cut ran across her forehead and her right arm was limp. "By the power invested in me by our great sovereign, I'm placing you under arrest."

Zall laughed and felt his ribs stab into his lungs. "What makes you think I won't just melt down your restraints and burn you as badly as I did your partner?"

"Simple," she responded. "You won't be awake."

The celenian swung her armored boot back and kicked the side of Zall's head with full force.

Son of Light

Ramji's father gave her a long stare and she could tell he wasn't exactly sure how to process her statement. The anticipation for a response continued to build. There were only two possible outcomes in her mind: either he accepted it, or he didn't.

That's a very straightforward way to perceive the situation, Shoroux chimed in.

It's the only way for things to progress, Ramji thought. *Father is a scientist like I am, and that means we both believe in absolutes. Backed by evidence, of course.*

Trescoise crossed his arms.

"How?" he finally uttered. "How do you expect to prove the validity of that statement to me?"

Ramji felt the tension release from her body. If he wanted proof, that meant he was willing to listen and to accept. It wasn't the outcome she was expecting, but it was a welcome one for sure. She went through the different routes she could take. Her hand waved across the air.

"*Rouwintou*," she said confidently as the air began to shift into steam. She waved it back across and changed the steam into a block of gold. It fell to the ground with a high-pitched ring. Before her father could respond, she tapped the gold.

"*Rouxalli*."

The block changed to a deep shade of pink, then purple, and finally settled on orange. Ramji stepped back and let her father observe her work. He timidly picked up the bar and looked it over from every angle. "This is beyond my comprehension. The particulate matter needed to assemble gold's composition shouldn't be able to manifest from the air. You've also managed to adjust the pigment of its natural chemical makeup."

"I basically tell Shoroux what I want to do and they help me break things down. I can see a variety of different forms of matter. It's all like clay in my hands," Ramji explained.

"And the engine? Did... Shoroux... tell you how to activate it as well?" her father inquired.

Ramji looked back at the shimmering ethereal door behind her. She recalled Shoroux's warning. "Yes, but they said that only I can know what's inside. I cannot relay any of that information to you, nor can you venture in yourself."

A look of skeptical displeasure crossed her father's face. She could tell that it hurt him to be left out of the picture, but that he also understood things were entirely out of his control. He placed his hands on her shoulders.

"Ramji, I will be straightforward with you. I don't trust Shoroux, nor any of the other gods. When one being holds so much power in our world, it's easy to use it all for the wrong things.

'Tomekeepers are not a blessing, my daughter. They are a curse. They're bound to serve. Do not fall so easily for the temptations of power that godhood can provide, for at the end of the day, you are mortal and they are not. They will revive, yet you only get one chance at life."

Ramji felt her stomach sink. She had miscalculated his actions and what she thought was a chance at approval. Trescoise traced the lines of his palm with his finger, once again deep in thought.

"That being said," he continued, "I cannot in good faith let you pass up this opportunity to observe a reality beyond our own. Even if I can't be there with you physically, I'm with you in heart and spirit. What I want most is for you to grow and learn. To develop your own experiences and your own hypotheses. Be your own scientist, Ramji. Go, while the gate is still open. I believe in you."

Ramji nodded in acknowledgement and turned to face the gate. Her assumption was right after all. She heard Shoroux's voice echo in her mind.

Are you ready to bear witness to the other side, Tomekeeper?

Ramji walked up to the gate and pressed her hand through. The light formed a thin membrane that broke as she pushed, then swallowed her hand into what felt like a cool gel. She took a breath, gave her father a small wave, and stepped forward into the unknown. The slime of the membrane slipped over her body and coated her as she entered a vast pale pink chamber. Purple and blue particles, no bigger than specks of dust, swirled with every step that she took.

"Welcome to my domain," Shoroux's voice reverberated around Ramji. The floor, ceiling and every wall seemed to be talking to her at once. It overwhelmed her senses, and panic set in as she realized she couldn't breath. Every breath she tried to take filled her lungs with the acrid-tasting gel.

"Please relax, Tomekeeper. There is no need for air here. Your body will adapt accordingly," Shoroux informed her. **"You will not be able to speak, as sound in the way that you understand it does not carry. I can still hear your thoughts, however."**

What is this place? Ramji mentally questioned. Her lungs felt full, but she tried not to pay attention to the unnatural lack of breathing. Her body as a whole felt like it was wading through an invisible ocean. *How am I able to survive here?*

"The aether adapts to all those that inhabit it," Shoroux put forth. **"It is life itself, melting and molding and manifesting. Such is the power and beauty of our existence. We are all filled with the cosmic matter that makes up the universe. Here in this realm there is no hunger, no thirst, no need to breathe. You exist, and that is all you need to do. Let me show you."**

The ground shook beneath Ramji's feet and made her body buzz. The ceiling pulled away from the walls, and Ramji realized she was on a circular platform. As it descended, the walls evaporated into brush-strokes of twinkling stars. She watched as the shining lights of the night shrank down into dotted landscapes coated in hues of red, blue, pink, and purple. Whole galaxies assembled like paintings before her eyes.

"Is it not beautiful?" Shoroux asked.

It's more beautiful than I could have ever imagined, Ramji answered in awe. *Is this what it's like when we look out into the sky? Is this what awaits us past our own world?*

"There's so much out there, Tomekeeper. It's more than you could ever see or learn about in a lifetime. To truly appreciate the

beauty of it all, though, I must also show you the darker side. The creatures that live in the shadows are more than a normal person can handle, which is why we must be careful."

Wait, what exactly do you mean? Ramji tried to clarify, unheard. The stars around her zoomed by and fizzled into a deeper black than she had ever seen before. The light that enveloped her, no doubt Shoroux's doing, was the only thing that broke through the shadows. That was when she first saw them. They were tentacled monstrosities with mouths that ripped open into three-pronged jaws and marigold pearls for eyes. Further beyond them were even more creatures, but Ramji's mind couldn't fully decipher their shape and features. She felt something worse than fear settle within her. It was frigid and lifeless, like her very soul had left her and was replaced by death's embrace. Tears formed in her eyes and a crushing weight sat in her chest.

Shoroux, I can't take much more, Ramji barely managed to think past the emotional distress. *I feel whatever this presence is eating away at me.*

"I understand, keeper. We will return once our connection has been strengthened."

The platform rotated and lifted back to its original position. The images, and the emotions attached to them, faded away into the pink of the chamber. Ramji tried to let out her breath and called attention back to the lack of air in her lungs. She had enough of the aether. The wall furthest from her slid open to reveal the gateway.

"Before you go, Tomekeeper, remember: no one can know what you have seen here today. All it will do is cause chaos."

Ramji pressed her hand against the gate. It was time to return to the comfort and safety of her home.

There's nothing to worry about, Shoroux, Ramji thought in response. *I couldn't subject anyone else to this.*

Silban waited patiently in the courtyard for Reveticus to join him. The sound of the birds chirping at the edge of the stone fountain mixed with the flowing water. Bright pink and yellow asters waved in the breeze, and travertine tiles made up the courtyard's flooring. Silban tapped his foot against the tile when the flap of wings from above caught his attention. He looked up and saw the glistening armor of his brother drop down in front of him.

Reveticus shook off his ultramarine wings, tipped with black and silver feathers, and created a gust of wind around them.

"Good morning, Silban. I hope I didn't keep you waiting for long."

"Of course not, brother," Silban responded. "I figured you would be busy. Thank you for taking the time to converse with me."

"I'll always find time for you and Trebellard. Speaking of Trebellard, where is our youngest counterpart?"

Silban pulled out a folded piece of parchment emblazoned with the crescent logo of the Vishwarn Military School and handed it to his brother. Reveticus opened it, glanced over the hasty handwriting, then tucked it inside of his chest plate.

"It appears he's going to outrank us both by the time he graduates. Quite an achievement," Reveticus chuckled.

Silban forced a laugh, but his heart wasn't in it. While he was happy for his younger brother, he couldn't help but feel a bit of envy at the same time. Reveticus was a hero in Silban's mind, and deservedly so, but Trebellard was the definition of failing upward. He was by far the least dedicated to the Awn family's role as the monarch's personal guard and constantly complained about wanting something different in life.

Despite his ungrateful attitude, Trebellard was hand-picked to attend Vishwarn. The cabinet of the school said his tactical brilliance was unparalleled. That left Silban stuck between a war hero and a military prodigy, the middle child often forgotten when the Awn's and their achievements were mentioned.

"That reminds me," Reveticus continued. "I wanted to give proper congratulations on leading the Banquet of Tomes. It's quite an honor indeed. I look forward to seeing your preparations in full."

"I'll do my best not to let you down, brother. After all, it's only a matter of time before our great goddess chooses you. I did have one concern, though, if I may share."

"Share away, little brother."

"I'm slightly worried that all these preparations will be for naught. I don't know about these other Tomekeepers, and I can't speak for their character at all. What if they decide they want to ruin the night or make a mockery of our kingdom?"

"Then it's up to you to put your foot down, Silban," Reveticus asserted. "The monarch chose you for this task because he sees your potential, much like he saw mine. You are strong, loyal and, above all, unyielding. Show them the might of the Awn family and keep them in their place."

Silban took a moment to reflect on the words of his older brother. They were short, but Silban could see the truth in them. There was no time or place for self-doubt when it came to the Banquet of Tomes. There had already been whispers in the air about the strength of the monarchy and Prodigium's continued hold as the capital of Lidaesea.

He needed to show all the Tomekeepers, and the nations that backed them, that Prodigium was still a kingdom of preparation, fortitude, and leadership.

"When you're back out of your thoughts, I have a request for you," Reveticus said to him.

Silban snapped back to attention. "What is it, brother?"

Reveticus drew his weapon, a longsword with a blade the same colors and style as his wings, and pressed it into the travertine.

"I want to see how much your sparring skills have progressed since our last match. It's been a couple of years, has it not?"

"Here?" Silban said as he looked around the courtyard. "There's barely enough space for us to move and talk, let alone swing a sword."

Reveticus let out a hearty hero's laugh. "No, of course not. I challenge you to aerial combat."

With that, Reveticus flapped his wings and launched into the sky with another gust. The force made Silban wobble slightly and the asters shoot into the air. Silban smirked and drew his arming sword, a standard among the forces of the Wingsong. There was nothing like friendly competition between brothers to build bonds. Silban stretched out his own wings and gave them a flap before launching through the cloud of pink and yellow flowers and into the azure blue above.

Kliev counted the stars that streaked across the midnight sky. The constant sounds of Selenti tickled his ears and the light of the city dulled the white and yellow gems that twinkled above him. The bench in the empty garden was a far cry from the nights he had spent atop his hut in Krijya.

Kliev remembered the tales his father had told him in his younger years. His father's gravelly voice would carry recollections of wintery battles and heroic accomplishments that echoed throughout the Krijyan woods. The campfire would crackle and pop, and the warmth would spread across the snow dusted fur of Kliev's ears. The journey of Mäcé, second Tomekeeper of Wogiwoj, had especially captivated him.

I never imagined I'd have a tale of my own, Kliev thought as his eyes drifted shut. *I wonder what they'll say of me.*

A flickering sensation ran along the interior of Kliev's ear and made him sneeze violently. He reached up with his hand and batted away the cause. Snickers erupted from I'el as she withdrew her vine.

"What kind of man falls asleep while his lady friend is away taking care of matters?" I'el said. "You could have at least waited to make sure I returned safely."

"Are we friends now?" Kliev responded as he stood and scratched his ear.

"That's the nicest way of labeling our situation, in my opinion."

Kliev cleared his throat and thought through his responses.

You can't let her mock your masculinity, keeper, Wogiwoj said in an unusually subdued tone. ***Find a way to turn the tide.***

"I was waiting for you, I'el, but I assumed that a woman as strong as yourself could handle her own. Unless you're saying you need me," Kliev grinned.

"Tell me something, Kliev—have you always been this daft or have years of exposure to thin mountain air wronged you?"

Oof, that one hurt, Wogiwoj commented.

Kliev laughed it off. "Sorry, I'el. I forget that you Phreeton are used to being protected by dragons and trees. You've never had to worry about fending for yourself."

"Fending for myself?" I'el fumed. "I don't need you to help me, bunny boy. I've said that before."

"Show me then."

"Show you what?"

"That you don't need me to protect you."

I'el rolled her eyes. "And how exactly do you expect me to d-"

"*Evogi,*" Kliev interrupted and pointed at I'el's feet. A ball of sparks shot out from the tip of his finger and popped as it hit the ground in front of her.

I'el let out a yelp.

"Not funny, Kliev!"

"*Evogi,*" Kliev repeated. He stepped closer.

I'el jumped away as another ball exploded at her feet.

"That's it!" she shouted. Her palms tilted up as she lifted her hands into the air. "*Cheenolavohpe!*"

A mass of dark green sprouted from the earth and slithered up Kliev's body. They yanked him onto the ground and continued to wrap around him until all but his head was encased in a solid cocoon. He tried to fight, but they only pulled tighter.

"Well, color me impressed," Kliev said.

Same, Wogiwoj agreed.

I'el smirked and twirled around on the tips of her toes.

"Told you," she said in a singsong tone as she walked away. "The cart will be delivered in the morning. Lady Bresha graciously paid for a room in advance, but alas, it's just the one. I'll be going to get some much needed rest."

Kliev pictured the singular bed that awaited them both and felt his cheeks and ears grow warm once again.

"Well, that sounds like a mighty fine invitation. You can let me go now, I'el."

The Phreeton stopped and turned around with a twirl of orange hair. A mischievous smile adorned her face. She tapped her index finger against her chin.

"I don't think my dragons and trees would let you get by."

"I'el!" Kliev called out as she walked into the distance. "Great joke! I get it now. I'm sorry for my comments. You don't need me at all. You're perfectly capable of handling yourself. I'el?"

Kliev let out a hefty sigh and let his head fall against the hard earth. His stomach churned.

Have I mentioned that I like her? Wogiwoj said.

Kliev fought back a smile.

"I do too, Wogi. I do too."

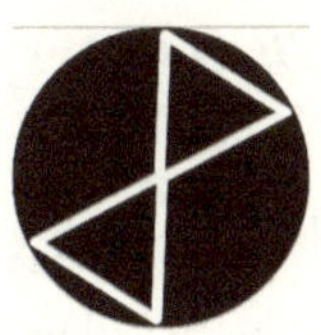

Utic pulled on his chains as Yonni froze them, snapping them with a loud crack. Her movement was still troubled, but her footing adapted as more time passed. He flung off the remains and thanked her before turning to the ladder next to them. There was no doubt that Orghov and his men had heard their escape and would make their way down at any moment. He signaled for Yonni to stay silent. The two crouched on the ladder's opposite end.

Loud thumps sounded from the deck, followed by shouts from whom Utic could only assume were Orghov's men. Utic glanced around the hull in preparation while Yonni inched closer, her head tilted upward to listen. Utic felt horrible for getting her caught up in their situation. They had just met, yet she had already gifted him her trust. While he couldn't have ever predicted Orghov's betrayal, he berated himself for not trying harder to protect Yonni from harm. He had to find a way to make things right.

The hatch above them creaked open and a body fell through the opening. It hit the ground with a thump and rolled. Utic didn't need light to know that it was Orghov's. Confusion arose.

A man in silver armor dropped down afterward, a magnificent broadsword coated in white flames gripped in his hands. He turned to face the two Tomekeepers, his eyes glowing with an identical magical energy. Yonni braced for a fight, but Utic wasn't sure if he should do the same.

There is no need to fear, Utic, Verna confirmed with unease behind her words. ***This one will not hurt you. It's against his better nature.***

"You two," the man called out. His eyes flickered back to a deep brown and his body relaxed. The sword in his hands lowered slightly and shifted back into a smaller form. "Are either of you hurt?"

"Tell us who you are and why you're here. Now!" Yonni commanded.

"I'm here to rescue you, of course," the man replied. Utic could feel a sense of magic emit from the stranger's body. The latter sheathed his sword and held his hands up. "My name is Tuvhe Vull. I'm a Tomekeeper as well. I was passing through when I felt your presence."

"How did you sense us?" Yonni pressed. "Why can we barely feel yours?"

"It seems that I've been more selective in my usage of our abilities. At least, that's what my god is telling me," Tuvhe said.

Utic stepped around and examined Orghov's body. He had been run clean through with Tuvhe's broadsword. Sadness and a sense of pity for the old man consumed him, and he wished things had turned out differently. Utic reached down and plucked the sapphire pin from Orghov's jacket while Yonni continued to question their savior.

"And what god is that? Who are you partnered to?"

"Eslen," Utic answered in Tuvhe's place. He had heard a few things about the god of judgment, as stories traveled through the dunes from Sennan settlers. They all had one thing in common: A trail of bodies was always left behind.

"The Betrayer?" Yonni exclaimed. "And we're supposed to trust that you won't take our lives as well?"

Tuvhe ran a gauntleted hand through his greasy hair.

"Eslen says that you can ask Drinex. The gods that chose you two are the only ones he considered, for lack of a better word, friends."

He's right, though the word "friends" is definitely a stretch of the imagination, Verna told Utic. ***I would instead say that our paths have been aligned for a couple of cycles.***

"Verna tells me he's okay, Yonni. But what about Drinex?" Utic asked her.

Yonni wrinkled her nose at Tuvhe.

"Drinex says you're fine, for now. But I'm still keeping a close eye on you. I've already been fooled once."

Tuvhe looked down at Orghov's body and turned back to Yonni.

"That situation has been taken care of. This Pyrolite and his friends have been judged accordingly for their crimes, many of which you don't want to know."

"So where does that leave us? We don't even know where we are," Utic piped in.

Tuvhe faced him. "You're in the Crystalands, but if you've been given the same task I have, I would think that you're both in need of a ride to Prodigium. Am I correct?"

Utic glanced toward Yonni and shrugged. He was more than happy to join forces with another Tomekeeper, especially one that had come to rescue them, but the decision ultimately rested with the princess. Whatever she decided, and wherever she went, he was determined to follow.

Yonni huffed and gave them both an annoyed look.

"I'll go along, but I'm keeping an eye on you, Mister Betrayer. One wrong move, and you're iced."

Tuvhe extended his hand toward Utic and Yonni. Utic shook it warily, as did Yonni while they introduced themselves.

"Now that the pleasantries have passed, I have a small favor to ask," Yonni said.

"What's that?" Tuvhe questioned.

"Would either of you be willing to help me up the ladder?"

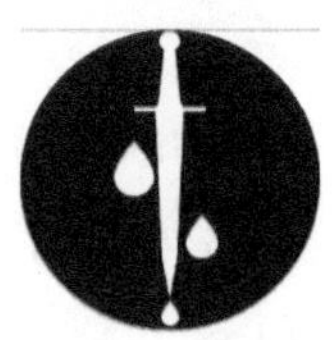

Verina impatiently tapped the side of the tiny boat as it slipped into the harbor. She had long heard that Prodigium was a city of vibrant sights that put even Selenti to shame, yet none of that mattered in the veiled shadows of its seedier districts. While it wasn't Verina's preferred way to enter the capital, it was a necessity. There was no way the Wingsong would let a Terrolaff waltz through the city's gates. It was too risky to all those inside and, to be fair, they weren't wrong. Fwen was smart to think about such things in advance.

The Noctide smuggler they hired in Selenti looked around to ensure the coast was clear. The bandage on his hand was stained with dried scarlet.

"It looks like you two are good to continue," he informed them. "The inn you requested should be around the corner."

Fwen stood up and stepped from the boat onto the dock without a word. Their entire trip thus far had been silent, not that Verina minded. The Noctide was too scared to talk, and Fwen seemed to be planning their next steps. Verina grabbed the two chests they had brought along and followed Fwen out of the boat.

"Hey, wait a minute," the smuggler called after them. "Your parents said that you would be the one to finish things up once we got here."

Fwen stopped.

"You're right," she said without looking back. "Verina, finish things for me, please."

Verina dropped the chests and faced the smuggler. He stepped back in terror. She could smell its sweet scent like the waft of a freshly baked pie.

The Terrolaff licked her lips, withdrew her dagger, and leapt toward the smuggler. He tried to run back to the boat, but she tossed her blade at his leg. It stuck and he fell against the dock. Verina yanked her dagger out and kicked the smuggler over. She slashed the blade against his chest.

"Scream for me," Verina ordered. "Scream as loud as you can, but know that no one will come to save you."

The Noctide begged and pleaded for mercy, his cries becoming louder and more desperate with every slash. Verina drowned him out with her own deranged laughter. She needed to release her pent up desires. She shoved the smuggler's body into the river after she had her fill of fun.

I'll leave that for the Wingsong, she thought. *A welcome gift of sorts.*

That kill was delicious, Tomekeeper, Istio commented. **You've starved me for too long, though. I need more to quell me. Much more.**

Verina could feel it too—the horrid pangs of a violent thirst unquenched. She slipped her dagger back into its sheath and followed after Fwen and the chests.

"Soon, my goddess," Verina promised. "Just let me get settled in first."

Verina caught up to Fwen as they rounded the corner and came to the door of the Inn. It was exactly what she expected for something in the less-than-reputable area of Prodigium: run down, dark, and a stone's throw away from something terrible happening. It was perfect, at least for the moment.

Fwen opened the door and went straight to the counter without looking around. Verina could tell her presence had potentially lured Fwen into a false sense of security. While she was happy to step in and handle any potential problems at the moment, she didn't want to be seen as Fwen's permanent hired muscle. There was no way she was going to be a pawn in someone else's game.

A thought nagged at the back of her mind. It was more than that. She wanted to be equals. Partners.

Fwen grabbed the key from the desk clerk—an angry older man with a crooked back and an eye patch—and waved it at Verina.

"Is the third floor alright with you?"

Verina affirmed and Fwen walked over to drop her chest off in front of her. Verina lifted it up and followed her fellow Tomekeeper up the stairs and to their room. As Fwen opened the door, the smell of mold and old carpet escaped. The room itself was a dusty square with barely enough space for the two beds inside, and a single window was boarded up in the middle.

"Do you think that's to keep things out, or keep us in?" Verina asked jokingly.

Fwen snickered and shook the dust from her cloak.

"From everything we've seen tonight, I'd say to sleep with one eye open."

I see you're spending time playing around when you could be finding our next prey, Istio snidely commented.

Verina's heart pounded a little faster.

My apologies, Istio. I'll leave now.

Verina dropped her chest off at the foot of her bed and started to make her way back toward the door.

"You're not going to rest?" Fwen asked with a touch of concern in her voice. "We're going to have quite a busy day tomorrow."

"I will, here in a moment," Verina responded. "I need a bit of fresh air first."

Fwen's eyes narrowed. "Was the air on the boat ride over here not fresh enough?"

Verina hesitated and thought her response through.

"I meant that I need to stretch my legs. There hasn't been much space to walk around on the ship, and that boat barely fit us as it was. I think I may have pulled something when I took care of our payment problem."

Fwen tossed her head back onto the rickety bed and closed her eyes.

"I understand. Just try not to be seen."

Verina slipped out the door and closed it. She let out a soft sigh on the other end. Her hands were shaking for some unknown reason.

Is there a reason you're so nervous, keeper? Istio hissed. ***You've been a little too obedient recently. Remember, this is not a job. We don't submit to anyone else.***

Verina tried to formulate a response to Istio, but couldn't create one that made sense. It was hard to explain something that she herself didn't fully understand. She squeezed her hands into tight fists and relaxed them. The shaking subsided.

It was time to hunt.

Fwen kept her eyes closed for a long while after Verina left, but her mind couldn't relax. She saw right through Verina's lies and the trembling of her hands. She was hiding something, and it was obvious. As long as she was out and about, most likely looking for another poor person to stab, she was a danger to their plans. Fwen had traveled too far across land and sea to get thrown into a Prodigium jail cell so close to the end of their journey. As helpful as Verina was to have around, Fwen had no hesitation in leaving her behind if the situation arose.

"I was worried you were becoming too attached to the pet," Netot said.

Fwen opened her mouth to reply, then realized that the voice wasn't in her head. She jolted up and looked around for the source. Her cloak remained undisturbed under her.

"I'm over here, Tomekeeper," Netot's voice drifted from the front of the bed. Fwen scooted closer and saw a collection of small purple particles mixed amongst the dust. It pulled together slowly but surely into a translucent ball. Fwen wasn't sure what was happening, or even how.

"You don't feel it, keeper? The energy radiating from Ghantei's castle?" Netot inquired. **"We're close to the tomes. I can pull energy off of the fringe of their power."**

"And that allows you to manifest in our realm?" Fwen tried to piece together.

"In a way. It wouldn't be conducive to be restricted to your inner thoughts, but only you can see me in my current form. Consider it a trait of our bond."

"Tell me, Netot: Does this mean that you'll be able to reach a full physical state again?"

Netot took a moment to respond.

"We've never been successful in attuning to our original forms. Ghantei separated us from our dying bodies. All we have is our spiritual essence."

"And no one has tried to find a way to help?"

"Many have asked the same questions you do now, Fwen Inati. All have failed in their efforts."

Fwen reached out and touched the orb body of Netot. Her hand passed through it, turning the particles of the orb into a dense mist. There had to be a way to bring Netot back, and Fwen was determined to find it. After all, having a god in the physical realm was much more powerful than just being their spokesperson. The orb reassembled and glided over to the other end of the room.

"I will be here while you rest," Netot informed her. **"Death sleeps for no one, and I have been locked up long enough."**

There was something morbid about the god of death watching over Fwen while she slept, but she also found comfort in the idea. Maybe it was the fact that she had been raised to worship Death as an entity, or maybe it was that she felt empowered over mortality because of her connection to Netot. Regardless, Death needed her. She laid her head sideways against the bed, wrapped her cloak around her like a blanket, and fell into a deep slumber.

Zall woke up on top of a thin, wooden cot that reeked of hay. As he rubbed his eyes, the orange haze of a candle by the bedside helped illuminate the granite walls around him. Water dripped from cracks above and gathered in pools on the cobblestone floors. A single wooden bucket was tossed haphazardly in the corner. The only way in or out was a door in the far left side with a slat in the middle.

Hey, the keeper's awake, Hilaster noted, his voice clear despite the loud ringing that plagued Zall's left ear. *It looks like we got tossed in the dungeons. They couldn't even give us a normal cell up top.*

"You just let them drag me down here? Why didn't you take over when I got knocked out and slaughter them all?" Zall questioned aloud, incensed.

I can't do that, keeper. There are lots of rules about taking over your body, even in emergency situations. I don't want to get on Ghantei's bad side. The best we can do is lend our power, but you're only able to receive about a quarter of that in your current state, Hilaster explained.

"So what's the plan then?" Zall pressed.

The same thing it has always been, Hilaster replied. *Get the tome, then burn Lidaesea down. I doubt these walls are strong enough to withhold a focused blast.*

Zall checked the room for options. The door seemed like the most obvious route of escape, and that most likely meant plenty of guards on the other end. As much as he yearned for bloodshed, Hilaster was right. There would be plenty of time for battle once he claimed what was rightfully his. The thought of what his abilities could do at full power made a sinister smile creep up his lips. He checked the ceiling, but it seemed to be too weak. Blasting it down would probably cause more harm than good, and perhaps even a whole structural collapse. Zall walked around the room, focused.

The feeling of chilled air tickled his fingertips as he ran his hands across the granite walls. It was a trace amount, almost unnoticeable, but it was definitely there. He dropped to a knee and ran his hands around the rough surface of the wall to look for the source. He felt a small hole, barely bigger than a coin.

"There's a draft, which means that air is able to pass through from somewhere up above," Zall deduced. "I'd bet that there's a way to get out of here on the other side of this stone."

Let's find out, Hilaster egged on. ***Bust it open.***

Zall held out his hand and closed his eyes.

"Hilasuun."

A spark of fire flitted from his fingertips and rolled into a ball that he slipped into the hole. It sizzled and expanded, cracking the wall until it exploded into a pile of gray rubble. Zall stepped through the breach and into a cobweb-ridden dirt tunnel on the other end. It stretched as far as he could see.

You were right, keeper. Well done, Hilaster complimented.

"They were fools to think they could keep me locked inside some dingy chamber," Zall said. He could feel the prickle of energy and anticipation washing over his body. "It's time to head to the castle and show them who we really are."

Ramji pulled herself through the gelatinous membrane of the aether gate and fell to the ground. Her lungs kicked back in and begged for air. She coughed heavily, gripping her body as the feeling of gravity settled back into her bones. It was like being born anew.

Trescoise sat in a crooked wooden chair, face buried in his hands. He seemed pallid and tired. He lifted his head up, then leapt up at the sight of her.

"Ramji!" he cried.

Ramji tried to pull herself up, but her legs couldn't hold her weight. She fell back to the cold limestone floor. Her father wrapped her arm around his shoulder and lifted her up, then accompanied her to the chair. She dropped into it with a heavy cough.

"Ramji, you're alive!" he said with bewilderment. "I had hope but I wasn't sure. The gate wouldn't let me pass, so I sat here and waited just in case you made it back through. My body wouldn't take much more."

Ramji gave him a puzzled look. The heavy bags under his eyes were confirmation that something was wrong.

"What do you mean? I've only been gone for a few minutes, father."

Trescoise sat on his knees and returned her expression with a dark stare.

"Ramji, you've been gone for almost a fortnight. Did it not feel like it on the other side? They've been waiting for your return, as have I."

Ramji wiped the slime from her glasses.

"They?"

The sound of metal on tile and the ruffle of feathers drew her attention to the doorway where five celenians entered with their swords drawn. The celenian woman in front placed both hands on her hilt. She was an imposing blonde with an asymmetrical haircut, jasmine eyes, and matching pair of wings clung to her back.

"Ramji Wrine, Tomekeeper of Shoroux. We've come to escort you from Casis to Prodigium on orders from His Excellency. Please come willingly, as I would hate to use force."

Prodigium

Verina leapt from rung to rung, hidden by the dark of night as she silently stalked her target. The woman that walked through the alley below was only a few years older than she was, tall and slender with a powder blue dress that stood out amongst the dull and dreary buildings. There was no good reason for someone with such an innocent air to have been alone in the early hours of the morning, but that was exactly what made the situation so enticing.

Verina made her way down the side of the buildings and dropped onto the stone of the alley with the softest of thuds. She slipped behind the woman and latched one arm around her waist and used the other to hold the dagger to her throat. Her skin was soft and the color of fine porcelain, and her lilac hair flowed down in sweeping curls.

"What's a pretty little thing like you doing alone at night?" Verina teased. The woman tried to break the hold and Verina tightened. "Don't struggle. As much as I like the fight, there's no need."

"No need? But I like to play too," the woman said and shoved her elbow hard into Verina's side.

Verina felt the sharp sting of pain shoot through her. She loosened her hold slightly, and the woman slipped out from underneath. Verina flipped her dagger around into a fighting stance, but the woman decked her across the jaw before she could progress. Verina tumbled to the ground, her dagger clattering down the alley.

Her lip burned and started to swell. She wiped it and looked down at her glove. Blood. A group of four men came around into the front of the alley, while another three shuffled in from the back.

"Oi, Elphana! Who's this sweet tart you brought to us?" one of the men in the front shouted. Verina mentally kicked herself. Of course it was a trap.

You couldn't tell? Istio criticized. ***It was incredibly obvious.***

Verina didn't respond, only fumed. She had been humiliated in front of her goddess, and it would be the last time she ever let something of the sort happen again. Her knees buckled under her as she tried to stand.

"You're going to pay for this," she growled.

"What was that?" Elphana mocked her with a hand pressed against her ear. She dropped down to face Verina. "I couldn't make out what you said past that busted lip, you sad clown-looking freak."

Verina shook her left sleeve and another blade, short and thin with a hooked tip, dropped into her hand. She slipped it between her ring and middle fingers and slashed upward. Elphana shrieked and fell back, hands wrapped around her face. Verina reached out, snagged a handful of Elphana's hair, and yanked her head back. She grabbed her dagger with her free hand, then sawed through Elphana's hair as roughly as she could. She tossed the chunks aside and kicked her face into the cobblestone.

Beautiful job, Istio said. ***Now, kill.***

The group of men charged in and swung wildly at Verina. She dodged their punches and rolled between them, slashing and stabbing at their arms and legs. The familiar feeling of magical power swept through her veins.

"*Pahszaraa!*" Verina yelled out. Spinning blades of etheric energy flew out of her sleeves, lodged themselves into the three men closest to her, and pinned them to the alley walls. One of the men stepped in to fill the gap as Verina slid under him and stabbed her way up his back. The remaining men scrambled away.

There was no room for mercy and no chance for escape.

"*Jehanasas!*"

Verina crafted three sickly green bubbles in her left hand and tossed them toward her attackers. They struck, melded, and expanded over the men's bodies until they were enveloped in a mass of sizzling acid. Each of them fought futilely against the goo.

Very inventive, my knife's edge! Istio praised Verina. ***Their suffering and screams will sustain me for now.***

A sense of pride built in Verina from the remark. She looked down at Elphana as she wept into the ground, then knelt down and ran the flat edge of her dagger against Elphana's neck.

"I'll spare you today, but only because I know that living with your shame will be a fate worse than death."

Verina drove the tip of her boot into Elphana's side and walked down the alley. Shadows crept up as dawn crested over the rooftops. Verina hopped onto a nearby cart and up onto the wooden rafters that stretched between the desolate buildings of the area. She hurried back to the inn.

Fwen was still asleep as she entered their room, nestled up within her cloak. Her light snores were the only sound in the early hours of the morn. Verina silently dropped into her bed on the opposite end and closed her eyes to rest. A sudden yawn caused her to flick them back open.

"Time to wake up, Verina," Fwen said groggily as she pushed herself to the edge of her cot. She rubbed her eyes and tried to pat down her messy hair. "We have to get ready."

Verina felt the temptation of a deep slumber beckon to her, but Fwen moved around the room with a boisterous energy that prevented her from succumbing to its call.

"I see you're covered in blood. Did you have a good night?" Fwen asked nonchalantly.

Verina giggled.

"You could say that."

Fwen opened up her chest and rifled through it. She mumbled something to herself and tossed the contents around. Verina watched as she continued to dig, surprised at Fwen's ability to pack so much in such a limited space. Fwen popped her head up over the chest's lid and tossed a cloak at Verina. It was made of black velvet with a dark green quatrefoil pattern weaved throughout.

"I can't have you going in front of the monarch in stained clothes, can I?" Fwen said. "A composed appearance can get people to let their guard down more easily."

Verina held the gifted cloak up to her own. It was definitely an upgrade, but one she wasn't sure she wanted. She rubbed the edge of her normal cloak with her thumb. It was special, and not in a way that she ever expected Fwen to understand.

"I don't have to get rid of this one, do I?"

Fwen popped back up over the lid, hair fixed and black makeup reapplied.

"I'm not going to tell you what to do with your possessions. You said never to speak for you, remember?"

Fwen disappeared into the chest once more, and Verina let a rare, genuine smile form for the briefest moment. She tugged on the strings of her cloak, removed it, and folded it with care into a square. Verina tucked it neatly into her own chest and picked up the cloak Fwen had given her. The new one felt light in her hands despite its heavier appearance. She threw it around her shoulders and tied it.

"It looks good," Fwen stated. "It accentuates your face nicely. While it's on my mind, do you want me to touch up your patterns?"

Verina hadn't thought about it, but figured it would be for the best. She nodded and Fwen popped back up, wax pencils in hand. She stepped close, closer than she had ever gotten, and retraced the patterns on Verina's face. Verina held her breath and tried her best to stay still despite the sudden burn in her chest and stomach. The soft wax melted against the warmth of Verina's cheeks.

"Done," Fwen said suddenly.

"That was fast, though I suppose you must be a professional at these things by now," Verina replied.

Fwen snapped her fingers in approval.

"One of the first things my mother taught me was the art of makeup and its many uses. I'm sure yours taught you as well?"

A sudden pang went through Verina's heart.

"I taught myself, actually. I spent lots of time studying the other Terrolaffs and drawing my own designs."

"Self-taught? I offer my praises. I don't have the patience for such things," Fwen responded. She closed the latch on her chest. "Are you ready?"

"Let's embrace our full potential," Verina answered. She followed Fwen out the door, chest in hand, and up the stairs to the inn's roof. Verina paused and looked around in confusion as they stepped into the sun. "Shouldn't we have gone downstairs to make our way toward the castle?"

Fwen placed her belongings on the roof and turned to Verina.

"Downstairs? Oh no! We're not going to them, Verina. Quite the opposite."

Fwen took a few steps back and hunched her shoulders forward. Her cloak billowed before it split down the middle. Each half spread outward and melted into skeletal wings completely coated in dripping black tar. They were sharpened and almost three times bigger than Fwen herself. Without another word, she rose into Prodigium's sky.

"What kind of bird is that?" Qio exclaimed as he pointed over the horizon. "I've never seen anything with wings that big!"

Irada placed his hand over his eyes and looked off into the distance. Far ahead, above the walls of Prodigium, was a dark figure with sprawling black wings. It flipped and spiraled over the cityscape before two golden streaks met it in the air. Something about the creature gave him an uneasy feeling.

"Qio, I don't think that was a bird," Irada told him.

Agreed, Heivara added. ***There's a trail of dark magic behind it.***
Qio scoffed.

"Come on, Irada. I thought those carrots you've been farming were supposed to help you see better. It was obviously a bird. What else could it be?"

"We're heading to Prodigium, so another Tomekeeper, perhaps?" Irada offered.

"Yeah, sure!" Qio said with a snort. "Last I checked, Zhonitas and Ghantei were the only ones that had any sort of flying ability."

Irada shrugged his shoulders, as he had at many points throughout their shared journey thus far. He'd come to realize that, more often than not, Qio just wanted to be right. Providing logical arguments or trying to have Qio look at things from a different perspective hadn't worked out at all. The Asceniate was hard-headed, probably more so than anyone else Irada had ever dealt with. It didn't really bother him, but he wondered how Qio managed to live amongst anyone less patient.

A wailing cry caught his attention. He looked off to the right side of the road and saw a girl tucked against a mound of red clay, hands over her bawling face. She was younger than Qio and Irada, most likely a teenager, and her tan dress was caked in the clay that she sat next to. She looked up towards the cart as the two approached and waved her hands wildly.

"Sirs! Please, I need help!" the girl shouted as she ran toward the cart. Qio looked at her, then Irada, and shook his head. Irada wasn't sure what that meant.

Qio must have registered the confusion on Irada's face.

"No. We're not stopping. The most important thing is that you get me to Prodigium, remember? We're not going to waste time helping some poor down-on-her-luck village girl that probably got dumped off by her lover."

Who hurt him? Heivara asked in surprise and concern.

I've been wondering that myself, Irada replied. *Qio has a lot of anger built up in him.*

Maybe you can get through to him at some point, Heivara suggested. **In the meantime, we have to help her.**

"Qio, we can't just leave someone on the outskirts of the city. There's too many creatures out there, plus she could be hurt," Irada told the Asceniate. He tugged on the reins and directed the horse toward the girl. Irada hopped down once the cart stopped while Qio pressed his face into his hands and let out an annoyed groan.

"Come on, you really can't be serious. She doesn't need help. I'd wager the whole thing is a trap," Qio complained. Irada kept walking. "I know you hear me! Irada. Irada!"

Irada heard Qio jump off the cart and walk after him. The girl waved again as she slowed down just a few feet away.

"Oh, thank you, sirs!" she said between heavy breathes. Her rounded face was bright red from running. "My uncle and I were out hunting shadowreeves when one of them caught us from behind. He got bit badly on his side and rolled down the mound. You have to help him!"

Irada took off toward the mound without hesitation. He had dealt with his fair share of shadowreeves before. They were nasty little creatures, half-dog and half-rat, that ate through everything they came across with their rows of needle-like teeth. If the girl's uncle had been bitten, they would need to move quickly to ensure his survival. Irada ran around the mound, Qio close behind, and found nothing.

The crack of the reins and the whinny of his horse made Irada swivel back toward the cart. The girl and two others, another girl around the same age and a slightly older boy, had hopped onto the cart and were darting down the pathway. Irada took off after them, but it was no use.

Qio ran past Irada and kept running down the road shouting curses before he eventually stopped too.

Irada met Qio halfway as the latter walked back in defeat. While Irada had tried to maintain a sense of peace despite his frustration, Qio held nothing back. He snatched the hat from Irada's head and tossed it to the ground.

"I told you it was a trap!" Qio snapped. "I saw that coming, and I warned you! You have to listen to me. I am a Tomekeeper. I know what I'm talking about."

Qio kicked Irada's hat into the air and it floated to the mound. Irada weighed going after it, but decided it wasn't worth the trouble. Instead, he watched as Qio walked around and ranted angrily to himself.

Tomekeeper, I sense something, Heivara interrupted.

Irada felt an odd tug and looked around before he caught sight of another cart coming toward them. He tapped Qio's shoulder to grab his attention. Qio turned and perked up when he saw the cart, then ran towards the road to intercept.

"Hey, you! Long ears! Get over here and help us out!" Qio yelled at the cart as it passed by. The Wojlidoj man driving gave him a scowl while the Phreeton woman seated next to him grabbed at her own ears in confusion. The man cracked the reins and their cart picked up speed as it passed them by.

Qio screamed in frustration and stamped the dirt.

"What the hael are we supposed to do now?" he asked Irada.

Irada shrugged once more and looked further down the road. Kephram's Keep was still about ten minutes by wagon, which meant it would probably be closer to a two-and-a-half-hour trek by foot. He tightened the strap of his bag and slung it over his shoulder.

"We do what everyone did before the gods gifted us the wheel, Qio. We walk."

"Man, that guy was an arse," Kliev said as he looked back over his shoulder at the pair in the distance. He noticed I'el had covered her ears. "Hey, you didn't think he was calling you that, did you?"

I'el felt the heat of embarrassment wash over her. Even if the man hadn't been talking to her specifically, she had already acknowledged that she believed the comment was directed toward her. She lowered her hands and rested them in her lap.

"What? No, of course not. Nope, definitely not," she said with a nervous laugh. "I just thought I felt something brush across them. It must be all the pollen in the air making them itch or something."

Kliev's expression lit up. "Yours itch too sometimes? I thought it was just because of my fur."

I'el couldn't help but crack a smile at Kliev's comment. She'd grown accustomed to the way that his words diffused the tension of a situation or just made her laugh for no reason. The thought of them eventually having to go their own ways made her a little somber. She studied the plains around them. The road to Prodigium cut through a mixture of grassy knolls with mounds of red clay protruding from flat patches of dirt. It made I'el yearn for the Hicarian forests.

"It's sad, isn't it?" she asked as she gazed into the distance.

"What is?" Kliev inquired.

I'el waved her hands out in front of her for emphasis.

"We're heading to the largest city in Lidaesea. Prodigium is home to some of the biggest and flashiest people, locations, and trends around. Yet the area outside of those walls cries out for love and attention. Just look at the grass. It's yellowed in some patches and dead in others. The clay is dry from a lack of moisture in the ground."

And there are no trees anywhere to be found, Noli added.

"And, there are no trees anywhere to be found!" I'el repeated with added concern. "Would it kill the Wingsong to fly over and sprinkle some seeds or water the ground?"

Kliev let out a hearty chuckle.

"I should have guessed you would be so passionate about the environment."

"I'm just saying that the monarch can make things happen with a clap of his hands. Why not spread some of Ghantei's love outside the city walls?"

"Maybe he's worried about having to take care of more than just the outskirts?" Kliev posited. "You know, the Krijyan mountains could use some love too."

I'el giggled.

"You mean you Wojlidoj have eaten all the grass up there?"

"Hey, hold on a moment," Kliev playfully huffed. "The idea that just because we have a rabbit's ears, and speed, and hop, must mean that we have a rabbit's diet is a gross misunderstanding. We don't eat grass. We eat hay."

"You do know that hay is just dried grass, right?" I'el snorted.

Kliev blushed.

"That's not the point we're trying to make here, remember? To be honest with you, though, I remember when I was a young boy. I would perch myself in a tree, usually dead from the frigid air, and look out down the mountainside to the Phreeton forests. They were always so vibrant and thick. A part of me always wondered what it would be like to actually explore them, but I never had the courage to."

"So what made you decide to come down from your mighty mountaintop, then?" I'el pressed. "You could have gone a number of different ways to get to Prodigium. Why through the Orchard?"

She watched Kliev furrow his brow in thought, and she wondered what about the question might have triggered the response. He opened his mouth to say something, then closed it again. After a long pause, he finally spoke.

"I'm going to be honest with you, I'el. I feel like I owe you that much. I was on the run."

I'el angled herself toward Kliev and leaned in. Quiet concern riddled her voice. "What do you mean? Did you kill somebody?"

"Woah, what? No!" Kliev exclaimed. "I set our gathering hall on fire. I was talking to the chief's eldest daughter, Totkoyova, and then I was chosen. I shot a lightning bolt from the sky. It all happened very fast."

"Did anyone get hurt when it burned down?"

"Totkoyova got burned by a piece of wood that fell, but that was it. It wasn't even a major burn."

I'el was confused. "Then why were you on the run?"

Kliev tapped his hands together awkwardly. "Well you see, the reason I was talking to her was-"

"Kliev, I'm a grown woman. I don't need you to explain your attempt to seduce someone," I'el interrupted before he could go into more detail.

Kliev scratched his temple. "No, I'el. That's not it. I mean, that would have been a plus. She's incredibly attractive, but we were supposed to get together that evening and talk about the truce our fathers were brokering."

I'el was even more lost than before.

"Truce? Your father made a truce with the chief of the Wojlidoj? How did he even manage to get that type of power, and for what?"

"The opposite, actually," Kliev clarified. "Totkoyova's father, Chief Vintar, made a truce with my dad, King Suhndher. I think he may have taken the whole lightning situation and harm to his daughter as a planned attack."

I'el sat back against the cart bench.

"Okay, I could see how that would make more sense," she thought aloud.

The realization struck.

"Wait. Wait! You're a prince?"

What was that I said before about unknown soils? Noli chimed in.

Not now! I'el snapped back at the goddess.

"I don't really like to share that out," Kliev told her. He was oddly subdued. I'el wondered if it was a point of shame rather than pride but, if so, she was curious as to why. She figured it was better to let it go for now.

"Your secret's safe with me, Prince Rorn," I'el promised with a soft smile.

Kliev bowed his head and looked forward, reins grasped firmly in his hands. The golden walls of Prodigium grew higher by the minute. Kephram's Keep, the city outside of Prodigium's main gate, was just within reach. That somber feeling tugged at her once more.

I'el, my sweet flower, I ask that you reflect on the situation. You have two men in very high positions that want your attention.

You would have to try really hard to mess this up, Noli commented.

I already told you that my heart belongs to my sweet Friston, I'el grumbled internally. *Why are you so invested in my love life, anyway?*

I love to watch all things grow, Noli answered. ***Especially the
seeds of love.***

The horses pulling the cart neighed and slowed as the duo entered
Kephram's outer edge. The change from quiet plains to bustling city was
almost instant. A crowd filled in around them, pushing and shoving one
another as Kliev followed other carts in the direction of the gate. I'el lifted
her head and soaked in the full size of Prodigium's wall. Something about
it made her feel insignificant in the grand scheme of everything—another
drop in the ocean or leaf lost to the forest—yet she knew in her heart that
there were big things in store for her on the other side.

"We finally made it," Kliev said with an immense sigh of relief. His
whole body seemed to deflate from the absence of tension. "So the
question now becomes: how do we get in?"

An endless line of carts, full of supplies and visitors, passed behind
Yonni as she explored the market square of Kephram's Keep with eyes
full of wonder. The way that the ribbons and flags hung from the rafters
and vibrant colors were splashed across every surface reminded her of
the Raftworks back home. She wondered if she would hear news of her
kingdom or whether she would be able to return anytime soon.

The weight of the accident that separated her from her mother weighed heavily on her mind. While Utic had tried his best to offer her solace, and Tuvhe his trust, nothing could replace the yearning she had to feel the salted waters of the sea embrace her. The sensation of being dragged down to the abyss knowing that it was not a place of fear, but home, was second to none. The weightlessness and freedom that came with being able to swim wherever she pleased was even better.

I miss it too, keeper, Drinex confided. ***We've been away too long. I can barely hear the water's call.***

I want to make sure the Queen is safe, Yonni told him. *After that, I would love to go wallu riding along the mineral wells. It would be nice to feel the current in my hair and see that diamond-like dust again.*

"Yonni, did you hear me?" Utic said from beside her.

The Anqualai had gotten lost in the sea of her oceanic fantasies and didn't realize he had approached. Her absent expression gave him his answer.

"Tuvhe says that we need to go," Utic explained as he grabbed her hand and pulled her along. "He's found a guard that may help us get in."

Yonni tugged against Utic's hand to loosen his grip. His palms were rough despite his young age. Her hand slipped out and she slowed her pace. While she had practiced walking plenty over the two days it took them to reach Prodigium from Orghov's barge, she still wasn't able to move as fast as she would have liked. Any attempts to speed up often resulted in her flat against the ground and both of her fellow Tomekeepers asking if she was hurt.

"Oh! I'm sorry, Yonni," Utic expressed. "I didn't hurt you, did I?"

Yonni shook her head. The curls of her hair bounced lightly.

"You're just moving faster than I can keep up with."

Utic apologized again, then looked around. Yonni felt it too. There was a heavy and negative sensation that rocked down her neck and into her stomach, like the sting of multiple jellyfish all at once. Her breathing intensified. It was a more extreme version of the sensation she experienced when Tuvhe first met them.

More Tomekeepers are nearby, Drinex informed her. **You may be feeling the culmination of our combined magical energy. I can sense... seven more nearby. One in particular has an abnormally large amount of magic currently pouring out of them.**

Can you tell who each Tomekeeper is connected to and where they are?

Everyone's magic is ebbing and flowing into one another's, Drinex explained. **I can detect all the gods except Heivara and Ghantei. As for where, the only thing that I can tell you is that Noli and Wogiwoj are somewhere in the immediate vicinity.**

Yonni met Utic's eyes as they looked around.

"Did Drinex tell you the same thing that Verna told me?" Utic asked. "About Noli and Wogiwoj?"

Yonni nodded in affirmation and scanned the crowd. Being able to navigate the flow of bodies was a massive task already, but trying to find two specific people in it seemed impossible.

Utic waved to get her attention.

"Bunny ears, three carts up. That's got to be them!" he suggested.

Yonni and Utic weaved through the crowds and carts until they reached the one that seated the bunny man and his orange-haired companion. Another strange vibration rippled through Yonni's body, one she could only assume was an indicator of their magical connection.

Outside of the Tomekeeper potential, the ears of both stuck out to her. The man's were tall and furry while the woman's were sharp and slightly tilted back. A Wojlidoj and a Phreeton, indeed. Yonni had heard many stories about both groups from her father growing up, but to her it was like seeing a mythical creature in person. She wondered if that was how others felt meeting her in all her Anquan glory.

"Excuse me," Utic called up to the couple. "You wouldn't happen to be riding into Prodigium, would you?"

The man looked down from the cart and looked Utic over. The woman leaned in and whispered something in his ear.

"Why are you asking?" the man replied to Utic with a guarded tone.

Yonni shuffled over to Utic's side. To her, there was no point in skirting around the topic. They looked displaced from their nations, had traveled to the city, and were an odd-looking couple to begin with. Either they were Tomekeepers, or they weren't.

"We're the Tomekeepers of Drinex and Verna," she informed them. "I have strong reason to believe you may be the chosen for Wogiwoj and Noli. Am I correct in that assumption?"

The couple exchanged a glance and relaxed.

"Drinex and Verna, eh?" the man replied. "A few of the good ones, I hear. Nothing like the off-kilter ones that surround us in the rest of Silnathum. I'm Kliev, Tomekeeper of The Woj."

Kliev reached across the cart and extended a hand that Utic and Yonni shook in good faith. He held his palm out towards the woman.

"I've never heard you call him The Woj before," she commented.

"He said he prefers it," Kliev responded.

"Alright, then," the woman said with a few heavy blinks. She faced Utic and Yonni, arms outstretched as she dipped into a small bow. "I'el Rivini, Tomekeeper of Noli. It's a pleasure to meet you two."

"The pleasure is ours," Utic replied as he returned her bow. "It's nice to acquaint ourselves with more Tomekeepers before the upcoming banquet."

"Banquet?" Kliev asked in surprise.

"Did you seriously forget about the Banquet of Tomes?" I'el asked him. "You know, the moment we all come together and officially acknowledge the centennial cycle?"

"I'll be honest with you, I'el. I don't recall much of the process. I just know if there's food and mead to be had, I will gladly be a part of whatever you need me to do."

Yonni tilted her head and tried to assess their new acquaintances. They seemed comfortable with each other, but both were awkward in comparison to many of the people she knew. Kliev came across as cocky and brash, a front to no doubt hide a more emotional side, while I'el was sweet, but flighty. They were an unusual mix that somehow managed to click.

"You two must have traveled quite a ways," Yonni said, breaking her silence. "I'd love to hear about your journey at some point. We just arrived ourselves and were trying to find a way into the city. Perhaps we can join together?"

"That's fine by me," Kliev answered.

"Same," I'el seconded.

Yonni let out an unnoticed breath. She had gone from all alone to a group of five strong, and thankfully all the Tomekeepers that she had met had been, from the outside at least, nice people. It was far from how she originally thought the situation and the journey would go.

"I see you two have made new friends," Tuvhe's voice startled Yonni from behind. She jumped and spun around to face him. He had an air of seriousness around him.

"Who's this?" Kliev asked Utic and Yonni.

Tuvhe offered a slight bow.

"Tuvhe Vull, Tomekeeper of Senna and the Devement."

"You mean Tomekeeper of the Betrayer, then?" I'el blurted. She stared at Yonni. "This is the company you keep?"

"Drinex and Verna told us to trust him, and we have," Yonni replied. "He hasn't steered us wrong. In fact, he saved us from a group of Pyrolites."

"The Woj is telling me that he was never proven to be the Betrayer," Kliev leaned over and told I'el.

"Well, Noli is saying otherwise," I'el said with crossed arms. "Something about weeds in a garden. Tell me, Tuvhe: Why should we trust you?"

Tuvhe stepped up to the cart and gave I'el a cold look. Kliev braced himself for trouble.

"Because if you don't, your options for getting into Prodigium reduce drastically," Tuvhe answered bluntly. "I don't suppose you would be able to grow a vine tall enough to stretch over this wall?"

I'el lowered her arms.

"To be fair, I haven't really had a chance to try."

"I understand your hesitation. I really do," Tuvhe said. "Yonni and Utic were the same, but I promise I'm just trying to help and get us to where we need to be."

Tuvhe waited for a response, then stepped back when there wasn't one.

"One of the guard towers next to the gate is helmed by a celenian named Coltiel. I told him about everything and he's offered to take us to the castle when we're ready."

"What made him believe that you were a Tomekeeper?" Yonni asked in surprise.

Tuvhe patted the hilt of his sword.

"I had to show him the only magic I can muster right now."

Yonni pondered asking more questions, then decided against it. The group looked at one another, then followed Tuvhe as he led the way toward the guard tower. It was bigger than Yonni had expected, a sturdy metal block that was raised high into the sky with the flag of Prodigium fluttering across the pointed tip. The celenians guarding the door stepped aside as the group entered and Tuvhe took them up six flights of stairs. They pressed on through a set of double doors and into a room with wood paneling along the floor and walls. An older Wingsong man with vibrant white wings and shaggy hair gazed out the tower's right side window.

"You've made it back," Coltiel said. "And with extras in tow. I take it you all are ready to head to the castle?"

He turned and Yonni let out an audible gasp. The tips of his entire left wing had been burned off haphazardly, as if someone had taken a sword to it and cut off chunks without regard to the final presentation. Black and dark brown lines ran along the edges. She didn't know it was possible to destroy a Wingsong's wings so badly.

"It's no worry," Coltiel said to Yonni, reading her expression. "I can't fly like I used to, but I can still hold my own in battle."

"Thank you for taking us to the castle," Utic said.

"Yeah, we weren't sure how we were supposed to enter," Kliev added.

Coltiel waved his hand in front of him.

"It's no problem, I assure you. We've been waiting for you all to show up, but, as you can imagine, we've also had to increase our security measures as a result. Word is spreading fast that the Tomekeepers have been chosen, and everyone wants to know who or claim that glory for themselves. I trust you can vouch for one another?"

Everyone nodded in agreement.

"Good, then we can proceed," Coltiel continued. He moved to the back of the room and pressed his hand against a hidden panel in the wall. It shifted back and he rolled it into the rest of the wood to reveal a doorway. "We're going to climb up onto the top of the wall and take the path around to the castle, then descend the bulwark to reach the courtyard. I hope that you all are ready for a walk."

Coltiel ascended a ramp into another stairwell, the group behind him. The rounded staircase spiraled to the top, but the lack of railing caused Yonni to cling to the stone wall as they ascended. They went through another door at the top of the staircase and emerged onto the paved pathway at the top. The wind blew fiercely against them all. While Coltiel was unbothered, the others flinched from the sudden blast of frigid air. Yonni felt like a strong enough breeze could even blow her over the edge. She shuddered.

The view of Prodigium from atop the wall was breathtaking. The mass collection of buildings, carts, and people all seemed so much smaller from Yonni's bird's eye perspective. The glittering rooftops and flags blended into a rainbow of colors that stretched across the city, and a massive grassy circle filled with man-made rivers broke up the infrastructure in Prodigium's center. The castle, tucked toward the back, was a multistory and sprawling work of architectural art made of five white quartzite towers that radiated in the sunlight. "Lidaesea's crown jewel", as it was often called, was the most fitting name it could have been given. It was truly a work only Ghantei herself could have created.

The bridge rumbled slightly as the gate below them opened up. Yonni looked over the edge to see the mass of carts had been parted to make way for a singular carriage covered in gold, silver, and blue tourmaline.

"What's up with the fancy carriage?" Yonni asked Coltiel. He stopped in place and tilted over to see what she had noticed. Another breeze threatened to blow her away as he looked back at her.

"Oh, that? That's another one of you Tomekeepers. I'm not sure who, though."

Ramji peered out of the carriage window and listened to the crank of the gate as it lifted. It sounded old, maybe even rusted. Probably in need of maintenance.

"You might want to have them run an inspection on that thing," she said to the blonde celenian seated across from her. F'jalla, as she had introduced herself, was not amused. She cracked her knuckles and remained silent. "I'm just saying," Ramji continued. "I wouldn't want to be the one to get a slap on the wrist for something that could be easily prevented."

"And what exactly do you think is going to happen?" F'jalla snapped. "You've been commenting on nearly everything we've seen or passed since we left Casis. Do you not stop talking?"

Ramji scooted back against the seat of the carriage and crossed her legs. "I thought you would have enjoyed the conversation. Clearly, I was wrong."

"Great Ghantei," F'jalla fumed. "I was told that you lot were supposed to be easy to work with. That you answered to the voices in your head and followed along. Nobody said anything about Tomekeepers being dense."

Ramji dropped her leg back down and shot F'jalla a deadly stare.

"I will not allow anyone to call me dense, or any other variation that dilutes my intelligence. I worked incredibly hard to get to where I am, much as I'm sure you have as well so, woman to woman, drop the shite and at least acknowledge that much."

F'jalla looked surprised, then a smarmy grin wrapped across her face.

"Oh, it looks like the Tomekeeper has some bite to her after all. Here I thought you were too buried in your books to know anything about standing up for yourself."

This one is quite the antagonistic force, Shoroux commented. ***I implore that we deduce why.***

Ramji agreed. "Why are you so spiteful towards me when I've done nothing of harm to you?"

"You think I'm going to spill my heart out to you? Tell you my tragic story and make you cry? Ha!" F'jalla mocked her. "The only thing you need to know is that I don't trust Tomekeepers."

"But why?"

"Because there is nothing you Tomekeepers have done that couldn't have been completed by everyday people. All of Ghantei's keepers were chosen because they had already done great things. Being a Tomekeeper never gave them the ability to do more than they had before. The rest? All power hungry or attention-starved louts that flaunted their connection to our almighty beings to gain favors."

Incorrect, Shoroux said. ***Gaddiel was one of the best Tomekeepers I've chosen and was neither of those things.***

"I don't believe that," Ramji responded. "I think you're being unfair in your assessment of what we are and do."

"And what exactly is that?"

Ramji ruffled the curls of her hair.

"Honestly? I have no idea yet. I won't until I receive my tome. I know I was chosen for a reason, though. Shoroux has already shown me that."

"If you expect me to believe that you, or any of the others, are not just using your connections to gain for yourselves, then I'm going to have to see hard proof. Actions speak louder than words."

"That's a trite phrase that offers little semblance of an argument," Ramji snarked. "You want proof? Fine. As a scientist, everything I do comes down to proving people wrong."

The ensuing awkward silence was filled by the clacking of the carriage wheels against the stone roads of Prodigium. Ramji looked out the window at the mass of people shopping, playing, and conversing around them. While she was sure it was paradise for some, she would much rather have been tucked away back in her lab.

There's solace in searching for the unknown, keeper, Shoroux told her. **That much I understand.**

Data makes sense, Shoroux, Ramji remarked. *People don't. I can understand the alchemic makeup of iron, or how to create a fuel for the propulsion of modernized vehicles, yet the actions of others continues to confound me.*

Life is a series of trials, Ramji. That is why I choose to explore what awaits us in the aether instead, Shoroux stated.

Ramji used her peripheral vision to see what F'jalla was doing. The clacking of the wheels now bothered her immensely. Ramji needed something to distract her and scratched at the tops of her nails. Meanwhile, the celenian rubbed a spot off the balled point of her hilt.

"You come across as someone who likes battle," Ramji noted. "Why work for the monarch instead of leading the troops?"

F'jalla stopped rubbing and looked up.

"Are you asking why I choose to serve His Majesty instead of chopping down naysayers?"

"If that's how you opt to take it, sure."

"That may be the only sensible question to come out of your mouth this entire ride," F'jalla teased. "The answer is simple. I love the thrill of battle. The feeling of my sword piercing through an enemy's armor is unmatched. The sounds of hundreds, if not thousands, of soldiers joined together and stomping across a battlefield is the only type of music I enjoy.

"Yet, I know the cost of it all. The sad truth is that when we go to war, the ones who pay the biggest price are the ones that never see the battlefield. The mothers and fathers of fallen sons and daughters. The widows left behind by their loved ones. The children that will never again feel the embrace of a parent.

"I've had to deliver news that nobody wants to hear too many times over to ever want to do so again. By serving the monarch, I can help prevent the wars that once ravaged our world from ever occurring again."

Ramji reflected on F'jalla's words. It wasn't the answer she had expected. In fact, it made the celenian seated across from her a little more human. War was an idea long forgotten to many of the people that inhabited Lidaesea. The last one, if Ramji recalled correctly, was in the third cycle half a millennia prior.

That was when we made the vow to never wage war again, Shoroux noted in her mind. ***We would resolve things peacefully, and by our own standards. No matter the cost.***

The carriage suddenly stopped as a loud explosion and screams of terror rang from outside. The pressure of the blast caused the windows to shatter across Ramji and F'jalla in a cloud of sparkling glass. The former covered her face and was too scared to move, but the latter wasted no time in getting out to investigate. Another explosion rocked the carriage.

"You really think you winged wimps can stop me?" Zall shouted as he tossed another marble sized explosive into the street. It ignited under a food cart and scattered an assortment of vegetables and fruit. Crowds of people ran to shelter around him as more celenians swooped down.

"Cease, by order of the monarch!" one of them howled.

Zall responded with a pillar of fire. Flames crackled and heat rose as the celenian forces stepped back.

"Come on! I thought you were supposed to be the best of the best here!"

Such a pity that Ghantei's guard has been reduced to this piddling mess, Hilaster added. ***It's almost as if they're too scared of having their wings crisped to fight back.***

"Everyone, step aside!" a blonde celenian commanded as she pushed through the gathered group of guards. Zall snickered. The woman at least looked like she could hold her own. She pulled out a lavish broadsword with light yellow edges that matched her wings and eyes. "I'll take care of this little whelp."

"Just who do you think you're calling a whelp?" Zall spat. His hands blazed a bright blue and his breathing grew heavy. "Let's see you talk after this one. *Evfuouun!*"

A barrage of small blue beads erupted from his hand and landed amongst the crowd. The smell of sulfur and smoke quickly smogged the air. The blonde looked down at them and snarled.

"Everyone, brace!" she warned. Her wings wrapped around her as the rest tried to follow suit. The beads glowed brightly and exploded in rapid succession, each one with the force of a cannon blast.

Zall let out a whooping cheer as the celenians were scattered by the blasts. He turned and ran through the overturned carts toward the castle. There was no one that could stop him. The celenians, the supposed toughest of the Wingsong, were weaker than many of the other Pyrolites he had faced in battle. The feeling of destroying them in battle was almost euphoric. The castle grew in size as Zall reached the outer courtyard.

"I'm here, Your Majesty!" Zall cackled. "This is what you wanted, right? Give me my tome and we can get this banquet off to a real explosive start!"

A sharp burst of wind blew past Zall, followed by the brunt force of a tackle. Zall and his assailant tumbled along the courtyard.

"Who the hael do you think you are to attack me like that?" Zall yelled.

Familiar white wings bristled and shook open.

"The same one that kicked your arse last time, you psychopathic punk," the celenian woman said as she stood and flicked her ponytail back. "My name is Qurena, and I'm here to send you back to the dungeons."

Zall let out a stifled laugh.

"Really? You got lucky last time. That won't happen again. *Evfuou-un!*"

Zall launched the same barrage of explosive beads that managed to get the better of Qurena's companions, but she was too fast. She ducked and dodged through the beads as they exploded around her, wings tucked tightly to avoid any burns. She jumped forward with a quick flap and put all of her force into a falling strike. Zall barely managed to grab her wrist and reverse the attack. He spun her around and tossed her sideways, but she threw her wings open and landed on both feet.

"Is that all you've got?" Qurena taunted. "I don't think I got lucky last time. I think you're just weak."

Zall felt the fiery magic within him blaze white hot and course through every part of his body. There was no way that he was going to let anyone get the better of him, especially the smug woman standing before him. He channeled the feeling of the hot cinders in his veins out into a physical form, and a wall of fire swooshed around him.

Yes! Hilaster exclaimed. ***We're close enough to my tome that I can pull some of its power. Lets burn this bird down to ashes!***

A hard metal slammed into the middle of Zall's spine. He felt his bones crack and the force sent him stumbling forward. The blonde twirled around his left side and smashed the metal sheath of her sword into the front of his legs. Zall fell to the ground.

"I had it, F'jalla!" Qurena shouted out at her companion.

"You were taking too long, Qurena! Threats need to be put down instantly. We don't play around this close to the castle," F'jalla argued back.

Zall let out an angry howl and propelled himself up with explosions from his hands. He was tired of the games. The wall of fire around him roared back into existence. He raised his fists to the sky and shouted as loud as his voice would allow.

"*Behfuohilasuun!*"

A tower of flame shot down from the sky like a bolt of lightning and swallowed Zall. Fireballs launched from the side like fireworks, burning and melting anything they touched. The tower expanded and the sheer heat made the travertine tiles of the courtyard sizzle underfoot. Qurena and F'jalla covered their faces and leapt back, using their wings to zip into the sky.

Inside, Zall felt the fires run over his body, but they didn't burn him at all. He had become one with the flame. The Pyrolite took aim at his circling attackers and launched a barrage of fireballs in their direction. Qurena dodged most until one managed to hit her shoulder, while F'jalla took four head on. Both dropped back down to the ground with a ringing clatter of metal armor.

Zall moved toward Qurena and held out his palm.

"*Dahfuohil*," he muttered as the flames assembled into a blazing red nifo'oti. He raised it over Qurena's head, gave her a malicious smirk, then swung its talon-like tip down.

Metal clanged as Zall's sword met the arming sword of another celenian, this one a young white haired male. He slid his blade against Zall's with the shriek of scraping metal. Zall tilted his weapon sideways, latched onto his opponent's sword with the hook and swung up to disarm him. The arming sword flew into the air where Zall caught it and melted the metal down into his palms. The broken bottom of the sword fell.

"That's it, then? Nothing without your sw-"

The man planted a gauntleted fist firmly into Zall's nose.

A flurry of stars blasted across Zall's vision. His opponent followed up with another punch into Zall's stomach. His concentration broken, the magical flames and weapon dissipated. Zall fell onto his knees, where Qurena offered a swift kick of her own into his ribs. He felt every bit of air shoot out of his lungs and he collapsed backwards. F'jalla limped over and slammed her foot onto his extended arm. Qurena did the same on the opposite side.

"Thanks for the backup, Silban," Qurena said wearily.

"We could've handled it on our own, though," F'jalla huffed.

Zall's head spun from a lack of oxygen, and his body felt broken in more than one place. F'jalla and Qurena kept their weight pressed down on him. He could feel the magical energy within him getting weaker. What was once a ravine of fire was now a mere puddle. Too much used too fast, he assumed.

Silban stepped forward and sheathed the remains of his sword.

"Welcome to Prodigium, Tomekeeper."

"Qurena, F'jalla, let him up," Silban ordered. He dusted the soot from his armor and shook his wings clean. The Pyrolite didn't put up any more of a fight as they lifted him up.

"The only reason you're alive is because Monarch Mivano deems it so," Silban told the attacker. He pressed his finger into the Tomekeeper's chest and watched as he winced in pain. "Pull another stunt like that, and I'll put you down. Do you understand?"

The Pyrolite let out a singular chuckle, followed by a shuddering breath.

"Your biggest mistake is letting me live. I took on the monarch's best, without a tome, and beat most of you with ease. I'll remember that. Next time, it won't be so easy to stop me. Do you understand?"

Silban wanted to punch the Pyrolite again, but knew the monarch wouldn't approve of his guests arriving at their celebratory banquet unconscious or beaten. The situation with the other two Tomekeepers that made a scene near the harbor district was already enough to deal with, and he hoped the three of them would be the only problems that needed to be corrected for the rest of the day. He rubbed his temple.

"Qurena, please escort the Tomekeeper inside."

"With pleasure," she said and pulled both of the Pyrolite's arms behind him. He cursed at her, and she pushed him toward the castle. "Come on, get to walking."

Silban turned to F'jalla and noticed the scorch marks on her armor.

"Where is your charge?"

"I had to leave her behind in order to help with the issue at hand," she answered. "He attacked our carriage."

"I understand. Go ahead and retrieve her. You can fly her back at this point, if it makes it easier."

"Of course," F'jalla responded and launched into the sky.

The ashes of the once vibrant flowers scattered to the winds. Silban reflected on the situation. Once the monarch had been notified of the two Tomekeepers brought in from the harbor, he demanded preparations for the banquet to be put into place immediately.

"If there are two here already, the others must have arrived as well," Monarch Mivano suggested.

As a result, Silban himself had spent most of the morning corralling cooks, dealing with the decorators, and scrutinizing security. Everything had to be flawless, yet the Tomekeepers so far seemed intent on making it anything but. He hoped for better as they progressed through the rest of the day, for the sake of everyone involved. The fear that not all of the Tomekeepers would be present also gnawed at his subconscious.

F'jalla dropped back down in front of him with her Tomekeeper frozen in terror against her armor. F'jalla peeled her off and set her down.

The woman tousled her tossed curls, pressed down her plaid vest, and pushed her glasses back up the bridge of her nose.

"I fail to see the logic behind flying me over here and causing unwarranted stress as opposed to letting me walk the remaining three-hundred-and-twenty-nine meters of my own accord and comfort," she complained.

F'jalla shrugged.

"We got here faster and it was more fun."

"For one of us," the woman scowled.

"Tomekeeper," Silban interrupted in the honeyed tone he had practiced for weeks. "Welcome to Prodigium! May I ask who I have the pleasure of greeting today?"

"Ramji. Ramji Wrine," she stated. "Tomekeeper of Shoroux."

Suddenly, the comment she uttered toward F'jalla made more sense in Silban's mind. According to his research, Shoroux had always favored thinkers and innovators in their selection, a group Ramji and her famous father seemed to fit into well.

"We're happy to host you and Shoroux, Ms. Wrine. F'jalla will accompany you to your quarters and help you prepare for tonight."

Ramji thanked him and followed F'jalla into the castle proper. Silban looked out past the courtyard's edge in anxious anticipation. The monarch expected eleven Tomekeepers, save for Reveticus, who was once again away in defense of the city. Only four had arrived, and Silban knew night would set in soon. He contemplated sending out more of the castle troops to comb the city in the event the remaining Tomekeepers were lost. As if Ghantei herself had heard him, Coltiel swooped down from the edge of the city wall.

"Silban Awn! Just the man I was looking for," Coltiel exclaimed joyfully as he drifted into the courtyard. He leaned heavily to the right side and his movement looked uncomfortable. He felt bad for Coltiel. Years in service of the monarch and his family, yet everything he built was almost ripped away at a moment's notice due to an injury.

"I came across a group of Tomekeepers over in Kephram's," Coltiel informed him. "I've brought with me Princess Yonni Sxem of the Anqualai, Tomekeeper of Drinex; Utic Delj of the Clawgraves, Tomekeeper of Verna; I'el Rivini of the Phreeton, Tomekeeper of Noli; and Kliev Rorn of the Wojlidoj, Tomekeeper of Wogiwoj."

"Yonni, Utic, I'el and Kliev," Silban repeated as he committed the names to memory.

Coltiel hesitated. "And Tuvhe Vull of the Devement, Tomekeeper of Eslen."

"The Betrayer," Silban grumbled. He felt the hairs on his neck stand at the mention. Eslen's Tomekeeper was no doubt worse than the other three troublemakers combined.

"Yes, he was the one that initially approached me," Coltiel explained. "I've been keeping an eye on him since the start. The Tomekeepers are assembled atop the wall, waiting to be brought down."

"Great work, Coltiel," Silban praised. "Continue keeping an eye on the Betrayer, but bring them down through the pathway that leads through the back keep. Have the staff direct them toward their quarters. I'll meet with everyone before the banquet begins."

"Right away," Coltiel said. He took off back toward the wall's edge with a few extra flaps. Silban let out a heavy sigh of relief. Nine Tomekeepers were accounted for, which meant that the Banquet would at least be well attended. The sun drifted behind a set of clouds, casting the castle in a shroud of gray. Silban sat in his usual spot and wished for the remaining two Tomekeepers to arrive.

An hour passed, then another. As the sun settled past the rooftops of Prodigium, Silban knew that he had to get back to the castle and finish out his preparations. The rest of the Tomekeepers needed to be visited as well. So much was still left to do, even though the triplet moons—black, white, and lavender spheres—had replaced the sun. Silban stood and stared at the set of sparkling stars that speckled the sky above him. He reached up and questioned if he could ever fly high enough to touch them.

"Hey, feather duster!" a voice hollered at him from the end of the courtyard.

Two men approached, covered in red clay and mud. One of them, dressed in Asceniate garb and an expression of the most reprehensible smugness Silban had ever seen, waved.

"Sorry to interrupt your daydream. Do you think you could make yourself useful and summon the welcome wagon?"

Silban stepped forward and crossed his arms.

"May I ask who you think you are to demand that of me?"

The Asceniate pointed his thumbs to his chest.

"It's your lucky day, you golden garbage can. You've been blessed with the presence of Qio Lod, Tomekeeper of Zhonitas! You'd do best to remember my name. You can share the story of how great it was to meet me with anyone you want."

Silban rolled his eyes. Another troublemaking Tomekeeper, and an arrogant one at that. It felt like something in the universe wanted him to suffer a little bit. The man next to Qio was calm and quiet, almost serene, a far cry from the likes of his travel companion.

"Who are you?" Silban asked him.

"I'm Irada Holst," he answered. "I'm the Tomekeeper of Heivara."

Twelve Tomes

Qio blinked multiple times and stuck his finger in his ear to make sure it was clean. He knew he must have heard Irada incorrectly.

"I'm sorry, what was that again?" Qio asked.

Irada turned to him with a face full of guilt.

"I'm the Tomekeeper of Heivara."

Qio smacked his lips and walked a few paces to the east. He took a deep breath, then let out a hearty laugh.

"Okay, Irada. You got me. You had me fooled for a moment there, because I would've been really upset if I found out you were hiding such a big secret from me the whole time."

Irada looked at Silban, then back to Qio.

"I'm not joking, Qio. I didn't want to tell you because I wasn't sure how you would react."

"Alright, Irada. You can stop now," Qio said. His tone grew more irate by the moment. "We all know there's no possible way that Heivara, or any of the gods, would have chosen you. You're just a farm boy nobody from backwoods nowhere!"

Qio could tell his words stung Irada, but he had to say it. Irada had forced his hand. Besides, it was better to be on the receiving end of some harsh truths than a total betrayal.

Irada swallowed and pursed his lips. He closed his eyes, clapped his hands together and then spread his arms out wide.

"*Acoquilhei.*"

A cloud of gray spores swept across the courtyard and clung to anything they could find, including the burned floral remains and Qio's own skin. They melted into the objects they covered, disappearing without a trace. Qio felt a supernatural warmth brush over him, like he had been covered snugly in a thick blanket or was seated by the flame of a campfire. It sunk deeper, moving past his skin and down into his bones. They popped and relaxed, tensions eased as the spores continued their journey. Finally, Qio felt a sense of relief deep within his conscience.

For the briefest of moments, the world around him—and all the troubles that accompanied it—faded into nothing. No pain, no anxiety, no fear. There was only peace of mind, body, and soul. The feeling of the world around him tickled the edge of his psyche, then formed into a trickle before cascading into a rapid of emotions and feelings that swept him away into the reality he so desperately wanted to escape.

Qio gasped for air, hands pressed against his chest. His senses screamed at one another, each vying for full control and attention. He had been blessed with total relief for the quickest of moments, then cursed with the reminder that such a thing could exist and was no longer attainable. New flowers sprouted from the ashes of the old, and the thousands of red and yellow petals that adorned them invoked the image of the very sun that gave them life.

For once in his life, Qio was speechless.

"Thank you for the demonstration, Irada," Silban said. "The monarch will be pleased to see his precious florals brought back to their full beauty. I take it you two are in need of rest and a cleanse?"

Irada confirmed while Qio's mouth still struggled to formulate the words that best matched his emotions. No matter how hard he tried, nothing would escape. The beauty he witnessed and the peace that he felt all seemed so exotic to him. It was natural and pure, for lack of a better word. He gave up and opted to follow Silban and Irada up the stairs and into the castle proper.

The candles within the castle's foyer flickered from the breeze that entered as Silban pushed open the castle's main doors. Their reflections danced among the crystal shards embedded in the cream-colored marble of the floors. Inside, three staircases broke up the space: a main staircase that ran down the center of the room, split at the bottom into three diverging paths, and two spiraling staircases that led to the towers connected on the left and right. A number of hallways extended out from underneath the staircase and along the walls, leading to a variety of rooms that Silban mapped in his memory.

The foyer itself was filled with an array of opulent furniture, statues, and rugs that covered almost everything. Silban had learned long ago to watch his step around the priceless artifacts, and proceeded to cautiously pass through them.

"Touch nothing," he instructed his followers.

Silban led Irada and Qio up the central path of the main staircase and to the second floor, where four hallways branched out in different directions, two on each side of another flight of stairs that continued upward. He moved down the hall on the far right side. Silban ensured that each of the Tomekeepers had been given their own space while at the castle, but he was careful to avoid placing them all in one wing. The doors to each room were made from the finest cherry-colored hardwood the Wingsong could find, and their handles were wrapped in a colored silk ribbon that correlated to each nation's coat of arms. He stopped at the third door on the left side of the hall, where the marmalade ribbon signaled Qio's quarters.

"Dinner will be served when the bell tolls nine times," Silban informed the Asceniate. "I trust that should be sufficient time to cleanse yourself?"

"I would prefer a little longer, but I'll take what I can," Qio voiced, as if Silban cared about his opinion. He pressed open the door for Qio and ushered him inside. "You'll find that fresh clothing in the style of your nation has been provided, should you choose to use it. If you need additional assistance, ring the bell and one of the castle staff will be along as quickly as they can."

Silban turned and began walking. He didn't want to give Qio the window to say anything else. Unsurprisingly, that didn't stop the Asceniate from trying.

"Irada, you fool! Don't think I'm letting you walk away without us discussing what you did," he shouted out into the hall after them. "I demand an apology for being lied to!"

Silban heard the door slam shut. He looked back at Irada as he continued down the hall and past another four rooms. "Did you have to deal with that the whole time you traveled?"

"More or less," Irada responded quietly.

Silban couldn't tell if the man was shy, or just used to being silent. He seemed to be wrapped up in his thoughts, or maybe conversing with the goddess that chose him. The idea of having a shared mental space with an ethereal being was absurd, in Silban's mind. He questioned the privacy, if any, that the Tomekeepers had in their lives.

"I imagine you must be a man of the highest levels of patience and understanding to deal with someone like that," Silban remarked.

Irada let out a soft, uneasy chuckle.

"Some would say that."

They approached the last door at the right end of the hall, the ribbon that ran along the handle a slate gray.

"Would you like me to repeat what I told your companion?" Silban offered.

"That won't be necessary," Irada answered. He bowed. "Thank you for your hospitality."

Silban opened the room and let Irada enter, then closed the door behind him. The Tomekeeper of Heivara came across as the most put-together out of the ones he had met. He swiveled and began the long walk back toward the foyer. Silban wanted to ensure that he had checked on each of the Tomekeepers before their impending meal.

The three troublesome Tomekeepers were housed in the next hall over. Silban stopped at the first room, marked by a mint green ribbon, and knocked. There was silence on the other end.

"Verina Hinlon," Silban called. "Are you available to talk?"

Silban waited a few minutes for an answer, then knocked again when there wasn't one. The idea of the Terrolaff being loose in the castle perturbed him immensely. Though he had only seen a brief glimpse of her as she was brought in that morning, something about the woman came across as deadly and undoubtedly unhinged. He ordered her to be kept under close watch, yet that had clearly failed. He admitted defeat, vowed to find Verina later, and moved on to the next room.

The purple ribbon of Fwen Inati's room had been moved ever so slightly, as if inspected and adjusted. Silban knocked, and was caught off guard when the Noctide opened the door immediately.

"I didn't request any aid," Fwen stated bluntly. "Please be on your way."

Silban placed his hand against the door as she tried to close it. She gave him a fierce look with her smoldering eyes.

"I'm Silban Awn, celenian in charge of the banquet," he told her. "I'm making rounds and checking on my special guests. Is there anything you require?"

"We're fine," Fwen answered succinctly.

"We?"

Fwen opened the door a little and nudged her head toward the Terrolaff seated by her bedside. Verina dug at her nails with the tip of her dagger.

"We were discussing proper dining etiquette," Fwen explained, pressing the door closed once more.

"I understand. I'll see you two downstairs at the ninth chime," Silban said and let the door close with a click.

Fwen was just as eccentric as her companion, but she at least had an air of nobility around her. He supposed that she was well-versed in a number of studies and protocols if the nation of To'tenkhar operated similarly to Prodigium. He made a mental note to try and ask about the politics of the region over dinner, then pressed on.

Silban rounded the L-shaped corner of the hall and came to a stop. Qurena was seated in a wooden chair outside a door with a crimson ribbon, one leg propped up on the other. She gave him a small smile as he approached.

"How's the Pyrolite doing?" Silban inquired. "Has he cooled off yet?"

Qurena groaned at the play on words. "You have to try better than that, Awn. As for our guest, he's fine now. I've kept him in line."

"Do you think he'll do anything if I enter?" Silban asked. Qurena's ability to detect danger was second-to-none and a skill he had always valued. If she sensed anything was wrong or dangerous, he wanted to know.

"You should be fine," Qurena replied. She tilted her head and her ponytail slipped out from the neck of her chest plate and down the side of her pauldron. "I genuinely think he's too tired to fight."

Silban stepped up to the door and pressed his hand against the handle. Qurena made a clicking noise to halt him.

"His name is Zall, by the way. Zall Destus. I don't know if you were ever told."

Silban looked back at her in surprise.

"You remembered his name? Did he leave that much of an impression on you?"

Qurena's cheeks reddened at the suggestion and she enclosed herself in her wings. Silban entered the room and found Zall on his back, sprawled out across the bed and hands linked together by a pair of metal cuffs Qurena must have placed on him. He stared at the ceiling and didn't move.

"This is quite the home you all have here," Zall muttered. "It would be a real shame if something happened to it."

"Are you going to behave or do I need to toss you back down into the dungeon?" Silban pressed with a sharp tone. He knew there was a strong chance he would have to fight Zall again by night's end. Pyrolites never respected wordy diplomacy, only physical altercations.

"You beat me fair and square earlier, feathers," Zall sighed. "I got a little caught up in myself. I'm not afraid to admit when I've been bested"

Zall sat up and Silban stepped back, hand close to his sheath, then remembered his sword was broken.

"I live by the fray conventions," Zall continued. "They state that when you lose two battles in a row, you're forbidden from another fight until you ask the Hilvundata for mercy. Last I checked, since you don't have an altar here, my hands are tied." He raised his cuffs up to Silban. "So, can you please take these off of me?"

Silban hesitated, then saw the guilt in Zall's eyes. The fierce embers that burned brightly during their earlier battle had dulled into pain and self-deprecation. Silban could tell he took these things quite seriously. Against his better judgment, he fished a key from his pouch and reached over to free the Pyrolite.

"What happens if you lose a third time?"

"I won't."

The cuffs rattled as they fell to the floor. Silban and Zall stared at each other, and the former prepared for the worst. The tension in the air was palpable. Zall threw himself back on the bed and closed his eyes.

"Miss no-nonsense outside said nine chimes, right?"

"Correct," Silban acknowledged.

"Then I'm going to get some sleep. Wake me later, will you?"

Silban turned without a response and left back into the hallway. At the very least, it seemed Zall wouldn't pose a threat like he originally thought the battle crazed Pyrolite would. Qurena looked the other way as he walked by.

"Take care, and don't let your guard down," Silban teased.

The distant chimes of the bell tower drifted through the windows, their sweet melodies like bite-sized bits of comfort for Silban's psyche. He counted them as he entered the third hallway. Eight chimes. That meant he had to speed up his visits and get back downstairs as soon as he could.

The first room in the third hall flaunted an ice white ribbon. Silban stuck his nose up and walked on by. Nothing would convince him to talk to Tuvhe. It was a waste of time for them both. Eslen's Tomekeeper needed to be monitored at all times and treated with the utmost caution. He was, in Silban's opinion, the most dangerous of them all. Silban continued to the next door, its ribbon dark green like the leaves on the trees of the forest nation it symbolized, and knocked twice.

I'el Rivini sheepishly opened the door. Bright orange locks covered half of her face. She looked like she was in the middle of a wardrobe change.

"Hello?"

Silban introduced himself and ran through his rehearsed lines. I'el turned receptive once she learned who he was, but there was still a sense of awkwardness about her. Small vines began to breach the underside of the door. He glanced down at them in confusion.

"Everything is fine!" I'el asserted in what came across as an attempt to curb any further questions. She promptly slammed the door.

Before Silban could digest the bizarre situation, the door to the last room in the hall opened and a blonde Wojlidoj man rushed out. He carried a handful of bottles and a pair of gardening shears in his arms. The man's ears twitched as he counted the number of bottles aloud, unaware that he was headed straight for Silban.

"Kliev Rorn! Halt!" Silban shouted.

The latter kept walking at a brisk pace, but looked up for the slightest of moments. Kliev registered the imminent collision and tried to stop his body, but the momentum carried. He smacked into Silban and dropped the contents of his hands onto the floor. The empty bottles all hit with glassy pings and rolled out, while the shears bounced across the ground.

"Hey, watch where you're standing!" Kliev grumbled. He knelt down to pick the bottles back up. "It took me far too long to gather all these things."

Silban crossed his arms and gave Kliev a stern look.

"Do you mind explaining what all is going on here?"

The door cracked open, just enough for a single vine to whip out and around the shears and yank it into the room. Silban jumped back in surprise. He threw his hands into the air.

"Nevermind. I'm sure whatever is going on, you two can handle it," he told Kliev. "Just make sure you're on time for dinner."

The more time Silban spent around the Tomekeepers, the more he questioned the gods' selection process. The Tomekeepers of the stories from his youth were adventurers and trailblazers, kings and queens. There were battle-hardened warriors and sages of peace. The collection of oddballs and impulsives that were assembled in the castle felt like a far cry from the image he had crafted.

"I guess not everyone can be like Reveticus," he mumbled under his breath as he reached the next room in the last hall. F'jalla stood guard outside the door and placed her fist against her chest in a military salute.

"Miss Wrine told me she doesn't want to be bothered," F'jalla informed him. "My apologies, Silban. She said that she's not feeling well and needs to rest."

Silban nodded in understanding. "No worries, F'jalla. I was just making my rounds to see if she needed anything. Keep me updated if her status changes."

F'jalla agreed and leaned against her wings. She pointed further down.

"The Clawgrave left his room a short while ago. He was already dressed and said something about needing some air. I'm sure you'll be able to find him nearby."

"Did he seem suspicious?"

"A bit blundering, but not dangerous."

"I'll let him have his space as well, then," Silban concluded. "No need for me to follow up."

Silban walked down to the last room in the hall, and the last Tomekeeper he needed to meet. He inspected the ocean blue ribbon strung along the handle. It had been retied into a larger, more elegant bow. His fingers caressed the silk as he admired the handiwork. The Anqualai princess certainly had an eye for décor. He tapped lightly against the door and waited for a response.

The door cracked, and he caught a flash of turquoise on the other end. As it opened fully, Silban was greeted by the most dazzling pair of emerald eyes he had ever seen.

Yonni stared at the Wingsong soldier in front of her, lost in the deep pools of cobalt that threatened to pierce her soul. She felt her breath catch in her throat and a nervous tremble strike her hands. Her eyes quickly traced over his sharp features, chiseled jaw, and broad shoulders.

"Princess Yonni Sxem, a pleasure to meet you," the man said in a voice that was resonant and crisp, bowing before her and sweeping his magnificent gray wings. White dots flowed across them in a stippling pattern that looked like snow dancing in the clouds of a storm. "My name is Silban Awn, the celenian in charge of tonight's banquet. I've come to see if you require any assistance."

Yonni's mind ran wild with ideas.

Tomekeeper, may I remind you we share a headspace? Drinex chastised.

Yonni blushed with embarrassment and lightly cleared her throat. She curtsied, pulling up at the fringes of the frilly pale pink dress that was left for her.

"It's a pleasure to meet you, Silban," she said. "My deepest thanks to your kingdom and monarch for having me here."

"The pleasure is mine, princess," Silban responded with a vivid smile.

He stepped forward and pulled a bundled scroll from the leather pouch at his side. Yonni looked up at him. She guessed he had to be at least a head taller than she was. He reached out and placed her open hand in his. Yonni felt him close her fingers around the rough parchment of the scroll. Their gaze never broke.

"I was told to bring you this message from Anqua as soon as you arrived. I apologize for being tardy on the matter," Silban told her. "I'll give you your privacy and let you finish your preparations. Please, let me know if you need anything. I look forward to seeing you downstairs."

Silban slowly pulled his hand from hers, but she still felt the warmth. A fluttering fire sparked in the pit of her stomach. He turned and took a few steps, then spun around.

"Princess, if I may be so bold," he stammered. "I would like to say that you look absolutely breathtaking."

Silban paused, as if his mind had caught up with his mouth, and bit his lip. Yonni could tell he was working on how to proceed. Her thoughts raced as well.

"Thank you, Silban," Yonni responded gracefully. "And please, call me Yonni."

"Yes, princ... Yonni," Silban corrected himself, cheeks rosy. His smile grew, and he was off once more.

I know I'm not one to talk, Drinex interrupted. ***I just want to say that romance, while a beautiful experience, can often cloud one's mind of the bigger tasks at hand.***

You're right, Yonni replied. *You're not one to talk, lest you would like Verna's opinion on the matter.*

Drinex let out a sudden, singular laugh. ***I see you've gotten comfortable with me. Fair enough, then, Tomekeeper. I shall keep such thoughts to myself, for now.***

Yonni closed the door and pressed against it. Her heart pounded in her chest. She shook her head to clear her mind and moved over to the full-length mirror at the room's other end. Yonni took a moment to look herself over from every angle. She loved how the dress looked on her. The flares and frills of its bottom reminded her of her tail, and the lack of sleeves made her feel free. The dress wrapped up and around her neck, and sweeping V's made of pearls encircled her waist. There was only one person who knew exactly what she would have liked.

Yonni moved to the bed and opened up the scroll. The fire in her stomach shifted to pangs of nervousness as she did. A small comb made from coral, silver and flecks of peridot fell into her lap. She turned toward the candles by her bedside for better light, and read the note aloud to herself.

"Princess Yonni, if you are reading this note, then you have arrived safely at the kingdom of Prodigium. We hope that you are unharmed and are able to appreciate your time amongst the surface dwellers. Please know that your mother, our gracious Queen Monalei, is back safely with us here in the castle. She sustained a few wounds, but we are working tirelessly to ensure her health. Do not worry about us. The queen requests that you focus on receiving your tome and make your return when you are willing. You have made us all incredibly proud. Sincerely, General Gandreke."

Good news, thankfully, Drinex noted. ***I'm glad your mother is safe, Yonni.***

Yonni agreed, rolled the scroll back up and held it close. It was an immense relief to have confirmation that the queen was alive, and the stress from days of being unsure finally fled her body. She looked forward to the moment she could return to Anqua and tell her mother, brother, and Gandreke all about her journey and the friends that she made. Her hands brushed across the comb, a physical embodiment of what she had to look forward to. Yonni stood, steeled with new resolve, and pulled her hair into a top bun. She slipped the comb into it to hold it in place, and took one last glance in the mirror. Satisfied with her appearance, she exited the room.

The sound of mixed laughter from down the hall caught her attention. She flitted past the rooms to investigate. As she rounded the corner, she was greeted by the presence of Kliev, I'el, and Tuvhe gathered near the edge of the staircase.

"Oh my!" I'el exclaimed as she rushed forward and grabbed Yonni's hands. Her dress was a singular and simple gown, a slightly darker green that evoked images of fresh seaweed, covered by a vast array of thin vines. Her brightly colored hair was pulled entirely to her left side with a headband made of knotted roots to keep it in place. "You look so stunning!"

"Same!" Yonni complimented I'el. "I love how you personalized everything."

"It felt right," I'el said. "Ever since we arrived, I can sense the magic pulsating in the air around us. I wanted to add a splash of life and the vines had a mind of their own. That Wingsong soldier scared me too. I thought I was going to get in trouble for using magic in the castle. Did he stop by your room as well?"

Yonni glanced to the side in a poor attempt to hide her affection, but I'el gave her a knowing look.

"So that's what you're into, hmm?" she teased Yonni. "I don't blame you. He's very handsome."

"Hey, I can hear you, you know. I'd like to think I'm quite the looker myself," Kliev quipped from behind her.

The Wojlidoj stood next to I'el, and Yonni noticed that his beard and mustache had been neatly trimmed. He was dressed in a long sleeved periwinkle coat that dropped down to his knees with a sharpened triangular edge. Gold and silver diamonds interlaced up the sides, and a line of brown fur ran along the collar. A bright white tunic popped out from underneath, tucked into navy leather pants.

"Oh, Kliev," I'el mocked in a dramatic, honeyed tone. "Any woman would be lucky to be graced by your stately visage and held in your strapping arms. Alas, my heart is still taken."

"Are you all ready to go?" Tuvhe asked in exasperation. His misery was poorly hidden.

A snow white coat trailed down his body into a black-edged U-shape behind his boots, and the dark gray vest underneath was covered in a silver lattice pattern that trailed down into his black pants. His brown leather sheath clung to his side, the faded material a stark contrast to the grandiose clothing Prodigium provided. Yonni could tell his discomfort was from a lack of armor.

I'el made her way to the stairs and stopped in front of him.

"It wouldn't hurt you to smile for once, you know," she nagged.

"Actually, it might," Tuvhe retorted.

I'el huffed and descended the stairs. Kliev followed behind and silently shrugged at Tuvhe as he passed. Yonni stepped up to the Devement man and adjusted his coat. He had a tired look in his eyes.

"Are you going to be alright?" she questioned.

"I worry that receiving our tomes will do more harm than good," Tuvhe answered honestly. "Are you not concerned about what could happen when we have the full power of the gods?"

"I'm not," Yonni replied. "I trust Drinex, much like I know Utic trusts Verna. I'el and Kliev appear to be aligned with Noli and Wogiwoj as well. The question I think you need to ask—and the one that I know everyone else is thinking—is if you trust Eslen."

Tuvhe ground his teeth and looked at the chandelier above them.

"I know that he isn't malicious," Tuvhe sighed, "just scorned. What worries me are the lengths he may be willing to go to prove to the rest of you that he isn't the traitor he was made out to be. Promise me something, Yonni."

"It depends on what it is, Tuvhe. But why me?"

"Because you have a good heart, and you're also cautious. You aren't quick to trust, but you're not quick to cast doubt either. You're pragmatic, much like I am."

"And what is it I'm promising?"

"That if I ever cross the line and hurt anyone that doesn't deserve it, or fall too deep into Eslen's quest for vengeance, you'll stop me. By any means necessary."

The seriousness of Tuvhe's request weighed heavily on her chest, but she understood why Tuvhe asked her instead of anyone else. He knew that she would if she needed to. She wasn't afraid. Yonni bit her cheek.

"Okay," she vowed. "If I ever feel the need to step in and handle you, I will."

Tuvhe ruffled his hair and let out another heavy breath.

"Let's move on to some lighthearted conversation and dinner, yeah?"

Yonni seconded and they descended the stairs to the foyer. She caught sight of I'el and Kliev flanked by a couple of celenians, as well as a few more individuals she didn't recognize ahead of them.

"Wait, where is Utic?"

"I saw him head toward the eastern tower, the one we first entered through," Tuvhe answered. "He should be back though, correct?"

We should check, Drinex encouraged her. ***Just to be safe.***

You could just say you're worried about Verna, Yonni responded. She gestured toward the east tower.

"I'm going to check and make sure," she told Tuvhe. "Go ahead and we'll catch up to you."

Yonni darted as quickly as her dress would allow toward the tower and up another spiraling set of stairs within. She passed one empty floor after another with no sign of Utic. Her legs quickly grew weary, but she pushed forward. A part of her heart felt like she had to. As she reached the top of the tower, she saw the hatch had been opened and a wooden ladder settled against it.

Yonni lifted the hem of her dress up with one hand and latched onto the rungs with the other, then wobbled her way up. Her footing slipped on the last rung, and she could feel the weight of gravity tug her to the ground. A hand reached out and grabbed her arm.

"Yonni!" Utic exclaimed. He pulled her up through the hatch and laid her out onto the tower floor. He was clad in a tan dressy tunic with citrine buttons, white pants, and an eggshell white cape draped over his left shoulder. "You shouldn't be climbing ladders. What are you doing here?"

"I came to find you. Something felt off and I wanted to make sure you were safe," she confessed.

Utic let out a nervous laugh.

"Oh, no I'm fine. I came up to look at the stars. I heard once that this was the best view you could get and wanted to compare it to the one back home."

"You came all the way up here to stargaze?"

"Yes. I mean, you can't really see much because of the vast amount of light below, but you can still make out some nice constellations."

Yonni relaxed and picked herself up. She dusted herself off, then walked over to the tower's edge. She could sense Utic's palpable anxiety as she leaned over the chest high barricade.

"Care to share? I haven't really had the time to appreciate the night sky."

"You've never seen the stars?" Utic questioned in surprise.

"Anqua is too far down to make a trip to the water's edge just for stargazing. Only those that needed to go to the surface for business or political reasons have seen them. My father used to tell stories about them to lull me to sleep."

"Do you miss home? I do. My family, at least. My sisters and my brothers. I often wonder if they've already moved on with me being gone for this long."

"I just found out my mother is alive, so I think that made me yearn to head back, yes," Yonni reflected. "I've enjoyed my time here, but I want to check on her, and see my brother again as well. He had just returned and I had to leave so suddenly, we never had a chance to truly catch up."

"I'm thankful to hear the queen is alive," Utic said. "I thought you looked a bit more spirited this time."

"Stars," Yonni reminded him. "Before we have to go."

Utic traced a design in the air with his finger.

"You see that big reddish ball?" he explained to her as he moved. "That one right there is Extansia, what many navigators use as their central point. It stands out pretty easily among the stars that surround it, so it's always quick to find.

"If you use Extansia, you can branch out and make Lodigen, the constellation in the shape of a lantern. People say it's the inspiration behind Ghantei's symbol. If you hop eight stars to the right, that's the beginning of Gentriol."

"It's a wallu!" Yonni realized. She couldn't help but embrace her excitement. The surface world still had so much beauty stored in every corner, and she longed to learn about it all.

"Exactly! I knew you would like that one," Utic beamed. "On the opposite end of Gentriol is Xemenicus. Can you decipher its shape?"

Yonni squinted.

"It looks kind of like a sword? Or some other type of bladed weapon."

"Correct," Utic confirmed. "You're pretty great at this!"

Yonni gave him a playful shove.

"Thanks, Utic. Maybe you can show me some more before I have to go back to Anqua."

Yonni thought she saw a flash of disappointment cross Utic's face, but it was gone after she blinked. She chalked it up to her imagination. He put his hands in the pockets of his vest.

"Yonni, in case I don't have another chance, I wanted to gi-"

The bell tower above them chimed loudly, the vibrations reverberating through Yonni's core. She covered her ears in pain.

"We can talk later," she shouted over the notes. "We need to get to the banquet before we're late!"

Yonni carefully dropped down the ladder and made her way to the stairs with Utic right behind. She counted nine chimes. They made their way back into the foyer where Coltiel stood in wait.

"Tuvhe told me you two may need someone to lead you to the banquet," Coltiel said cheerfully. "If you two are ready, we can be on our way."

Yonni and Utic, both out of breath, tried their best to confirm. Coltiel flapped his wings once and gently blew the dust off of them, then gestured for them to follow. They traversed down a hall and into another open courtyard, where they turned down a diagonal path and followed it to another large building. Travertine pillars held up the awning of the building, while the five steps leading up to it stretched the entire length. They climbed and stopped at a pair of gold trimmed wooden doors bigger than anything Yonni had ever seen. Coltiel knocked twice, and the doors slowly opened.

The bright light within the hall bled out into the dark of the courtyard and swallowed up the three. Coltiel ushered them inside and pointed to their spots at the large square table their companions were seated at. Six chairs of gold, silver, and red fabric were placed on each side of the table, and an appetizing feast had been spread across every inch of it. Food from each of the various cultures were repeated at least three times over to ensure there was more than enough for all, and porcelain dishes were placed neatly in front of everyone. Anywhere on the table that food wasn't present was filled by stunning floral arrangements in an assortment of colors and shapes.

Silban observed the room from a few steps up, standing next to the throne that Yonni presumed belonged to the monarch. Behind him, tucked in the corner, was a seven piece orchestra playing a variety of string and wooden instruments. Their tranquil music brought an aura of calm across the hall. Yonni studied the seating arrangement of the table and the other Tomekeepers she had yet to meet.

Kliev and I'el were placed next to each other in the middle of the table's right side, with Tuvhe and a woman with large messy curls and circular glasses to I'el's left. The woman scribbled and sketched on a piece of parchment in front of her with a charcoal stick. Across I'el was a man of subdued demeanor with long brown hair that swept down to the middle of his back. He twiddled his thumbs and kept to himself. Two empty seats were on each side of him, one for Yonni and another for Utic.

The remaining four positioned at the table's end were all new faces. To Kliev's right were a sullen Noctide woman and a snooty Asceniate man who seemed to be talking aloud to no one in particular and gesturing to himself. Across from them were another man and woman, but Yonni had a hard time determining who looked more deadly. The woman, clearly a Terrolaff from her facial paint, stared daggers at the Asceniate, as if waiting for the moment to pounce. The Pyrolite next to her dug his hands into the table and bounced his leg rapidly. Yonni could tell he was getting more furious with each passing moment. She rounded the table and took her seat across from Tuvhe, then looked up to Silban, who had been watching her the whole time. She gave him a warm smile that he returned, then realized there was still an empty seat next to her.

Drinex, is Silban the Tomekeeper of Ghantei? Yonni asked, hopeful.

To be honest with you, Yonni, I don't believe Ghantei has chosen anyone yet. Her magic would be far too powerful to conceal, Drinex answered. ***The idea that there isn't a Tomekeeper of light thus far concerns me.***

The orchestra transitioned their music into an triumphant march and pulled everyone's attention to the throne. The wall behind the throne parted, and a swarm of celenians entered. Silban stepped up to the throne's side and monitored the others as they broke away and revealed the monarch of Prodigium, dressed in a flowing bronze robe and covered in a number of jewels that mimicked the colors of all twelve nations. Yonni stood and bowed along with Tuvhe, I'el, Utic, Kliev, the man next to her, and the Noctide woman. She was shocked that the remaining Tomekeepers didn't show the same respect that they did, and that the monarch didn't immediately call attention to it. Instead, he waved to them all.

"Welcome, my most sacred of guests," the monarch said in a booming voice. He outstretched his wings and sat upon the throne, where Silban handed him a goblet full of red wine. "I am Monarch Cason Mivano, and I would like to propose a toast to open this glorious celebration."

Mivano raised his goblet toward the Tomekeepers.

"Sit, please. A toast to all that have assembled in these hallowed halls to celebrate the dawn of a new age. We, in keeping with the traditions of those before us, choose to come together and feast with one another in the ideals of peace and Lidaesean prosperity. I offer my humble thanks to all of you, selected by the gods and goddesses of our world to carry out their will. It is not an easy task, nor should it be.

"You are the future. You will change the very face of the earth that we walk on. Our future generations will look back on every decision that you make, much as you now look back on those of your ancestors, and either thank or curse you for it. It is a beautiful thing to shape the future, but it must also be a task embarked upon with the mindset of permanency. There is no going back to change or redo the choices that you will make for your great nations.

"I start by offering a welcome to the Tomekeepers from the province of Voncarn: home of sand, sea, hearth, and snow. May you please stand and be recognized."

Yonni scrambled to stand again, caught off guard by the request. Tuvhe, Utic, and the man next to her stood as well.

"Yonni Sxem, Utic Delj, Tuvhe Vull, and Irada Holst. A pleasure to see you. Next, let us welcome the Tomekeepers from the province of Silnathum: home of shadow, storm, fire, and war."

The Noctide, Kliev, Terrolaff, and Pyrolite stood. Kliev looked wildly out of place in the group. I'el giggled quietly next to him.

"Fwen Inati, Kliev Rorn, Verina Hinlon, and Zall Destus. Most of you have caused quite the stir in my nation today, but I offer open arms and a hope that peace will continue through the night. And finally, let us welcome the Tomekeepers from my own province of Pradarek: home of air, light, aether, and forest."

The cocky Asceniate, curly haired woman, and I'el stood. The remaining Tomekeepers glanced toward the empty chair, then to Silban in confusion.

"Qio Lod, Ramji Wrine, and I'el Rivini. May you who reside as our neighbors never be strangers," the monarch concluded. "You may have noticed we are missing a Tomekeeper, but I promise he will be along shortly. With that, I only have one thing left to say. Let the Banquet of Tomes begin!"

Kliev lurched forward and snatched the leg of mutton he had been eying from the sterling silver platter it rested on. His teeth ripped into the meat, the taste savory and juicy. The top of his right ear twitched in happiness.

Don't forget to try the brauthon rib, or the finchrel eggs, Wogiwoj over joyously advised him. ***The tastes of the world are before you, keeper! Be merry in my stead!***

Kliev had died and ascended to the highest of the heavens. There was great food with new friends and a beautiful woman on each side. He grasped a tankard of ale and chugged down the malted magic, then reached for another, and another after that. He caught Fwen's look of disgust from the corner of his eye, and opted to give her the biggest grin in response. No one was going to sour his mood, especially the prissy Noctide.

"Want to try one?" Kliev asked as he offered her a bite of a half-eaten brauthon rib.

"No, thank you," Fwen answered back with a grimace. "I don't eat meat."

"Then you haven't lived!"

Kliev declared and pushed the tray of ribs closer to her.

I'el slapped his hand.

"Try to behave, will you?" she reprimanded him under her breath. "Fwen and Verina are trouble. You remember what happened last time we ran into them."

"Oh, I remember quite well," Kliev responded loudly. He turned to Verina, who had been staring coldly. "You think I didn't catch you watching me, 'Nirave'? What, are you going to threaten to stab me again? Cut my neck and serve me on a platter with an apple in my mouth?"

That's right, keeper. You tell her what for! Wogiwoj commended.

Verina stood and reached for her sheath within her cloak, but Fwen placed her hand up.

"One moment, Verina. Give me the chance to speak."

Verina let out a frustrated groan and sat back down. Zall snickered while Qio remained in a conversation with himself. Fwen turned to Kliev and stared him down. Her gaze was intense, but warm. It reminded him of the bonfires that used to heat Krijya in the coldest winter months. Her flared purple ball gown popped out from under the table, and lacy black frills ran up the edges to converge into a solid black bodice that accentuated Fwen's slender figure. She leaned closer, crescent moons dangling from her ears.

"My deepest condolences for our earlier behavior," Fwen said. "My lady-in-waiting has been trained to fight first and question later. I ask that you won't hold her upbringing against her."

"Your lady-in-waiting happens to be a Tomekeeper as well?" Kliev replied with a raised eyebrow. "Fancy that."

"My family wanted to ensure my safe travel, hence Verina's false name and unfriendly demeanor. I, myself, like to keep things close. I'm sure you understand that, as well," she explained, then dropped her voice to a whisper only loud enough for Kliev's ears to pick up. "Right, Prince Rorn?"

Kliev felt his blood run cold. He coughed, then took a long drink from his tankard, unsure of how to respond.

"I do."

"Then all is forgiven?" Fwen asked in her normal volume. Her eyes grew big and she gave him a slightly pouting look. She ran a finger along the side of her head and brushed her hair behind her pointed ear. "I'd quite like for us to start on much better footing. You know, as fellow Tomekeepers and in the name of peace, and all."

Kliev rubbed his temples. He knew he was being toyed with, but a small part of him enjoyed it. Fwen twisted her hair around her finger and waited for a response. He downed the last of his drink and wiped his mouth clear with the top of his coat sleeve.

"Sure," he said. "To new beginnings."

"What exactly are we beginning?" I'el jumped in. Her tone was sharper than Verina's dagger.

"Oh, nothing that concerns you. I was just about to tell Kliev that it would be nice for him to come by To'tenkhar after all of this is done. I would love to show him around. After all, it isn't often that we get visits from our snuggly next door neighbors," Fwen leaned over the table and told her.

I'el clicked her tongue.

"Ah. I see. So, Kliev? What are you going to do?" she staunchly asked him. "Do you feel like dipping your face in a puddle of ink and putting fifteen holes in your ears?"

"At least there's culture in To'tenkhar. Or would you rather spend your time rolling down hills and picking off twigs and ticks from your body?" Fwen snapped.

Kliev raised his hands up between them.

"Hey, now. Peace is nice, right? Is that not the theme of tonight's banquet?"

"You're right, Kliev. My apologies. I promise I'll be good now," Fwen said with a wink and a mischievous smile, then engaged in conversation with Verina.

I'el ripped the leg off of a roasted hen and bit off a mouthful. Kliev nudged her with his shoulder, but she looked the other way.

"I'el, I've actually been doing a lot of thinking."

"Yeah?"

"Yeah. After tonight is done, I don't really know where I'll be headed next. It's damn sure not back to Krijya."

"Sounds like you've already got an offer on the table."

Kliev held his breath and hoped for the best.

"Actually, I was hoping I might be able to go to Farnen's Grove for a while. With you."

Ooo, talk about an exciting development, Noli commented. ***Is this the blossoming of something special?***

I'el was stunned by Kliev's request and started to stammer. In the half-second it took her to respond, she went through hundreds of different thoughts.

What does he mean? Why? Where will he stay? What are his intentions? What about Friston? Will he think there's something going on? What if his parents don't approve? I'el pondered.

I'el, just say yes! Noli yelled at her.

"Yes!" I'el blurted. She could feel the others glance her way at the sudden outburst. Even Kliev himself jumped slightly from the energy. I'el recomposed herself. "I mean, yes, that would be fine. I know you need a place to go, so who am I to turn you down?"

Kliev's eyes lit up and he put a firm hand on her shoulder.

"Thanks, I'el. You're the greatest."

I'el felt a sense of solace take over. She didn't realize how much she dreaded the idea of Kliev leaving. She had felt sadness about their future parting, yes, but the anxiety was a new component that she wasn't expecting. The worry of heading back to Hicaria alone shifted into a fear of how the rest of the Phreeton would react, but I'el knew there would be plenty of time to think through all of that in the future. The vines on her dress crept up onto her shoulder and over Kliev's hand. He pulled back and laughed, striking a deep embarrassment in I'el.

Why did you do that? I'el cried to the goddess in her head.

That wasn't me, I'el, Noli claimed. ***I don't have the ability to control your powers for you.***

I'el flicked the vines off and buried her face in her hands. She refused to talk to Kliev any further until she had figured out what was going on.

She turned to Irada, who had been sitting silently across from her, before Kliev could say anything else.

"Irada Holst, right?" I'el asked, hoping the attention would fade from her as quickly as it came.

Irada nodded his head.

"It's a pleasure to meet you, I'el," he said, barely audible over the conversational roar of the table.

"I imagine you're from Varlan?" I'el inquired. "What was your journey over here like?"

"It was fine, for the most part. I traveled with Qio over there," he said and pointed to the loudmouthed Asceniate in the corner.

"Oh! I'm sorry," I'el replied. "I'm sure that wasn't the most peaceful trip."

"I found if you let him talk it out, he's pretty alright," Irada told her. "The company was nice, anyway."

I'el opened her mouth to ask another question, but the blare of horns pulled everyone's attention back toward the monarch. He stood and waved his left hand across the room. The table went silent. The doors to the great hall were thrown open, and a Wingsong man with stunning blue wings entered.

"Tomekeepers, I would like to announce the arrival of our dearest Reveticus Awn— Hero of Kephram's Keep, purveyor of righteousness, and chosen by Ghantei's light to serve in her most special of roles," Mivano praised.

Awn? Is he related to Yonni's boyfriend? I'el questioned.

Reveticus moved around the table and took the empty seat next to Yonni. Silban looked on with an expression of pride. I'el saw Reveticus say something to the Anquan princess, but couldn't make out what it was.

I'm concerned, I'el. Ghantei's light isn't so easily hidden, and I don't sense it anywhere around him, Noli shared.

Are you saying he's not a Tomekeeper? That would imply the monarch is lying.

Or protecting something. Or someone.

I'el rested her chin on her hands and observed the shift in mood. Noli was right. She heard the clack of Kliev setting down his twelfth tankard next to her.

"Well, it's about time you graced us with your presence, lightkeeper," Kliev taunted. "You sure know to keep the rest of us waiting."

Reveticus was unphased, but Silban stepped forward.

"Watch your tongue when addressing my brother, Rorn."

"Or what, birdbrain?" Kliev spat back as he leapt from his seat. I'el tugged at the back of his coat in a failed attempt to make him sit. The last thing they needed was a fight in front of the monarch. She caught the look of concern in Yonni's eyes as well.

"Gentleman, please," Mivano pleaded from the throne. "Let us take a moment and remember why we are gathered here. The in-fighting and ultimate betrayal of our great goddess Ghantei is what led to the destruction of the gods' physical form and the collapse of society through the Discordance. It wasn't until the first selection over a century later, through the channeling of the gods during the Reset by the power of in-carnacy, that the nations have been able to find some semblance of peace. It is up to you, as the Tomekeepers chosen in this cycle, to keep that peace. You will need to be leaders for your people and make impossible decisions. You will need to stand tall when life tries it's hardest to knock you down. Do not yield."

Ramji had long since passed the point of annoyance with the monarch and his haughty speeches. If he genuinely cared about the people of Lidaesea and their well being, he wouldn't have stifled her father's attempts at a better transportation system or shut down the efforts of the Alcheknight society to develop new defense systems for the many cities. Instead, Reveticus got to play hero and the city of Casis was branded as a place of dangerous ideas.

A king is only as powerful as his followers allow him to be, Shoroux warned.

He doesn't understand the severity of what's on the other side of the veil, Ramji added. She continued to furiously scribble the signs and diagrams that Shoroux had burned into her mind. *All this talk of peace is nothing but a stopper in the sands of what will inevitably come.*

Just remember that it is not our job to prevent. We must merely watch, Shoroux clarified. **This information is for you to better handle that task.**

"That is why you have the power of the gods bestowed upon you, and the tomes will only unlock that power further," Mivano continued preaching. "You must use incarnacy only for the greater good of those that you are indebted to protect. Do not abuse it."

Ramji's charcoal snapped in half and smeared across her light brown vest and the white blouse underneath.

"You talk about abuse, Monarch Mivano, but you fail to mention the numerous times that the Tomekeepers of the past have made selfish decisions for the so called 'greater good'," she shouted out. "Incarnacy has been, and always will be, a means to an end. Do I need to remind you of Jahailah's fall or the sins of Ashamonte? Your idea of peace is to put people in the corners and silence those that dare to speak out against you."

"That's enough!" Silban shouted. "His excellency will not sit here and be slandered!"

"Especially by one so warped in the head that she sits and scribbles like a toddler," Verina quipped from across the table.

"Says the one that paints her face in the name of her goddess, as if she actually gives two shites about you," Ramji snarled.

Verina stabbed her dagger into the table, but Ramji refused to show fear. She had seen far worse than a temperamental Terrolaff with a stabbing fetish.

"Geez, way to kill the mood," Kliev commented from the side.

"No, she's right," Qio chimed in. His marmalade robe, accented by a golden key pattern, swayed as he motioned to Reveticus. "You really want me to believe this pompous fool is Ghantei's Tomekeeper?" His hand moved to Verina. "Or that this one wasn't a mistake chosen simply because her name is one letter off from Istio's older sister?"

"Do you ever shut the hael up?" Zall exploded. He slammed his fist against the top of the table. Unbridled fury bubbled within him. "You're the pompous one, if anything. You've been talking non-stop and it's driving me crazy. Do you even have anything worthwhile to say, or is spewing nonsense all you do?"

That's right, keeper. Tear him down! Hilaster cheered.

"You think you can take me on, you fire obsessed fraud? I'm the only one here worthy of the title of Tomekeeper," Qio argued back.

Zall tightened the three black belts that went across the sleeveless crimson tunic he had been given. He cracked his knuckles and stood. There was no way for him to fight, not until he did as the fray conventions commanded, but Qio didn't have to know that. In fact, he was sure he could scare the wannabe weakling before a single punch was thrown.

"Boys, please. Have some respect for yourselves and the rest of us," Fwen interrupted. "We are in the presence of the monarch of Prodigium, in the very hall our gods gathered in. There is no need for all of this ridiculous behavior."

"There's no need for you to open your mouth and tell us what to do, either," Zall barked. It was clear that Fwen only wanted attention. "Back off, before I make you."

He watched as Verina flipped onto the table, knocking off the platters of food, and pressed her dagger against his chest. The tip dug into the space between his ribs. She clicked the heel of her boot against the table to reveal a hidden blade and swung it out toward Qio's throat.

"I'm getting rather tired of all the disrespect being thrown our way," she seethed. "One more comment, one more move, and I start sending people and their gods to the afterlife together!"

The situation had spiraled out of hand faster than Fwen would have liked. She had been carefully laying out her plans, yet Verina was about to throw it all away for the sake of bloodshed. Her gaze turned to Mivano, his mouth agape at the scene that unfolded before him.

"Salvage this. Now," the floating orb of Netot spoke to her. **"We need to ensure that those tomes are opened by the end of the night."**

Fwen ran through eight different plans in her head, then opted to go with the simplest of them all.

"Your Majesty," Fwen called as she pushed her seat back. "Tensions are clearly high amongst us right now, and I believe it's because we're all so anxious to get our tomes. The magical energy in this castle is much unlike anything we've experienced before and it's quite overwhelming, to say the least."

Monarch Mivano stroked his beard as he listened.

"A part of me understands the nerves. You are, without a doubt, being asked to handle something far greater than most people would even have to consider in their lives. It's only natural to remain in a state of uncertain turmoil until you know what the gods ask of you. That said, a number of you have shown me great reason to be wary of extending out such power. I do not want to be the one bearing the guilt of what may happen by giving it to those who simply are not ready to wield it."

"Tell him that he knows what will happen if he doesn't," Netot ordered.

Fwen wasn't sure what he meant by that, but she knew better than to question. "No. Instead, you will be the one to bear the guilt of what will happen if you don't, Your Majesty. We both know that."

The Monarch furrowed his brow and a look of subdued anger crossed his face. He placed his goblet down and stood up from the throne. Silban immediately rushed to his side and knelt while the rest of the Tomekeepers looked at one another, trying to gauge if anyone else knew what was going on.

Fwen remained perfectly still.

"I can taste the fear spilling from him," Netot told her.

"Very well, then," the monarch said softly. He tapped Silban on the shoulder and gestured for the Tomekeepers to come closer. "We will descend down to the sacred vault, home of the twelve tomes of Lidaesea. Come along, and do not prove my fears correct."

Mivano moved around to the back of the throne and unsheathed an arming sword with a white, jewel encrusted hilt. Gold lined the blade's edges. He turned it upside down in his hands and slid it diagonally into the back of the throne. The ground shuddered and quaked.

Fwen felt the excitement bubble within her, but couldn't tell if it was Netot's or her own. The throne produced a blinding yellow light. Fwen shielded her eyes with her hand. She was just a few moments away from the ultimate power she craved. The throne spun around in a slow circle to reveal a spiraling staircase leading deep into the ground. The monarch entered without another word, followed by Silban and the celenians that had joined them.

Reveticus was the first to leave from the table. As the others joined, fear crept into Fwen's stomach. Specifically, the fear of having to embrace destiny. If her future wasn't what she wanted or expected, there was no way to turn back. All she could do was try her best to see her plans through.

Fwen ascended the stairs and reached the edge of the new staircase. She looked down into the cavernous, inky tunnel, lit only by the miniscule balls of candlelight that bounced toward the bottom. The dark called to her. She took her first step down the staircase, and embraced the shadows.

The walk down was silent, marked only by the occasional cough or scuff of a boot. Fwen guessed that the other Tomekeepers were just as nervous about slipping off of a step and falling into the pit below as she was. Netot's orb floated next to her, it's weightless form hanging over the depths, as if mocking her. A tiny light at the bottom grew more luminous with each passing step, and the celenians—along with the monarch and Silban—had gathered into a waiting crowd.

Fwen reached the bottom, glad to be on solid ground once more. Mivano waited for Zall and Ramji behind her, then pressed his sword against the limestone wall in front of them. It rippled, then dissipated to reveal the obsidian door of a vault.

"Obsidian? Mined from Hilaster's Peak, no doubt," Fwen heard Zall mumble from behind her.

The vault opened with a loud whoosh of air that shot past the group. Inside, a massive library composed of mahogany bookshelves stretched from the floor to the vaulted ceiling and as far back as Fwen could see. Circular shards of crystal floated around between the bookshelves and against the walls in matching intervals to provide a source of light. In the library's center was a rounded platform centered around a stone statue of all twelve gods.

As the group moved further into the library and toward the platform, Fwen caught sight of a handful of glass cases running along the room's sides. Weapons and armor of previous Tomekeepers, like the axe of Quifad and the helm of Binavi, were nestled safely on the other side. It was a whole sanctum dedicated to the Tomekeepers of the past.

"Do you feel it? That intoxicating pull of dark magic?" Netot asked her.

I feel more than that, Fwen thought in response, concerned the others would hear her if she answered aloud. *I can feel everyone's magic. The flow of different forms of power.*

The twelve types of magic phased through her in their own unique patterns. Every particle in her body buzzed rapidly, victims of the intense energy waves. She spotted Tuvhe alone at the group's fringe and made her way over to him.

"Laying out more plans, Tomekeeper?" Netot inquired.

Crafting back ups, if need be, Fwen corrected.

Fwen sashayed over to Tuvhe and peered over his shoulder.

"It's all so beautiful, isn't it? The magic in the air and the pieces of our past assembled before us?"

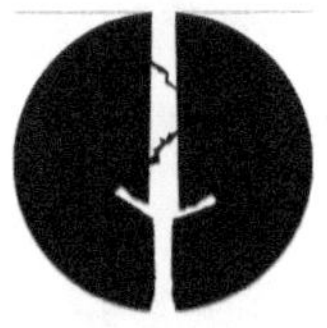

Tuvhe shuddered slightly as the chilled air of death crept up upon him.

"I see what you're trying to do, Fwen. It may work on Kliev, and many others, but rest assured when I say I will not fall for your ways."

Fwen circled around him and stared him down with a look of displeasure.

"Hmph. I thought the adjudicarum were supposed to be men of chivalry. Clearly, I was wrong."

Fwen departed to the other end of the statue as the monarch made his way to the front of the group. He turned at the statue's base and looked at each of the individual Tomekeepers. Tuvhe could feel Silban's gaze burning through him from behind, but opted to pay him no mind.

The only one here worthy of judging others is myself, Eslen crowed. ***And you, keeper, by extent. The rest will learn very, very soon.***

Monarch Mivano tapped his sword against the base of the statue, which lowered with a resounding clunk. Hidden inside were twelve crystalline chests, each containing an ancient text. Tuvhe felt his muscles tighten. Seeing the tomes in person was like living in a vivid dream. The celenians formed a line, grabbed a chest, and met up with each of the different Tomekeepers. Coltiel brought Tuvhe's chest up to him, grasped tightly in both hands.

"Please form a circle, Tomekeepers," Mivano instructed. "We must now perform the unsealing ceremony."

The group spread out into a circle in front of the statue as ordered. Tuvhe analyzed the expressions of the other Tomekeepers: fear, worry, excitement, and malice. Coltiel opened the chest and pulled out Tuvhe's tome. As he placed it in Tuvhe's hands, the latter couldn't help but feel that the book itself was eerily light. Despite its immense size, closer to an atlas than a normal book, it weighed no more than a singular piece of parchment. It was almost as if its physical form didn't truly exist. The ice colored leather-bound surface was worn, the etchings on it faded by time. Tuvhe cracked the book open and peered down into it's pages.

Blank. Every single one.

"I see the concern on many of your faces," the monarch stated. "Worry not. Only by assembling all twelve Tomekeepers and using their combined magical energy can the tomes be read. Please, place your hand on your tomes and channel your powers."

Tuvhe held the tome in his left hand and placed his right on top of the yellowed pages. He felt an instant connection to the deep magical energy surging within. It beat against the barrier of the tome, like a caged animal longing to be released.

Say it, Eslen commanded. **Now.**

Tuvhe took a deep breath.

"*Xera.*"

A ribbon of light poured out of the pages and into the middle of the circle, followed by more as the rest of the Tomekeepers followed suit. The ribbons blended and swirled, creating a whirlpool of colors that rose into the air. Suddenly, it sputtered and the ribbons unraveled into threads.

"What happened?" Yonni asked.

"It would seem that we were unsuccessful in our attempt to unseal," Ramji noted.

"I've never heard of this happening before," Mivano stated. "Not once in all of the unsealing ceremonies thus far has it been unsuccessful."

Fraud, Eslen called out from within Tuvhe's mind. **Lying filth.**

Tuvhe looked around to see who Eslen was referring to when Silban let out a guttural howl from behind Reveticus. The latter stumbled forward, then swiveled in surprise.

"No," Reveticus muttered. "I was trying so hard. No! It should have been me!"

Silban grabbed his head and fell to his knees. His wings stretched out to their maximum length.

"Make it stop!" Silban begged. "Please! The voices. The pain. I can't handle it!"

Yonni moved to help, but the celenian beside her held out an arm.

"The pain! Someone plea—**Tomekeepers!**" His voice shifted into a higher, metallic pitch. Golden light flooded his eyes. Tuvhe knew Silban was no longer in control of himself. The sheer magnitude of magical energy that flooded the room dulled all of his senses.

Ghantei had arrived.

"You have gathered. Welcome, all. Let us break the cycle once more."

The tome flew out of Irada's hand and onto the floor in front of him. The pages fluttered, then the gray ribbon materialized once more. It slithered into the whirlpool like it had before, this time joined by the golden thread of Ghantei's light.

Irada couldn't believe it. It was stunningly beautiful, yet utterly horrifying. The whirlpool flattened out into a wheel that snapped and popped.

Irada sensed a hard tug on the front of his body, then the ripping of what felt like his soul. An orb emerged, the same color as the magical ribbon that fed into the wheel. He noticed Heivara's absence immediately.

Orbs emerged from the rest of the Tomekeepers and settled onto their respective tomes. Pillars of light grew, and with it, the shapes of the gods themselves. Irada watched in awe as the light molded and bent into the featureless body of Heivara. He reached out, and she reached back.

Silban stood, wheezing heavily, while the rest of the celenians and Monarch Mivano knelt in respect. The light mold of Ghantei's body stepped forward from the tome and stopped when she was directly under the wheel. It gave one last pop, then finished spinning.

"**Tomekeepers,**" Ghantei announced. Her voice was calm and sweet, like the most relaxing of musical pieces to Irada's ears. "**We are finally here. You have been selected by your respective gods—my friends—to help them achieve a task of utmost importance. Every century, we choose, gather, and assign. It is the completion of these tasks that allows us to slowly recreate our physical bodies until we are one day whole again. With our arrival comes that of the astral nexus, a point where all realities converge temporarily. Failure to complete your task by the peak of the next astral nexus means that there will be too much magical residue. If the realms converge in this state, they will all cease to exist.**"

The group let out a collective gasp. Irada felt his heart drop and his hands shake.

"**The next astral nexus will occur on the sixth moon of the eighth month, fifteen years from now,**" Ghantei continued. "**Please, Tomekeepers. We cannot let this reality and those within die. My friends, I ask that you help your Tomekeepers and assign them their tasks. May we all walk in the light together.**"

Heivara's light mold bent over and picked up the tome, then placed it back into Irada's hands. He felt her spirit coursing through and around it.

"**We are together now. Fully as one,**" Heivara told him. "**Now that we have made the connection, my whole pool of knowledge and magic is at your disposal. Please do whatever it takes to complete the task I have for you.**"

"Of course," Irada said.

Heivara's light mold formed an orb in her center and melted into it. The orb lifted and dropped into the tome with a flicker of ethereal dust. Irada watched as the orbs of the other gods followed suit. The eyes of each lit up in the statue beside them until all twelve were illuminated. Complete, the statue released a flash of white that filled the library.

Irada blinked away the flash and looked down into the open pages of his tome. Scribbled in elegant handwriting across the pages was a singular sentence: *Train the Golden Wing.*

Hey, Heivara. What does that mean? Irada wondered. *Who is the Golden Wing?*

Heivara's orb poked out of the tome. **"I cannot tell you, Irada. That is for you to learn and achieve when the time is right. Any additional information in the matter could sway your actions. Just know that I chose you for a reason, and that I trust your heart."**

"Then I'll make you proud," Irada replied.

Verina stifled her laughter beside him. Irada thought she was laughing at him at first, but when he turned, he saw that she was in her own world.

"This I can do," she said aloud to herself.

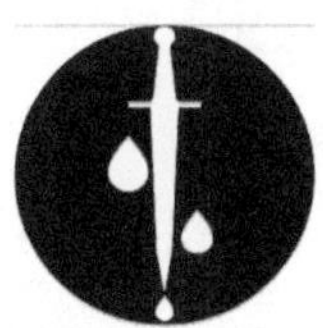

Verina closed her tome and fought back a malicious smile. She hated that she had let doubt creep into her mind. Istio had always had her best interests at heart.

Fwen inched over to Verina and opened her tome carefully, ensuring that no one else could see. Emblazoned across the pages in dripping black ink were the words *"End it all."* She shut it immediately after.

Yonni let out an audible noise of disgust from across the circle.

"What? No. This has to be a poor attempt at a joke, Drinex."

Verina glanced at Fwen, who nodded. She took advantage of the chaos and slinked behind everyone, then worked her way around to Yonni's position. I'el had started a private discussion with the princess.

"I don't understand, I'el," Verina overheard Yonni complain. "I don't want to bear the monarch's child. That's a gross abuse of power. It's my body. No one and nothing gets to tell me how to use it."

I'el clasped her hands around Yonni's.

"Maybe it's all just a weird misunderstanding. Perhaps it isn't something we should take at face value. Mine is to 'craft the alliance', whatever that means. What alliance? With whom? Why? There's too many questions to answer right now, but I'm sure it will become clear for both of us. We have plenty of time, after all."

Verina weaved between the crowd on her way back to Fwen. If what Yonni and I'el said was true, then they were both assigned with potentially world-changing tasks. That would make her job that much more difficult, but she relished a challenge. Her palms itched and a familiar thirst gripped at her throat.

"Vull!" Silban called out from his side of the now-fractured circle. "Share your task with us so we can ensure it's not built around our betrayal."

Verina stopped, and her eyes flicked back and forth between Tuvhe and Silban. The former swept his hair back and straightened his posture. He stepped into the center of the circle.

"That's a lot of courage from one so freshly chosen," Tuvhe said dryly. He pulled out his tome, opened it for the others to see, and read the words aloud. "'Reveal the truth.' Nothing more, nothing less. Does that suffice?"

Interesting, Istio commented. *I wonder what dear Eslen is trying to show us.*

"What truth is Eslen referring to, Vull? Does that mean that you're hiding something?" Silban pressed.

"Lay off him, Awn," Qio interrupted. "He clearly needs to find out what this truth is. Don't you have more important matters to tend to? Your fraud of a brother, for example?"

"Everyone, please!" Utic yelled from behind Tuvhe. Verina never noticed him move. In fact, he had been silent and, by extent, invisible the whole banquet. She pulled the hood of her cloak tight around her face.

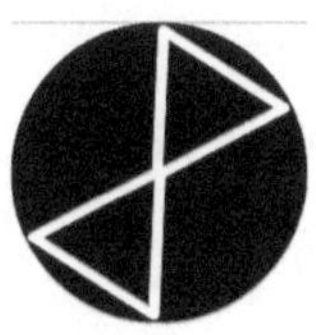

Utic didn't want to hear the infighting any longer. It was painful to listen to the other Tomekeepers tear each other down over dinner, and the tension had only increased since then. There was a need for someone to step in and defuse the situation. If he could handle his siblings, he could handle the other Tomekeepers.

"I suggest we share all of our tasks aloud with one another," he voiced. "If we are to stop this astral nexus from destroying our world, doesn't it make sense for us to work together? Our tasks could be aligned, or even be in a specific order."

"Not happening," Zall muttered.

"Agreed. To share would only allow others to use it as a weakness against us," Ramji counterpointed.

"I have no intention of putting my kingdom in jeopardy," Silban argued.

"I couldn't read mine if I tried," Kliev stated. "Vision's too blurry."

"Sorry, pal. Not happening," Qio joined.

Utic's disappointment built with every response.

"Look, everyone, I understand the desire for secrecy. These are your tasks from your god or goddess. But what we need to be fully aware of is that it's more than us we need to worry about now. Think of all the innocent people we serve that could be hurt, or worse, if we don't accomplish what's been delegated to us."

"Tell us yours, then," Fwen encouraged. "Perhaps if you share, the rest of us may feel better inclined to."

Utic gulped as everyone in the library focused on him. He saw Yonni give him a smile of encouragement from behind I'el. With a crinkle of pages, Utic opened his tome.

"Truth be told, I was hoping that if we all shared, I would be able to get a better grasp on what mine means," he confessed and showed the inside off to the Tomekeepers, celenians, and monarch gathered around him. "It's not a lot. It just says to 'be the first.' The first what?"

"I can answer that," Verina's voice drifted from the circle.

Utic took a sharp breath as he felt the plunge of a blade enter through his back. It pressed forward and ran him through. He looked down at the tip of the bloodstained dagger and tried to reach for it, but his body was in too much shock to move. Everything slowed around him. Drops of scarlet life splashed across the pages of his tome, a punctuation to emphasize the end of his journey.

I'm sorry, Utic. It had to be done, Verna said, voice heavy with regret. ***I hope that you understand.***

Utic felt the blade withdraw, and he fell to his knees. The heat of his body seeped out of the wound, replaced by a bitter void. His vision tunneled, and his strength gave.

"Arrest her!" Utic heard the monarch yell as his head hit the ground. He rolled onto his back.

Verina jumped over Utic's body and rushed the celenians that marched forward to attack.

"*Pahszaraa!*"

Spinning green blades embedded themselves in her foes. Utic's hearing started to muffle, and he missed her next incantation. A volley of acidic bubbles shot from her hands and into the crowd.

Monarch Mivano cried out in pain as he took one directly to the left side of his face. Silban and his companions leapt forward and engaged in battle, but Verina was too fast and too skilled with her blades to be bested. She weaved through them and into the stairwell, where she ascended out of view.

"After her, now! Show no mercy!" Reveticus shouted to his fellow soldiers. A sea of golden armor formed around Mivano, while a smaller squadron broke off and approached the staircase.

Utic felt his conscience slip and his eyelids grow heavy. They closed.

"No! Please. Stay with me," a familiar voice begged.

Utic opened his eyes and saw Yonni above him, silhouetted in the crystal's glow like the angel he knew she was. Tears formed in her eyes. He tried his hardest to comfort her with a smile.

"Don't worry about me," Utic said through pained breaths. Each word took more energy than the last. I'el dropped next to Yonni and wrapped his torso in a tight vine, while Kliev and Tuvhe tried their best to support. Utic reached into his tunic pocket and, with what remained of his strength, pulled out the gift he had desperately wanted to give Yonni earlier that night.

"Utic, please. We're trying. Just hold on," Yonni pleaded.

Utic knew there was nothing more they could do.

"At least I. Got to show. You. The stars." Utic pieced together.

He placed the turquoise water lily, edges stained red, in Yonni's hands and gave in to the darkness.

On Bridges Burned

Verina's pulse pounded and adrenaline shot through every muscle as she entered the great hall. The sound of metal boots clambered up the steps behind her, interwoven with furious and frustrated yells. Bloodlust continued to build, and Verina's body heat intensified. The feeling of her blade as it pierced through Utic, the idea that she had claimed the life of her fellow Tomekeeper, and the fact that there would be much more bloodshed to come made her feel a sense of elation she had never encountered before. It was the purest form of bliss.

A mint orb rose from Verina's tome and swirled around her head.

"No more hiding," Istio said. **"We are one now. We must strike swift and true against all of our enemies. Let them drown in their cries as we rend the flesh from their bones!"**

Verina reached the doors of the great hall and swiveled around to face her pursuers. She tugged her hood down.

Let them see me in all my glory, she thought.

Istio's orb moved in front of her face.

"You should feel my power coursing through you. Do not hold back. The more magic you use, the more my consciousness merges with yours. Incarnacy is on the horizon."

"I understand, my goddess," Verina replied. Lidaesean words of old increased in her memory. Combinations and powers unimagined came to light. The tome dissipated into a shower of magical flecks. Verina outstretched her arms as Istio's magic ebbed and flowed over her hands.

The celenian guards filed into the great hall and spread out. Swords and spears raised into the air. A single celenian male with spiked brown hair and yellow eyes approached.

"Verina Hinlon, stand down by order of the monarchy!" he ordered. "Give yourself and your tome over willingly, or we will use full force to subdue you."

Verina cocked a crooked smirk.

"*Jehalafuoist.*"

A resounding boom and a symphony of shrill screams from the top of the staircase pulled Ramji's focus away from the chaos that unfolded around her. She felt the room closing in and pressed her hands against her ears to try and center herself. Her tome dropped to the floor and burst into a cloud of pink dust. Each sound seemed amplified to the umpteenth degree.

Breath, Ramji. Focus on my voice, Shoroux guided. *Focus and feel. Istio has given her keeper terrifying power. Do you sense it?*

Ramji shuffled through the overwhelming sensations that rattled her mind and searched for the specific one that Shoroux had mentioned. A tendril of darkness wriggled at the edge of her conscience. She closed her eyes and tried to picture it. The chamber around her and all those within it dissipated into clouds of pink smoke that reassembled into a square chamber the same color. The air thickened into an opaque gel.

Ramji held her breath and slipped her hands forward through the viscous fluid. Each motion and twinge of muscle compounded in weight and force. The fibers of her corporeal form snapped with every passing second.

A few steps ahead, a black string the width of a grass blade and around two feet in length stuck out from the wall. Ramji grabbed it, wrapped it around her palm, and pulled back. More of the string slipped from the wall, thickening every couple of inches. The wall around it finally crumbled away to reveal a throbbing mass of black vines and vibrant red veins that made Ramji nauseous.

Just as I feared, Shoroux stated. *There are darker forces at work here. What is Istio playing at?*

Ramji gingerly reached toward the mass, which pulsed shades of red and violet as she approached. Her hand stopped midway. She tried to move it, but it stayed frozen in place.

I'm sorry, Ramji, Shoroux said. *I cannot let you proceed. The risk is too great right now.*

Ramji bristled in annoyance.

I understand your interest, keeper, but your priority is not the aether and its creations. Not yet, at least. We will return.

The room melted away and Ramji was thrust back inside the madness of the underground chambers. Another wave of celenians rushed up the stairwell, led by Silban. Smaller groups now encircled Monarch Mivano and Verna's Tomekeeper, who's name escaped her. Blood from both pooled along the floor.

There's no way that psychopath survives an attempt on the monarch's life, Ramji thought. *Tomekeeper or not.*

To her right, the Betrayer's chosen charged up the stairs, followed by the rest of the Tomekeepers. Only two lingered behind. The elf and Anquan—I'el and Yonni, she recalled—had been pushed away from the celenian crowd. Strips of ripped green fabric stained with dried blood, torn from the hem of I'el's once magnificent dress, and withered vines rested beside their feet.

"Are you sure you want to stay?" I'el asked Yonni. "They'll do what they can for him. We need to help capture Verina."

Ramji watched as Yonni pushed her way back into the crowd of celenians. Something was clasped tightly in her hands, and only flecks of turquoise and red peeked out from her fist. Yonni's demeanor was drastically different. It wasn't the shy or friendly expressions she had retained during dinner, nor was it the look of disgust that took over when she opened her tome. Her expression was much darker.

Seething.

Vengeful.

"Go," Yonni said succinctly.

I'el nodded and rushed toward the stairs, stopping to grab Ramji by the sleeve. The soft cotton of the tunic threatened to give.

"What are you doing?" Ramji cried out. She pushed her glasses back up her noise. "Unhand me!"

I'el tugged harder and the sound of her green leather flats clacked against the steps. "We need to help! However we can!"

Ramji let out a groan of annoyance and followed I'el up the stairs. The situation at least gave her a chance to study the nature of their newfound strength a bit further. They stepped back into the great hall and I'el let out a sharp gasp ahead of her. Ramji took off her glasses to make sure she was seeing things correctly.

The right wall of the great hall had been smashed away completely with nothing but a few scattered lumps of stone left behind and the light of Lidaesea's moons seeping through. The bodies of an entire celenian squad were strewn against the remaining walls and across the table and chairs. Blood and acid spattered the room. It was a massacre the likes of which Ramji could never have imagined.

That Terrolaff did this? Ramji thought, face frozen in horror. *She murdered them all.*

My fear was correct, Ramji. Verina has claimed the ultimate power we provide, Shoroux said, their voices colder than normal. **How she was able to access it this quickly, and at what cost, is beyond me.**

What power? How do I utilize it?

Incarnacy. The ability to become one, as Mivano had mentioned earlier. We haven't yet achieved the full mental symbiosis needed to activate it. It normally takes months, even years, to obtain such a connection.

How did Verina do it then? What does she know that we don't, Shoroux?

I don't think it's some grand revelation, keeper. Rather, I believe it to be some form of combined bloodlust.

A small green orb fluttered between I'el and Ramji.

"We must leave here at once," Noli unknowingly interrupted. **"The magical energy of Istio and her chosen are rippling from outside the castle walls. It's building."**

Ramji nodded and followed I'el and Noli as they passed through the open wall. A stabbing sensation pierced through her core, followed by a shuddering wave of anxiety. The air outside of the great hall was as thick as the air within the aether.

How do we even begin to fight this, Shoroux? Ramji panicked.

We do what we both know best, Ramji. We study, and we create.

Zall spat on the castle tile and trudged past the screaming crowds of Prodigium. On one hand, he appreciated the terror that Verina had managed to instill. The people of Prodigium were pompous, ignorant fools who deserved to be knocked down a peg or two. On the other hand, he was upset that he wasn't the one to do it.

"We had a pretty good show ourselves, keeper," Hilaster said as his orb, a swirling mass of red and yellow, floated beside Zall's ear. **"Cooked a couple of birds, made a mockery of the Monarch, and w-"**

"It's not enough," Zall said, his tone harsh and distant. "We should have been the ones to attack Mivano. The city should be covered in flames, not poison and acid."

Hilaster floated in front of Zall's face, slightly above his eye level. The yellows appeared to twist and flicker like that of a candle's flame. His voice dropped to a slow, menacing rumble.

"Do not interrupt me again, Tomekeeper."

Zall cracked his knuckles and gently pushed Hilaster's orb to the side.

"I'm not scared of you, Hilaster. You've given me a task, and I intend to complete it. Help me help you. Give me the power I need to finish the destruction Verina's started."

"The conventions forbid you from starting another fight, keeper. Lest you forget."

"I'm still wounded from before Hilaster. I don't plan on fighting."

Hilaster spun around Zall, then floated back a few inches.

"Interesting."

The tome in Zall's hand crumbled, and magical words dripped into Zall's mind, a gift from the god of fire. The Pyrolite stepped into the center of the street, feet away from the castle's exterior walls. He held out his hands and focused on the warmth that developed in his palms.

"Cavfuohilas"

Embers drifted from Zall's hands and down onto the tan paved streets of Prodigium, where they accumulated into dancing flames. The flames crackled and twirled into funnels that stretched up into the sky. They wriggled furiously and doubled in size as they warmed the air.

One funnel split into two, then two into four. Each continued to rotate and snap until a group of fiery tornadoes encircled the Pyrolite. Zall waved his arms out in a grand gesture and sent the tornadoes spinning into the streets. Carts were launched and bodies swallowed into the funnels as they passed through. No one could escape their immolating glory.

"That should keep them busy," Hilaster said. **"Now we find the assassin."**

Silban soared through the skies of Prodigium, followed closely by F'jalla and Qurena. A deep hatred he never thought possible had engulfed his heart and mind.

Verina Hinlon would not leave Prodigium alive.

The navy of Reveticus' wings darted by mere feet below them.

Seems he feels the same way, Silban thought.

Silban, you must not let vengeance cloud your mind, the sound of Ghantei's voice pierced through his thoughts.

Silban winced in response. He had not yet adapted to the intruding voice or the idea that he carried the great goddess of the pantheon within himself. He was more than frazzled.

A golden orb wrested itself from his chest and settled in front of him.

"I hope this suits you better," Ghantei said. **"You need not worry about my position amongst the gods, nor your performance in front of me. I chose you for a reason, Silban."**

Ghantei's physical appearance before him, even in the form of a glowing ball, worsened his nerves.

"Pardon my question, but why me, my goddess? Why not Reveticus? He is the hero amongst us. Just as you have chosen those like him in the past, we were sure that he would be your vessel this cycle. I do not have half the accomplishments he does."

"Yet," Ghantei responded. **"I did not choose your brother because his heart is not as pure as the one that resides within you. You**

are the one who fights when no one is watching, and who serves with no expectation of reward. Do you believe that those of the past started as the heroes you now know them to be? Ostoiray, or Naveah, or Hannigan? No. They rose to legend with me by their side, just as you will."

Silban still refused to accept her decision and said nothing in return.

"You are stubborn, but we will break that. I know your emotions are not born of malice, but regret."

"Regret?" Silban finally said. "I do not wish for you to believe that, my goddess. You have decided, and spoken on that decision. I can only hope to become the person you believe me to be."

"You will, Silban. Of that, I am sure."

Silban looked back at Qurena and F'jalla, who had become engaged in a conversation of their own. He adjusted his wings to settle into a dive toward Prodigium's center. The increasingly heavy pulse of magical energy called to him.

"May I ask one more question, my goddess?"

"You may."

Silban hesitated. "You tasked me with creating a new nation. What exactly does that mean?"

Ghantei bounced softly before him. **"There is much to learn, young Awn. The nexus approaches and many secrets—and many more dangers—have yet to be discovered. You will need strength that Prodigium in its current form cannot provide. That is all I shall say for now."**

Silban cleared his throat and posited his follow-up, but the air grew hot. His wings blew a gust to halt him in place as a funnel of flames rose where he would have been. It spiraled into the clouds and whipped toward him.

"Qurena! F'jalla! Evade!"

The funnel dipped toward Silban as more rose into the sky. He propelled himself to the left and dropped into a nosedive, his wings angled as he spiraled around the intense flames. Heat glazed the edges of his feathers.

"Silban, those flames are tearing through the city! Your orders?" F'jalla asked as she and Qurena pulled up behind him.

Silban gave Qurena a knowing look.

"You've had the most experience with that hardheaded Pyrolite, and you're the fastest. Do you think you can handle it?"

"My boot's been aching for another round," Qurena grinned.

Silban nodded in acknowledgement and pulled away from the funnel of flames. F'jalla followed suit.

"Would you like me to assist Qurena, commander?"

"No need, F'jalla. Qurena can handle it. Besides, I sense there will be more trouble ahead."

The two celenians descended to the streets and dropped into the hectic crowd with hefty thuds. Small fires crawled across the top of the wooden market stalls. Silban opened his wings and flapped them into a mighty gust to extinguish the flames.

F'jalla drew her sword and held it against her chest, examining the faces that ran by.

"Do you think she's around here?"

Silban's eyes darted across the terrified crowd before a strong prickle ran along the back of his neck. He felt a pull, like the hand of an otherworldly spirit was beckoning him from the distance.

Not a spirit in the normal sense, Ghantei told him. ***You're sensing Istio's violent nature. It's tempered, which... worries me.***

A trap, then? Silban thought in return.

Perhaps. We cannot let that deter us, though. She must be stopped before more innocents die.

I promise you, she'll be brought to justice.

I do not need those types of promises, Tomekeeper. Such thoughts are what got Eslen in trouble.

My apologies, Ghantei.

You are alright. Also, Silban, a word of warning?

I am listening.

I sense more than just Istio and her chosen. Something dark is feeding her its power. What it could be is beyond my understanding for now. Just be wary. And do not kill the Hinlon woman. Too many have perished already.

I understand.

Ghantei's presence dulled and Silban turned his attention back toward F'jalla.

"You looked deep in thought, so I thought it best not to interrupt," she told him while she continued to examine the crowd. Her hands were clutched to the hilt of her sword, as if awaiting the chance to strike.

"I have a plan, F'jalla."

F'jalla raised an eyebrow in interest.

"I should preface," Silban added, "that you're not going to like it."

Qio couldn't believe the amount of betrayal that had occurred since he stepped foot into Prodigium. As he wandered through the city streets, his annoyance steadily increased. First, Irada had completely destroyed his trust by revealing his Tomekeeper nature and stealing the attention Qio had rightfully earned. Then, Silban, the uptight celenian, had placed him in a room just above the horses' stalls. The smell had yet to leave his nostrils. The less to say about their supposed celebratory banquet, ruined by the incessant chatter and fighting of the other Tomekeepers, and the literal backstabbing of that forgettable Clawgrave by the court jester in training, the better.

Why pursue them, then? Zhonitas said, finally breaking his silence.

"Simple, Zhonitas," Qio said. He followed the trail of smoke and screams to the city's market. "This is the perfect chance to make ourselves known."

So, to rephrase, you crave the attention. Remember this: he who seeks the praise of all obtains the praise of none.

Qio paused.

"Who said you could speak?"

The marmalade orb that contained Zhonitas' conscience whipped around Qio's chest with a light gust. It glided from side to side.

"You did, Tomekeeper, when you read from my very tome. I have let you address me crassly thus far, but it is my power that you now feel flow through your veins. You have a task. It's time for you to take it seriously."

"Yeah, Yeah. I don't know what this ghost you referred to was, but I'll handle it," Qio waved.

The Asceniate pushed past the stream of people leaving the market, the scent of burnt oak thick in the air. Red funnels of death and destruction rampaged through the rest of the city. A smoldering upturned cart rested along the other side of the market entrance, and the stalls were scorched and smoking from recently extinguished fires. The touch of death stabbed into his tailbone.

"What is that?" Qio asked as he searched for the source. It radiated from the right side of the city, just beyond the market. His sense of self-preservation screamed to avoid it.

"We can't," Zhonitas responded from his side. **"That feeling is only going to get more powerful. If you want to have the love and praise you desire, you have to help stop Istio and her keeper."**

Qio took a breath and tried to shake the sensation out. It pierced deeper into his back and through his stomach, prompting reflux. He pressed forward to the edge of the market.

An explosion of concussive pressure burst from the neighborhood just beyond the market and rippled through the streets, ripping up a tidal wave of brick and tan stone as it went. Qio threw both of his arms up in front of his face and turned his head.

"Ivesafuoita!"

The debris stopped a couple of feet short of Qio and amassed into a shield that spread around his sides. The explosion passed and Qio exhaled, letting the debris fall to the ground. He wiped dust from his hair.

"How did you know that would work, Zhonitas?"

"The building materials here are composed from a number of natural stones and minerals. Despite us being on what is essentially a giant island, you should be able to fight using the roads and homes. Even the smallest particles of dirt can be molded into the mightiest of castles."

"A bit of an overstatement," Qio said. He cautiously stepped over the brick and stone and out of the market. "I'd refuse to live in a castle of sand, no matter how mighty it may be."

The sight on the other side of the market was worse than Qio could have imagined. Rows of homes were toppled and twisted beyond repair, and the streets were replaced by trenches of dirt. As Qio worked his way through the devastation, his eyes crept over every inch of broken wood and shattered stained glass.

I can't imagine anyone would have survived this, he thought. *I can only hope these homes were empty.*

Qio stepped on a piece of wooden frame that snapped in two. He looked down to avoid breaking it further when a tuft of light purple caught his eye. He knelt and pulled a child's stuffed toy, a torn and tattered rabbit, from the mess. Dread filled him.

Please, gods, let these homes be empty.

Qio tucked the rabbit into the belt of his tunic and stood up, legs shaking. Zhonitas surveyed the damage and returned to his side.

"There's no one here, keeper. We can rest assured by that, at least," the orb bounced as it talked.

Qio stepped through the remains of the house and continued to follow the increasing discomfort that sludged up his soul to the edge of the neighborhood. He stopped and held his hand up. The ground ahead curved down into a crater that Qio guessed was at least an acre wide.

"There's no possible way that clown could have caused this, right, Zhonitas?" Qio asked in disbelief. "How did she get this much power?"

"Istio should not have this much, not after we..." He trailed off.

Before Qio could press his god for an answer, a cry caught his attention.

"Do you hear that?"

Qio looked around fervently for the source and tracked it down to a destroyed home along the western edge of the crater. He ran along the rim of the crater to the home, entered what was left of its decimated interior, and searched through the remains.

"Please, help!" a woman cried out from the center.

Qio moved further in and knocked over a thick mahogany beam. The woman, barely visible, rested underneath a pile of debris from what Qio assumed was originally a grand staircase. He grabbed pieces and tossed them to the side.

"Don't worry," he said in a voice full of false bravado. "Your rescuer is here!"

"Hurry!" the woman cried again.

I've never seen you move so fast, Zhonitas noted.

Qio grabbed the side of another beam and tugged, but the weight was too much. He planted his feet firmly against the floor, tightened the muscles in his legs, closed his eyes, and pulled. The beam slid with ease this time and tumbled down the pile before it slid across the floor. Qio couldn't help but develop a grin that stretched from ear to ear.

"Great job, Qio! Miss, are you alright?"

Qio's eyes shot open and his grin shifted into a snarl.

Irada stood in front of him, knelt down with his hand outstretched to help the woman up. The woman reached out to accept it, but Qio wouldn't allow it. It was his rescue, and he had done all the hard work. Irada was not going to steal another moment from him.

Qio took a step forward, pulled his arm back, and launched his fist into the side of Irada's jaw.

Irada tumbled back and smashed against the debris. A jolt of pain speared through the right side of his teeth, and the metallic taste of blood made itself known. Irada put his hand against his cheek and could feel it swell underneath.

"What was that for, Qio?" he said in a huff. Uttering the words made the pain worse.

The gray orb of Heivara rushed out from Irada's chest and stopped in front of Qio.

"What exactly do you think you're doing?"

Another orb, orange, drifted from behind Qio's head.

"I'm with the others, keeper. We do not fight those that are on our side. A man cannot stand on bridges burned."

Qio brushed past the two orbs and grabbed Irada by his collar, sliding him up the wall and back to his feet. He slammed Irada's body against the wooden frame, a look of hatred burning in his amber eyes. Another punch went into Irada's left side and forced the air from his lungs.

"You won't take my moment!" Qio yelled at Irada, his face flushed with anger. "Do you know how hard I worked for this? For the chance to be acknowledged for once?

"You swooped in and took that away at the castle. Pulled the rug right from under me with your little secret, but you're not doing that again! I'm taking credit for this rescue. My name will be the one that people praise!"

None of what Qio was spouting made any sense to Irada. He didn't want the fame or the recognition of being a Tomekeeper. He simply wanted to help. Irada shook the hair from his face.

"You're too busy trying to fight me over nothing," he told Qio. "If you want to help, just help!"

Qio slammed him against the wall once more.

"Quit the good guy act! I see right through it! No one is as calm or as caring as you are. No one! Unless you're some sort of psychopath like that damn harlequin, you must be faking it. But you're not going to fool me, or make me drop my guard. I should've taken you out back when you said you were Heivara's."

"What do you mean by that?" Heivara rushed in. She buzzed around Qio's head like a fly hellbent on annoyance. **"Leave him alone!"**

"Stop this nonsense, keeper!" Zhonitas shouted in support. **"Irada has done nothing wrong!"**

Irada's feet slid against the floor as Qio pulled him off the wall and tossed him to the floor. He hit with a loud thump and rolled again. The muscles in his left arm clenched from the hard impact.

Qio's gone crazy, Irada thought. *But what do I do?*

"You two shut up!" Qio screeched at the orbs of the gods. "I'm tired of being told I'm in the wrong. Tired of being looked down on. I'll show you. I'll show you all that I was chosen for a reason!"

Qio rushed toward Irada, but the latter was ready. He snatched a plank of wood with his right hand and smacked it against the side of Qio's head. The blow sent Qio back a few steps and cut him from the tip of his eyebrow to the helix of his ear. Maroon dripped down the side of his face.

"You want to fight? Come on!" Qio shouted, fists raised.

Irada stood warily, but his mind was on defense. He pushed his forearms together in a makeshift shield and circled around. Qio swung, and Irada defended.

"Fight me!" Qio yelled. "At least give me the pleasure of bashing your lying teeth in!"

Qio moved in for a gut punch and Irada reacted accordingly. Qio smiled and shifted his motion to the side, landing an uppercut against

Irada's exposed chin. Irada stumbled back and tripped on an iron rod. He tried to regain his footing, but the quick turn sent him slamming against the window frame instead.

"Quit it, you dolts!" the woman shouted, free from the rubble. Her asymmetrical blonde hair and jasmine eyes rang a bell of familiarity in Irada's mind. Light yellow wings spilled from the back of her white shirt and ruffled in irritation. "You're ruining our plan!"

Plan? Irada repeated.

Qio lunged toward him with a howl, consumed by his rage. Irada raised his arms again, but Heivara's orb intercepted Qio and emitted a flash of light in front of his eyes. The Asceniate lost his footing and batted Heivara away as he stumbled forward. Irada stepped to the side and pushed Qio into the cracked stained glass that clung tightly to the frame. It shattered as Qio went through headfirst and crumpled over the frames edge.

"Are you okay, Irada?" Heivara asked. Her orb circled him, inspecting his wounds.

"I'm fine, Heivara, but I want to apologize to Zhonitas," Irada said. He faced the orange ball hovering on the other side of the room. "I didn't want to do that to him. Is he... alive?"

Zhonitas bobbed. **"He's alive, but unconscious. You may want to do something before he wakes. As for apologies, that is on me, Tomekeeper. I did not think my chosen was capable of such violence."**

Irada looked at the deep purple bruises forming on his arms and shook his head. "Neither did I."

He shuffled behind Qio and put a hand on his back.

"Piyelcahacone"

"Why are you helping him after all he's done?" Heivara asked bluntly.

"Because it's the right thing to do."

Irada turned to the woman.

"You're one of Silban's group. F'jalla, right? Why is a celenian hiding under a pile of rubble?"

F'jalla scoffed. "I'm not hiding, Tomekeeper. I never hide."

"Then why make it look like it?"

"Because Silban and I are hunting, and you just walked into the trap."

Irada slicked his hair back. The horrid sensation that had drawn him to the house returned, filled with even more malicious intent. He physically recoiled.

What was left of the ceiling splintered apart in a thunderous crack as Silban crashed through it and into the ground between them. His wings went limp and his head slumped over.

"Silban!" F'jalla yelled and dropped to his side.

The sound of sizzling filled the air like a horde of hungry cicadas. Irada looked back to the rooftop and saw two thin green lines cut through the top of the house from each side. They met in the middle, and the rooftop was ripped off with a deafening snap. Irada fell on his back and looked at the creature encased in metal that hovered above the house.

Not a creature, Irada corrected himself. *A woman. Verina?*

"What do we have here?" Verina said, her voice distorted by a metallic echo. "Three Tomekeepers to take off my list, and an extra toy to play with after, all in one space."

Verina descended and Irada was able to get a better look at what the Terrolaff had become. Moonlight glinted off the fitted mint green armor that encased her whole body, highlighted by edges of black and silver. A black cloak was draped around the armor's raised collar and billowed in the wind. Across her smoothed chest plate, leather straps created a net that was linked together at the center by three silver drops of blood. Spiked pauldrons flared from her shoulders, and matching blades jutted from the back of her elbows.

In her left hand was an ornate dagger with a hilt of green sapphire and a silver blade so perfectly crafted no blacksmith in Lidaesea could recreate it. Three sharpened crossguards ran down each side directly underneath the blade and merged into a gold grip. Acidic green magic swirled in the palm of her right.

Her helmet, however, captivated Irada the most. It was in the shape of a standard armet, yet two hollowed eyes and a slivered smile were carved in silver into it. Gold decorum, much like the kind Verina had on her usual face paint, was spread across the remaining free space. Twin dials rested on the sides, and a pointed blade in the shape of a feather ran along the top.

"Hey Heivara, what the hael is that?" Irada asked, jaw sorely agape at the sight before him. The ground shook below his palms.

There was a moment of silence, as if Heivara was too frightened to speak.

"Incarnacy."

Through Cinders and Ashes

Fwen took a brief moment to bask in the glow of the moonlight and listen to the chaotic cacophony around her. It was shrill, sweet, harmonious havoc. As she followed the intoxicating chill of Verina's discordant energy through the destroyed city streets, she thought about how simple everything had been.

At this rate, my task will be done by tomorrow, she mused.

"Do not think so highly of yourself," Netot crowed as his orb slinked up Fwen's back. **"You have been having Verina carry out most of the work. It's time that you stepped in to ensure its completion."**

There was a silence between both parties.

"Unless you are too fearful of your own inability to carry through," Netot added.

Fwen ground her teeth.

"That's not the case, and you know that. I'm merely here to make sure that your task is carried through. I cannot do so if I've become one with your domain."

Netot chuckled.

"No, you are right. You cannot. Otherwise, I would do it myself."

Fwen rolled her eyes and looked out to the horizon where a vast crater had marred the landscape. A gleam of mint green hung in the air above the remains of a home. Fwen shifted between admiration and envy of Verina's newfound state.

"It was so easy for her to achieve. Why can't we do the same?"

"Because we are not supposed to be able to at this moment. Whatever is going on with your companion is beyond my comprehension. Her strength is unmatched."

"She's not my companion," Fwen said. "She's a pawn. Nothing more."

Yet deep within her mind, Fwen knew she was lying. Verina had been more loyal to her than any she dared to call a "friend" in the past, and her time with the Terrolaff had been pleasant. She knew that it would have to come to an end, though. There was no room for attachment where she was headed. Attachment was a weakness that could be easily manipulated, and she refused to be manipulated anymore.

That includes by you, Fwen thought, knowing that Netot would be listening in.

The god of death let out another chuckle.

"I see no reason for mind games. All are welcomed into my arms at one point or another. I simply wait."

Fwen continued her walk toward the house. Verina had descended down through the broken roof, no doubt finishing off whoever was unlucky enough to be trapped inside. She could sense three presences, but who they were was still unknown. Regardless, with Utic dealt with and Verina on her side, that only left six more Tomekeepers to handle after.

Halfway there already, Fwen smiled. *I can convince that rabid Pyrolite with ease, and sweet little Kliev is clay in my hands. The rest can take a quick trip to an early grave.*

"Netot," she said aloud. "Do we have to wait for the nexus for things to end? Is there not a way to hasten the process?"

Netot hovered in place.

"The conjunction is on a set timetable. It is out of our hands."

"Shame."

"Is there a reason you want to see things fulfilled so quickly? I don't mind, of course, but it's rather curious in my opinion."

Fwen looked away, as if the action guarded her thoughts and her heart. Her right hand lifted up to the center of her chest and closed into a fist. Pain threatened to overwhelm her calm composure.

"I don't want to live on this plane anymore."

Netot moved closer and she could feel him poke through her memories.

"Ah, I see now," he whispered. **"That's why you've been so eager to help."**

Fwen pushed him back, eyes blazing. She raised her index finger.

"That is the one and only time I will allow you to search my mind. God or not."

Netot didn't respond. His orb inched closer to the house. Soft white light blinked from deep within his core.

"There's something amiss."

Netot was right. Verina should have been finished with the others. Fwen looked toward the house in time to see a cloud of gray spores erupt from the house and settle over the land. Grass and flowers sprouted from the previously dry soil.

"What is all this?" Fwen said in disgust.

Verina busted through the wall of the house, pushed out into the air by a beam of golden light. She spun and regained her balance, settling in the sky. Silban flew out of the house after her, molten gold dripping from his wings. They clashed among the starry night, sending shockwaves out with every blocked blow.

Fwen hunkered down to avoid the mighty gusts and heard a sputtering behind her. She spun around as the funnels of flame ravaging the rest of Prodigium flickered out of existence.

"No, no, no," she muttered. "This isn't how it should be."

"We provide assistance, then," Netot said in a low tone. **"Call upon the dead."**

Fwen heard the words and placed her palm against the soft grass. She could sense the lives of those long past echoing through the dirt, energy flickering like the last ashes of a burnt out fire.

"There's not many here. This place is on a bed of rock, after all."

"A few will do fine, keeper."

Fwen nodded and closed her eyes. She focused on the flickers, imagining them rise back into radiant flames. Purple smoke poured out of her palm and across the land.

"Danudwennet-"

A thick vine wrapped around Fwen's wrist with a slimy thwick and yanked her hand off the ground.

"Not tonight, inkblot!" I'el shouted.

I'el tugged down on her vine whip and dragged Fwen to the ground. The Noctide cursed, then dug her heels into the dirt. She stared at I'el with an expression of sheer hatred.

"Ramji, help me out here!" I'el called to the flustered Tomekeeper beside her.

"Ok, um..." Ramji glanced down. Her eyes darted from left to right repeatedly, as if reading a book only visible to her.

"Ramji!" I'el called again, but the moment had passed.

Fwen wrapped the vine around her forearm and grasped it. A devilish smirk crept up her lips.

"Net."

Smoke sprayed from her palm once again and swirled up the vine. As it passed over the surface and toward I'el, the vine withered and dried. Fwen snapped it in half and shook the crumbling remains from her wrist.

I'el let go of what remained from the whip and watched as the smoke destroyed the remainder. She aimed both hands at the grass below Fwen's feet.

"Nolavohpe!"

A pair of vines broke through the ground and wrapped around Fwen, but the effect was the same. The Noctide recited her magic and killed them without hesitation. She stepped closer to I'el and Ramji.

"That's it?" Fwen goaded. "A few measly vines and a girl who's stuck in a daydream? That's how you're going to stop me?"

"Kill them. Now," Netot rumbled beside her.

"I see what you're doing, Fwen," I'el responded. "You want me to get in close so you can touch me with that death smoke of yours. Not going to happen."

"And why is that?" Fwen laughed, ever closer.

"Because all I need is a few measly vines to kick your ass, honey. *Vreefuonolacaaska!*"

A line of vines sprouted from the ground and encircled Fwen, then snapped up and started to attack in a barrage of quick hits. Fwen yelped in surprise and reached for the vines, killing what she could. More rose from the surface.

"Got it!" Ramji said suddenly, startling I'el. She pushed her glasses up her nose and counted the spells on her fingertips while she rattled them off. "*Rouwintou. Rouqeri. Rouwintou. Minhenfuosho.*"

I'el watched as four clouds of pink dust flew from Ramji's body and toward their attacker. The first cloud split and shifted into a pair of fuchsia blocks that wrapped themselves around Fwen's hands. The second stretched into a rectangular door that twirled and swallowed Fwen, spitting her out seconds later covered in a jelly-like slime.

Fwen coughed up transparent fluid, her eyes the size of saucers. Skeletal wings sprouted from Fwen's cloak. She pulled them back, preparing to take flight. The third cloud wrapped around and split amongst the vines, changing them into metal chains that snagged Fwen and held her to the ground.

"Stop this!" Fwen gasped between coughs. Her hair had fallen in front of her face, and the slime caused her makeup to run. "You're going to beg for mercy when I catch you!"

"I'd like to see you try," Ramji quipped. She snapped her fingers and the last cloud lifted into the air. It rumbled and materialized into a bottomless cage of shimmering pink energy that dropped on top of Fwen.

"You are dead, glasses. Dead! Do you hear me?" the Noctide screeched.

I'el tried to hold back a snicker as Fwen struggled aimlessly against the chains. She turned towards Ramji.

"Nice job," she complimented.

Ramji shrugged.

"I just needed to calculate the correct order of operations, and contemplate the organic makeup of the materials that I shifted, but thanks."

I'el's eyebrow twitched. She glanced back down at Fwen, helpless inside the cage. Her wings shifted back into fabric around her. I'el crouched down to meet her gaze.

"You're obviously working with Verina. How do we stop her?"

"Stop her?" Fwen laughed. "She's in a form the rest of us can barely understand, let alone touch. I give the winged boy scout ten minutes before she tears him to shreds. The rest of you even less." She spat at I'el. "Honey."

Tuvhe scraped his sword against the tan pavement of the street to emit a shower of sparks, then pointed it at Zall.

"I don't want to fight you," he announced from across the street.

"Why are you hesitating? You've witnessed his crimes," Eslen hovered.

"He's hesitating because he knows that I can't fight back, Betrayer," Zall responded. "He'd be striking down a civilian."

"I'd hardly call you a civilian."

"And I'd say you're not worthy to judge others, Betrayer," Hilaster swooped in.

Tuvhe sighed and placed his sword back in his sheath. His head pounded from the unnecessary conversation. Zall was right. He had managed to utilize his knowledge of the city layout to catch the Pyrolite, and wanted to avoid any further destruction if he could. The people of Prodigium had suffered enough.

"Look, Zall. I understand the need to adhere to your conventions," Tuvhe said. "You've stopped your fires, so I shall stand by my own code as an adjudicarum and merely bring you in. No fight. No punishment. It's out of my hands at that point, but if the celenians find us, they will not hesitate to make you pay for what you've done."

"Is that an offer, adjudicarum? You expect me to hand myself over to the puppet of the Betrayer, and to walk out of this alive?"

"You don't trust me, Zall?"

Zall paused.

"You? Maybe." He pointed at Eslen's pulsating white orb. "Him? Never."

Hilaster zipped around like a toddler out to play.

"It's been great seeing you two, but we have to depart. I'd love to say we'll miss you but that's a hael of a lie."

Tuvhe watched as Zall spun around on the ball of his foot and started to walk away.

"Stop."

The Pyrolite let out a heavy sigh.

"I'm not standing around and waiting for any of these Wingsong to come in and save the day, Tuvhe."

"That wasn't me," Tuvhe replied, confused. He searched for Eslen, guessing that the command had come from the god himself. Eslen, however, was nowhere to be found.

I'm taking over, Tuvhe. I have to do what you refuse to.

Tuvhe's eyes grew wide with realization and he moved to discard his sword.

"Zall, ru-"

The distance between him and Zall elongated. Blue ribbons streaked along the corners of his vision, then froze over into sheets of ice. They merged to create a semi-transparent wall, and a navy blue sphere developed around him. Tuvhe opened his mouth to speak, but no sound emerged. His adjudicarum armor formed around him.

Is this my conscience? he thought instead. *You've trapped me within my own body?*

It was easier when your mind slept, Eslen grumbled. ***I'm being forced to hold you back whilst trying to complete my duty.***

Tuvhe watched through the frosted wall as his body moved of its own accord and drew his sword once again. He placed his hands, as transparent as the wall in front of him, against the ice, yet felt no cold. His physical body moved closer to the street.

"I told you I don't have time for this," Zall's words echoed through the navy chamber. "I already said I'm not fighting you either."

"**Shame,**" Eslen said in return, fully in control of the body outside the wall. **"Kneel, then, and take your punishment accordingly. Do not make this difficult for me."**

Hilaster emerged with a snicker.

"Eslen. Poor, misunderstood Eslen. All these cycles and you're still using the same old tricks? If you keep having to take control of your keepers, maybe they're not the issue."

"Easy for someone who never takes responsibility for their own actions to say. I will only repeat myself once. Kneel, before I make you."

Zall let out a grunt of frustration and waggled his fist.

"You're lucky I can't bash your damn face in right now! I don't kneel to anyone. I never will."

Tuvhe watched the situation unfold with a sense of unease. Eslen was in full control of his body, and the navy sphere he stood in appeared to compress around him by the minute. Tuvhe punched the wall with a gloved fist, scraping deep grooves within the ice.

You believe you can break through? Eslen's voice filled the chamber. *I won't let you intervene.*

New sheets of ice spread across the wall and filled in the grooves. Tuvhe punched the ice again and reeled his fist back in pain. The impact had been more akin to punching the side of a stone castle.

Watch, and take note, Eslen continued. *Truth requires sacrifice.*

Tuvhe's physical body charged at Zall, sword raised above his head. The latter took a step back and raised his hands to block. Wisps of flame rose from his palms. Eslen stopped the sword and swung Tuvhe's leg out, catching Zall off guard with a hefty kick to the ribs. Zall slipped back, and Eslen followed up with a horizontal slice aimed for the Pyrolite's neck.

"No!" Tuvhe shouted as he pressed his hands against the wall.

The sharp ring of metal resounded through the chamber and rattled Tuvhe's armor. He peered through the frosted wall to see a marine longsword interlocked with his, mere inches from Zall's body. He followed the length of the blade up to the scowling face of Reveticus.

"He's mine, Tomekeeper," Reveticus snarled.

Kliev hopped over the destroyed rooftop, hand placed on one of the split wooden beams for extra support. He landed on the other side with a soft rustle, ears twitching as he followed the sounds of a nearby battle. His heart ached from the senseless destruction he traversed.

"Lenitehnweh!" Kliev heard Tuvhe's voice shout from the other side of the market.

An arc of crackling white magic swished past the rooftops and carved through the buildings it crashed into. Kliev felt an overwhelming amount of magical residue sweep over him. The hairs on his ears raised, and a bolt of his own magic sparked overhead.

That isn't normal, Wogiwoj informed him. ***It's too much pure magic for even a fully unlocked Tomekeeper.***

"I'm not sure what that means, Woj, but it sounds like trouble to me," Kliev responded. He leapt to the rooftops and rolled into a crawl. The rough surface of the stone scraped against his palms and clothes. "Let's see what our friend is up to."

Kliev peered over the rooftop's edge and caught sight of Tuvhe, sword clashing against his opponent's in a shower of hot metallic sparks. Kliev gasped.

Reveticus? Wogiwoj asked in disbelief.

"Why is Tuvhe fighting the 'Hero of Kephram's Keep'?" Kliev added as Wogiwoj's orb lifted from his back and moved to his side.

"I don't think that's your friend anymore, keeper," the god of storms responded with a subtle bounce. **"Look at his eyes."**

Kliev focused on Tuvhe, his body thrashing like a madman as he tried to land a strike against Reveticus. The Woj was right. Tuvhe's eyes glowed in a brilliant white that he had never seen before.

"So the Betrayer has betrayed us, yeah? Who would've guessed."

Reveticus sliced at Tuvhe, who dodged with a side step. Tuvhe swung his sword in retaliation, only to lock blades with Reveticus once more. The Wingsong flapped to produce a gust that sent Tuvhe skidding back, sword grinding along the stone as the Tomekeeper tried to maintain balance.

"I thought you Tomekeepers were supposed to be powerful," Reveticus taunted. He flicked his sword down and readied his stance. "This fight is nothing more than a training session. Maybe Ghantei, in her good graces, spared me from boredom."

Tuvhe shook his head in disgust.

"You are a disgrace to your crown and the great goddess' name."

Kliev realized that the tone of Tuvhe's voice had changed as well. It was harsh and hollow. His movements were rigid, like those of a marionette. Reveticus took to the air in front of him.

"*Lenitehnzei!*"

Chains of white spilled from the sleeves of Tuvhe's coat and wrapped around Reveticus' wings and arms, tossing him back to the ground.

"Let go of me, Betrayer!" Reveticus demanded.

"Silence!" Tuvhe yelled in response. Embers of white flaked from the sides of his face. **"Reveticus Awn, thine judgment is nigh. For the crime of dishonesty to the crown, and the aiding and abetting of a dangerous criminal, I hold trial. What say you?"**

"I say that the only disgrace here is you," Reveticus spat.

Tuvhe stepped back and let out a single deep laugh.

"You plead guilty, then."

The sound of wings flapping in the distance caused Kliev to gaze up in the sound's direction and away from the informal trial ahead of him. A celenian woman with a brunette braid circled around before torpedoing into the scene. She withdrew her sword and flared out her wings upon landing.

"Release him, Tomekeeper. Now!" she demanded.

Tuvhe said nothing, merely staring at her in response.

She part of the brother's group, correct? Wogiwoj asked. *Ghantei's new Tomekeeper?*

I believe so, Kliev thought, careful to keep his silence in the intense moment.

Reveticus struggled against the chains beside her, his wings crushed against his back.

"Don't worry about me, Qurena!" he ordered. "The Pyrolite ran further into the devastation without putting up a fight. Do not let him escape!"

The chains wrapped around Reveticus' throat and mouth, muffling his words. Qurena stepped back, nodded, and slid her sword back in its sheath, then looked at the rooftop that Kliev rested on. Their eyes locked.

"Help him," Qurena said. "Lest you continue to idle by."

The celenian took off with a running jump and flew into the city remains. Tuvhe and Reveticus, confused by Qurena's statement, pivoted to see Kliev for themselves. A sense of embarrassment filled him as he stood.

"Tuvhe! Or rather, Eslen, I should say," Kliev mumbled in a tone of false enthusiasm. "Release Reveticus. He has done no wrong."

Solid performance, Keeper.

"And if I refuse?" Tuvhe laughed. **"What are you going to do? Tickle me with your tail?"**

The orb of Wogiwoj, as blue as the skies above Krijya, slipped out from Kliev's coat.

"Eslen, you pernicious crow, stop this nonsense! You're only feeding into the negative identity that's been cast upon you."

"*Lenitehnzei.*"

Another set of white chains clambered up the side of the building and wrapped themselves around Kliev's feet. They yanked him to the ground with substantial force and dragged him over to the possessed Tomekeeper. Kliev grunted through the pain while more chains snaked and tightened around his body.

"Yet another who has failed to stay out of my way," Tuvhe said, mouth upturned and warped. **"Shall I call the sword of justice down upon you both?"**

Tuvhe pulled Kliev closer, then stopped. His head tilted to the side and the white flames dissipated from his eyes. Brown irises blinked back into existence.

"Kliev! I need your help. I managed to break through, but I'm not sure how long it will last. You must take me out. Hit me hard. Please, while you still ca-"

Tuvhe dropped his head, then lifted it back up. The white enveloped his eyes once again.

"That was quite the nuisance," Tuvhe said, his voice hollow like before. Eslen had returned. **"I won't allow that to happen again."**

Wogiwoj orbited around the trio.

"Eslen, please. I know we can figure this out together."

"No! The time for talk is long past, old friend. The time for action is now. I will not wade through countless cycles twiddling

my thumbs any longer. You will know the truth. She must pay. They must all pay.”

Kliev felt the chains squeeze him, his ribs and shoulder blades threatening to crack from the increased pressure. He tried to breathe, but his lungs refused to fill. Thoughts of I'el caressed his mind as his head swirled from lack of blood flow.

Don't give up on me, keeper, Wogiwoj mentally encouraged. ***I didn't want to do this, but we have no choice.***

Kliev uttered the word Wogiwoj gave him with the last of his breath. *"Ogen...phal."*

A wave of blue particles lifted into the night sky and accumulated into a cloud. It rumbled and swirled, producing numerous blinding bolts of lightning and cracks of thunder that shook the very ground. Tuvhe looked up at the sight as four bolts struck him in rapid succession. The chains released, dropping Kliev and Reveticus to the ground as a fifth bolt, larger than the rest, zipped across the sky. It made contact, and Kliev's vision gave way to a wall of white, followed by the sweet comfort of unconscious black.

Yonni sat on the edge of the celenian circle, the petals of the water lily tickling her palm. Its scent, soft yet sweet, drifted against her nose and blended with the soured metallic smell of blood. Utic's, to be precise.

The sea of red cascaded over the lands of travertine tiles and filled the ravines of grout between them, staining them all with the shadows of violence. Nails dug into skin as Yonni clenched her free hand into a fist.

The celenians separated and carried Monarch Mivano on a leather stretcher, bandages wrapped around his face and angled to cover most of his scalp. He had passed out from the pain, but Yonni had been too deep within the prison of her own mind to know when.

Bear the monarch's child.

The words were imprinted on her psyche and repeated endlessly in hushed whispers. The sight of Mivano as he passed by drew nothing but disgust from within. Prickles of energy rippled along her spine and shoulders.

I cannot do what is asked of me. This man is far too old, there is no connection, and I have too much respect for myself. I outright refuse such an offensive task, she bristled.

Yonni, I know that this may be difficult to process, but I wo-
Silence, Drinex. Your explanations are not welcome here. Not now.

Yonni turned her attention to the remaining celenians and watched with bated breath as they slipped Utic onto a stretcher of his own. The look of peace upon his paled face scared Yonni to her core. She bit her lip, unsure of what, if anything, she could do.

"Wait!" Yonni cried out as the group walked past her. She shuffled between the confused celenians carrying the stretcher and placed the water lily on Utic's chest, centimeters from his heart. She held back a sniffle and exchanged glances with them all. "Please make sure that stays with him."

The celenian closest to her, a young brunette woman carrying the head of the stretcher, nodded.

"We'll see to it, ma'am."

Utic and his entourage ascended the stairs and out of Yonni's sight. She clenched her other fist. A singular drop of blood dripped down from her hand and into the pool that collected beneath her feet.

"Drinex," Yonni said aloud, the only one left in the chamber. "Reveal yourself."

The navy orb of Drinex spun into existence beside her. Guilt was heavy in his voice.

"Yes, keeper?"

Yonni refused to look in his direction, opting to keep her gaze forward.

"I cannot forgive you for what is asked of me, but I need your help."

"I understand your rage, Yonni. Trust when I say there is a reason. A plan."

"Will you help me or not?"

There was a pause.

"Will you be willing to work with me if I do?"

Yonni closed her eyes, fighting the scowl that crossed her face.

"We have been bound, Drinex. For fifteen years, it seems. Despite my rage, as you so put it, I understand what's most important right now."

"And that would be?"

"Stopping Verina before more fall victim to her hand."

Drinex floated up to Yonni's eyes.

"On that, we can can agree. Istio and her keeper must be stopped. I sense other parties at play as well. Hilaster, Netot, and… something else. I'm also catching lingering waves of light. Ghantei's magic, perhaps?"

"If Silban is using Ghantei's magic, then that must mean trouble, right?"

"I would feel comfortable in assuming so, Yonni. The amount of power Ghantei is using right now is concerning."

Yonni nodded and made her way up the stairs, swift yet careful in every step that she took. The muscles in her legs burned as she rose into the great hall and observed the destruction.

"I don't know why surface dwellers like to use stairs for everything. It's such an unnecessary exertion of energy. Drinex, how far is Verina?"

"The other end of Prodigium, from what I can tell. Such a journey would take you quite a while."

"We need to get there, now."

Yonni timidly examined the corpses around her, careful to maintain the respect of the dead. Dread ate away at her mind.

"I have a potential solution, though it requires a significant pull of magic."

"I'm prepared to do whatever is necessary, Drinex," Yonni responded. "We need to help, no matter the cost."

The image flitted into her mind with the smell of salt and the caress of a gentle ocean breeze. She focused on the magic Drinex had gifted her and held her arms out, palms aimed at the sky.

"Drinobant."

Flecks of moisture rose from the ground and spiraled into a small wave. It ebbed and flowed, growing larger with each motion until it became a liquid rail. Droplets fell from underneath.

Yonni examined the rail, perplexed.

"This is fascinating, Drinex, but how does it help?"

Drinex dropped another word into her mind, one brimming with unfettered power. Yonni looked at him through squinted eyes.

"Will this work?"

"Only if you trust me in this moment."

"Do I have any other choice?"

Drinex floated in silence.

"Fine," Yonni said and closed her eyes fully. She focused on the word and the image of a glowing cerulean crystal that it projected in her thoughts. The crystal spun in place as the color spilled out of it and spread across the cavernous floor beneath it. She imagined herself beside it as the fluid pooled at her feet. It latched onto her and made a steady climb until it enveloped her mental body.

"Dahafuodrin."

The power that followed was overwhelming. Yonni dropped to her knees with a gasp as she felt the press of the fluid against her physical skin, chilled like the waters of the Idlieldev Sea. The fluid compressed against her skin and solidified into an opulent suit of cerulean armor. Metal creaked as sharpened boots and cuffs of silver developed around her feet and wrists. Diagonal waves etched themselves on her chest and over her rounded shoulders.

Yonni reached up pulled her mother's comb from her head. The magical energy consumed it within her hands and reconfigured it into a helmet with a soft pop. She rolled it around, examining it thoroughly. Black glass covered the eyes, supported by a triangular mouthpiece that stretched past the chin. Gold gills ran along the smoothed sides and bled up into a golden headdress that adorned the top. The spikes of the headdress itself were reminiscent of a crown made of fish bone and coral. It was breathtakingly stunning.

"There's one more piece, Yonni," Drinex uttered as he moved closer. His orb elongated and molded itself into a weapon that stayed afloat in front of her. She placed the helmet on, then reached out and held it in her hands.

Yonni felt the engraved waves and ridges of the weapon's cyan shaft beneath her gloves. It was a thin pole around five feet in length with a single black grip around the center. The remains of two golden trident points, snapped off into jagged blades, surrounded the still intact middle blade to form a spear.

"The Spear of Drinex," Yonni uttered in realization.

You are the Spear, Yonni. Take my power, wield me as a weapon, and stop Istio. This is the true state of incarnacy.

"Does this form return you to my mind?"

Only for the duration. Now make haste. Extend the spear.

Yonni did as instructed and pointed the spear ahead of her. The rail of water reacted, tracing after the tip. Yonni smiled in understanding. She swept the spear sideways to create a spiral of water and placed a gilded boot at the edge. Her boot clung to it, held in place by the water itself. She pushed off against the ground with her other foot, using the momentum to cling to the rail. Her body slid along it effortlessly, as if she was carried by the tide itself.

A holler of excitement left Yonni's lips as she crafted the rail's path out of the castle yard and into the sky over Prodigium. She ascended to heights she never believed an Anqualai could reach and peered out over the clouds to see the destruction of the city. Her vision swept the landscape in an effort to find Verina. Sparks of golden light and balls of mint green magic drew her attention to the smoldering neighborhoods at the city's outskirts, and she descended toward their origin.

Yonni passed through the clouds, armor coated in condensation, and listened to the wind whip around her. It was a deafening roar, yet she felt no fear. As the ground grew closer, she swung her arm up and crafted a loop that she rode into a roll. Buildings zoomed by her peripheral while she weaved between the wreckage.

As she neared the city's outer wall, the sound of clashing metal reverberated through the skies. Yonni caught sight of Silban ahead, sword locked against Verina's silver dagger. His wings flapped violently to try and hold him in place.

Despite Ghantei's light, the sweat that beaded Silban's brow and his pallid skin betrayed his exhaustion. Dark bags formed under his eyes. It wasn't the same spirited Silban from hours before. This Silban was a warrior betrayed, ready to die for his king.

Verina's incarnate form twinkled under the light of the stars as she dashed forward and threw her knee up into Silban's stomach. He tried to brace, a moment too late, and let out a grunt as he took the hit. He spiraled back into the air, regaining his balance with another flap. Verina didn't let up, pressing her assault with another kick, then a forward strike. The image of the moons reflected off her dagger, colored circles in the arc of a smile.

Yonni painted a rail of water forward and launched between them, catching Verina's dagger on her spear. The dagger twisted, hooked between the spear's center blade and its broken left. It flew up as Yonni used the force to spin the spear in a full circle.

"Drinivesa!" Yonni shouted as a wall of water spouted up between her and the armored assassin. She turned to Silban. "She's distracted. Go! Now!"

Silban blinked in awe. "Princes-I mean, Yonni?"

"Go!"

A sliver of mint green sliced through Yonni's water wall, erupting it into a shower of rain. Verina blasted through the mist and tackled Yonni, sending them into the crater, where a cloud of dirt and rubble rose from their point of impact.

Careful, Tomekeeper. We may be stronger, but we are not in-
vincible, Drinex warned.

"Noted," Yonni responded through gritted teeth. She pulled her knees up and pushed Verina off of her.

The Terrolaff flipped back and landed into a crouched position, re-coiled and ready to strike. She traced into the dirt with her dagger, as if in thought. Her posture relaxed and she stood, rotating her shoulders.

"It looks like I'm not the only one that can take this form," Verina said through her helmet. "Interesting. Tell me, Anqualai—why did you choose to fight? Why bother stepping in my way?"

Yonni stabbed the spear into the ground and lifted herself up. The armor around her felt as light as the seaweed clothing she would wear, despite its heavier appearance. A pang of anger rose in her stomach.

"You stabbed my friend. Left him bleeding on the floor of the castle. I won't stand by and watch you escape with this power. I cannot let you harm any others."

"Such a noble cause," Verina hissed. "You really embody those princess ideals, don't you? I'll be straightforward with you, fishtail. If you truly believe that you'll be able to stop me, you're just as deranged as I am!"

Verina broke out into an unsettling cackle, made worse by the lack of features on her helmet. She raised her dagger toward Yonni and mo-tioned forward with her other hand.

"Come on, then! I'll slice you from toe to throat and watch your color splash across the dirt. I've always wondered if you mermaids bleed blue."

Yonni huffed and charged, spear aimed at Verina's torso.

One swift motion, she thought. _Follow Gandreke's training and strike._

Verina sidestepped the attack and swung her dagger at Yonni's back. Yonni rotated the spear in her hand, then held the shaft up behind her to block. Metal clanged.

Yonni rotated on the ball of her foot, following up with another disarming maneuver, but Verina stepped back and tossed the dagger into her other hand to avoid it. She slashed toward Yonni again, grazing the side of her armor. Yonni exhaled, thankful the armor held, and stabbed the spear into the ground.

Yonni leapt and used the body of the spear to spin into a kick that connected with the side of Verina's armored head. The Terrolaff stumbled and held out her hand for balance.

"Enough playing. You're mine now!" Verina yelled, her voice soaked in frustration. "*Jehanasas!*"

Acidic bubbles launched from her hands at Yonni. The latter yanked her spear from the dirt and pointed the blade along the ground, crafting another water rail. She swerved between the bubbles, careful to avoid their touch. One sizzled against the corner of her armored shoulder.

Verina hopped to the left and sent out spinning blades of acid next. Yonni dropped as they flew overhead, causing the air to crackle and pop. She swung her spear in an upward direction, crafting a small wave and sending it crashing into her opponent.

You're learning fast, keeper, Drinex lauded.

She's keeping me on my toes, for sure, Yonni responded.

The Anqualai hopped on her water rail once more and careened past Verina. She swerved into a tight turn and readied her spear for a final attack.

Verina clasped her hands together and slowly pulled them apart. A single acidic bubble formed between her palms. She widened the space between her hands until the bubble was the size of her torso, then shot it forward. Yonni tilted to the left to avoid it and banked back right to regain her balance.

"I thought you clowns had better aim!" Yonni taunted as she pulled her spear back.

A heavy weight splashed against the width of her back, followed by a searing heat, as if the lava flow of Mount Hilaster itself had been thrown on her. Yonni fell from the rail and tumbled across the ground, coming to a stop with her face against the dirt. The Spear of Drinex rolled a few feet away. Yonni clambered back up, but the burning intensified, cutting through her armor. Droplets fell onto her back, and she felt small circles burn into her skin. Yonni cried out in pain.

Verina stepped over and kicked Yonni in the side, then pushed the Anqualai onto her back. Verina kneeled beside her and raised her dagger above her head.

"Istio and I are tired of these games. With your sacrifice, I'll usher in a new era built on your friend's blood and your bones."

"*Vreefuonolacaaska.*"

Vines sprung from the ground and whipped toward Verina. She somersaulted back and returned the attack, slicing and stabbing any that tried to entrap her. Verina stomped the ground and sprayed a cloud of acid from her foot, disintegrating her pesky foes.

I'el ran over to Yonni and tried to help her back to her feet. She let out a hefty grunt.

"Goddess, you're heavy."

"Thanks?" Yonni replied with a small laugh. Her back stung from the acid, but she could feel the holes in the armor resealing themselves with every passing second.

Verina dashed at the duo, and Yonni could sense the immense fury radiating from her. A cage of fuchsia magic dropped onto her from the sky. Ramji stepped into view, hands on each end of a pink cloud.

"You two figure out a plan while I hold her," Ramji said.

"Too slow," Verina quipped. She carved a triangle into the cage bars and kicked it open. The bars shattered in ethereal dust. "Did you really think your low level magic could hold back a goddess incarnate?"

Verina reared her hand back and flung more acid disks at Ramji. The latter let out a yelp as she dodged them and pushed her glasses back up her nose.

"I have tricks of my own, incarnate or not," Ramji replied. "*Fawintou.*"

The cloud in Ramji's hands morphed into a duplicate of Verina's acid disk. Ramji pulled back and flung it at the unsuspecting Terrolaff, who took the hit directly to the mask. The sound of ripping metal filled the air. Verina's head snapped back and she stumbled. Her hands reached up to cover her face.

"Damn you!" Verina shrieked. "You'll pay for that!"

Yonni caught sight of Verina's face before her mask reformed. Blood rushed from a large cut that had spread from her nose to her left ear, mixing with her skeletal face paint. Her eye was completely black, but Yonni couldn't tell if it was from Ramji's attack or Verina holding it closed.

Verina's helmet finished reforming and she cracked her neck. She crouched and dashed once more, a blur before the eyes of Yonni and her allies. Verina grappled Ramji by the throat and lifted her, pushing her back toward Yonni and I'el. She tossed Ramji into I'el, then dropped down and swept Yonni's leg out from under her. Verina threw her dagger at Yonni's body.

Yonni rolled to the side and the dagger thunked into the dirt. Verina planted another kick, this time to Yonni's chest, and grabbed her by the headdress. She smashed her fist into Yonni's helmet and sent her back to the earth. The impact sent a hollow ring through Yonni's head.

Verina retrieved her dagger and wiped the dirt from it. She stomped on I'el as she made her way back to Yonni.

"Any last words, princess?"

Yonni crawled back, racking her mind for a plan of attack. Gilded wings grew in the distant sky—Silban's, she presumed. She glanced at I'el and Ramji, doubled over in pain beside each other. She couldn't risk anyone else getting hurt.

Yonni had to stop Verina. She was the only one that could as long as Verina had the power of incarnacy on her side. Yonni reached toward her spear, clasping the edge and swiping it in Verina's direction.

"Let's take this fight elsewhere."

The water rail formed and knocked into Verina, then doubled around into a loop. Verina tracked it's movement, allowing Yonni a second to draw the line back down to her and stab Verina in the shoulder with the spear. She hopped on the water rail and forced it to keep moving, Verina stuck on her weapon. The latter swung at Yonni, unable to get a hit in.

I have to get to the castle, Yonni thought. *It should be empty by now.*

Yonni and Verina glided over the market, where a mass of celenians were tending to injured civilians and the damaged structures around them. Yonni caught sight of Silban's brother among them, and two more stretchers holding Kliev and Tuvhe, their eyes closed. She hoped they were merely unconscious.

Verina grabbed the spear's blade and tried to burn it, thwarted by a thin film of water Yonni kept applied for the very situation. They approached the side of the castle and blasted through the wall. The rail dropped off, leaving Yonni and Verina to tumble toward the floor. They leapt away from one another.

Yonni landed back on her feet as Verina did the same. She studied the room around them. It was a library, adorned in red and gold accents with shelves full of books that stretched up to the vaulted dome of a ceiling. The colored spines ranged from ancient to brand new, in every shape and size.

Careful, Yonni, there's a lot of history...

Verina sent an arcing wave of acid across the room that Yonni jumped to avoid. It splashed across the library's priceless contents.

Here... Drinex sighed, disappointed.

"Why won't you just die?" Verina yelled. She leapt and swung in another attack that Yonni blocked with the shaft of the spear. Yonni tilted the spear down and stabbed at Verina's feet, missing each time. Verina dropped onto her back and launched herself back up with her hands, planting both feet firmly into Yonni's neck and sending her through the dome.

The library roof cracked and crumbled as Yonni busted through and into the tower beside it. She rolled down a handful of stairs before catching herself against the wall. She looked up at the tower's spire. It was the same one her and Utic had stargazed out of mere hours before.

Yonni lost what little patience she had left. Verina leapt into the tower after Yonni, but the latter was prepared. She slammed the shaft of her spear into Verina's side, then followed up with another quick whack of the blade against Verina's helmet. It disappeared briefly before it reformed.

I can't get past the armor, Drinex. It recovers too quickly, Yonni thought.

You won't be able to finish this fight with weapons, Yonni. Istio is far too advanced in such skills. We need a workaround.

Yonni nodded under her helmet, a plan developed.

"Come on, Verina! I thought you would have killed me by now. What does your great goddess think of your incompetence?"

"Silence, fish!"

Verina headbutted Yonni into the tower wall and slammed her arm against Yonni's chest. The two continued their clash up the tower steps, a dance of blades and fists, until they reached the top. Verina backhanded Yonni against the barrier.

"You will not speak ill of Istio, especially when I overheard your own task and reaction. I handled the monarch accordingly, so you should be thanking me that it's no longer a concern."

Yonni scowled, face hidden.

"Stay out of my business, Verina! What my task is doesn't concern you."

"Are you scared, princess? Worried that I'll decide to take out your dear queen mother next?"

Yonni swung at Verina and missed. Verina swept in and placed her dagger against Yonni's throat, then pressed her back against the barrier.

"One wrong move and that's it, princess. I'm going to kill you, then your mother, your precious friends, and anyone else who stands against me and Fwen."

"Doing so won't make her love you," Yonni argued. "You don't think it was easy to see your feelings? You hide them with the grace of a blind goat. You're nothing but a lapdog to her, and you'll never be anything more. So why don't you go fetch?"

Yonni tossed her spear behind Verina, who followed the motion with a turn of the head. The grip on the dagger loosened in Verina's hand,

and Yonni used the distraction to grab and shove it into the bottom of Verina's helmet. It sliced through the neck of her armor, barely avoiding her actual throat. Verina stepped back in surprise, her armor healed, and raised her dagger.

"You missed your one chance," Verina growled. "I won't."

"I didn't miss, Verina. I just needed an opening."

Yonni raised her hand and focused on the particles of water magic that she had slipped inside Verina's helmet. She pulled the moisture from Verina's breath and sweat into them, forming a mask of water big enough to cover the Terrolaff's mouth and nose.

Verina dropped her dagger and clawed at her helmet, suddenly silenced.

"You have a choice, Verina: either drown under your helmet, or discard your incarnate form. What speaks louder, I wonder? Your devotion to your goddess, or your own pride?"

Verina fell to her knees, scratching at her neck and face. It was a fruitless attempt at freedom. Yonni held her breath as she waited for Verina's decision. Time slowed. Finally, Verina's armor melted away. She fell onto the tower's tile, unconscious.

Yonni removed the mask and approached Verina with caution. She pressed her hand against Verina's throat. The Terrolaff was breathing, thankfully, but out cold. Yonni let out a heavy sigh of relief. The battle was done, and Verina would be taken into celenian custody. It was a victory for sure, if only temporary. Yonni stared at her boots and the swirls on her armored palms.

"What do we do now, Drinex?"

We wait, Yonni. We wait, and we take a much needed rest.

A Leap of Faith

Yonni gazed across the city of Prodigium as the sun rose from behind the wall. The sounds of the city folk starting their routine began to trickle up toward the tower. It was odd how quickly the denizens of Prodigium had returned back to their normal life despite all the destruction around them. Those that still had their shops and homes, at least. She pressed herself against the barrier and felt the breeze against her face. It didn't sting anymore.

Her thoughts wandered to Anqua and her family. Her task was a monumental one that could shift the entire power structure of Lidaesea. She wouldn't be able to hide it for long.

Yonni shook the thought out of her head. That would be a problem for tomorrow. Today, she had to celebrate the small victory she was allotted.

Drinex floated up beside her.

"You said before we would have to spend the next fifteen years together, Yonni. I hope that we won't remain estranged for too long."

Yonni didn't respond. Drinex had helped her and, as a result, wanted things to return to normal between them, yet there was so much that still seemed wrong about the task he had heaved upon her that full forgiveness seemed further than he probably would have liked.

It wasn't impossible, though.

The flap of wings sounded from below the tower's edge. Yonni peered over, and caught sight of Silban ascending toward her. She stepped back as he rose in front of the barrier. Golden light glimmered from the edges of his wings.

"I was searching for you," Silban said quietly. "I didn't know where you had gone."

"I wanted to get some air," Yonni explained. "Or needed to, I should say. The fight last night took a lot out of me. It's been quite a stressful time here in your kingdom."

"Certainly not the impression I wanted you to have. By the way… I haven't had a moment to tell you, but I'm sorry about Utic," Silban expressed. "I don't know how best to say it, but I feel like he was the strongest of us."

"Is," Yonni corrected. "I'm still holding out hope."

"Even given his lack of response?"

"If there is something that you should learn about me right away, Silban, it's that I don't give up on others so easily. I fight for those I believe in."

Silban flapped his wings.

"I gathered from your battle with Verina. It takes a lot of courage to go blade to blade with a killer, much less one empowered by an equally psychotic goddess."

Yonni rubbed her arm.

"I get the feeling there was something else, Silban. Something more than Istio. I can't really explain how, but it felt... different. It wasn't the same type of magic that we carry."

"We'll figure it out, Yonni. Verina's not going anywhere."

Yonni cleared her throat, unable to shed her discomfort.

"Monarch Mivano... how is he?"

"He is under the best care, so fret not. He extends our deepest gratitude for your assistance and kindness. Reveticus, meanwhile, will lead in his stead." Silban examined her expression, then looked out across the city. "Hey, Yonni... You said you needed air, right?"

Yonni stepped forward.

"What are you suggesting?"

"A leap of faith," Silban stated, hand outstretched. "For the future."

Yonni took his hand, stepped onto the barrier, and stared deeply into Silban's eyes.

"For the future."

Irada sat on the edge of the courtyard and observed the flowers that had bloomed from his magic. As they fluttered in the breeze, the smell drifted under his nose. It was sweet, yet mild, a scent that would go unnoticed amongst the rest of the courtyard's floral arrangements except to those with a highly trained sense of smell. The composition, however, was better off for it. Not everything needed to be flashy and at the forefront to be special.

Irada heard a shuffle of footsteps and caught sight of Ramji descending the courtyard steps, pad and charcoal in tow. She sat across from him, deep in thought, and scribbled down illegible words.

"Did you come out here to clear your mind too?" Irada asked, slightly louder than a whisper.

Ramji's head snapped up in awareness of her courtyard cohabitant.

"Quite the opposite, actually. I came out here because the flowers remind me of my mother, and that spurs my mind. I'm working on a problem, but I can't quite determine where to start." She wrinkled her nose. "There's another scent as well that's permeating the grounds. It's clashing with the arrangement that's already here."

"Clashing, you say?"

"Well, not quite. Perhaps I'm too harsh in that deduction. I believe a better phrasing would be that said scent is trying to blend, when it's better off on its own. Does that make sense?"

Irada let out a soft chuckle.

"More than you know. Are you returning to Casis, Ramji?"

"As soon as I deduce this starting point," she answered, nose buried back in her pad. She scribbled a couple of unknown symbols and tapped the charcoal against her lips, leaving a small smudge. "You?"

That's a good question, Irada. What are we doing, anyway?

You said we need to train the Golden Wing, right, Heivara? I suppose I should figure out what exactly that means.

Irada looked at Ramji, who raised her head at his silence.

"I'm going to go off on my own for a bit."

Qio studied Irada and Ramji from the opposite end of the courtyard, jealousy bubbling within him. The top of his head stung from the multiple stitches used to seal up his wounds. His once perfect hair had been mangled to choppy pieces by the blades of the surgeon that worked on him.

Qio's eyes locked onto the rabbit that still sat tucked in Irada's belt.

Such a wasted opportunity, he thought. *That child is probably distraught, and it's all Irada's fault.*

His thumbs rubbed the parchment held within his grasp. Qio glanced down at it once more, and re-read the contents.

Qio Lod, Tomekeeper of Zhonitas,
Your presence in front of the Aiguille has been mandated. We look forward to addressing your crimes against the Asceniates in front of a jury of your peers. If you still refuse to make yourself present before our great council, we shall exhaust every resource and connection to find you.
You cannot run, Tomekeeper.
Make haste,
The Aiguille

Qio crumpled the parchment up and tossed it over his shoulder. He could run to the farthest corners of Lidaesea, but the letter had been placed on his bed before his arrival. Someone in the castle knew he would be there. Whatever connection that person had to the Aiguille was inconsequential. He had no choice.

Qio had to return home and clear his good name.

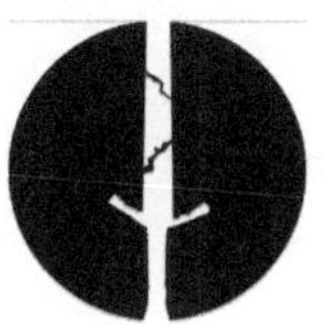

The bells around the castle rang ten times to signify the change of the hour. As their song swept across the castle grounds, Tuvhe stirred from his forced slumber. Blurry vision focused into a smooth and slightly yellow ceiling.

Tuvhe tried to roll onto his side, but the harsh zap of static electricity forced him to stop. He let out an exasperated sigh, and the scrapes of metal along the floor responded. The tips of swords and spears pressed into his space.

"He's awake!" Tuvhe heard a man's gruff voice yell out. "Keep yer weapons readied, all!"

Four celenians crept into Tuvhe's view, weapons held tight. Tuvhe stayed motionless.

"You don't have to worry about me. I understand the situation, but I am in full control of myself, not Eslen."

One of the four, a man with a scraggly beard and tired eyes, inched closer.

"That's exactly what Reveticus said you would tell us," he said, his voice the one Tuvhe had heard yell just before. "We don't take kindly to the Betrayer here, Tomekeeper, nor do we appreciate the way your actions played into the destruction of our beloved city."

Tuvhe knew where the conversation was headed.

"So what now? You smother me? Pretend I died in my sleep? Or do you take turns running me through with your weapons?"

"Exile, actually," the man sneered. "Far too light for my liking, but you had a friend vouch for you."

"A friend?"

"Aye. Ol' Coltiel's word goes far here. He seems to think you're not as bad as we've been lead to believe." The man spit on the ground beside Tuvhe. "I still don't buy it."

Tuvhe closed his eyes and took a moment to mentally thank his celenian savior. Eslen's voice was nowhere to be found. There was a small trace of his presence that lingered in Tuvhe's body, like the trickle of a blocked stream. There was a noticeable difference—an absence. Eslen was locked away, but how it happened remained beyond Tuvhe's understanding. He tried to think to the moments before Kliev electrocuted them both and came across a mental block.

"You said exile," Tuvhe said as he opened his eyes and turned to the man. "It wouldn't be the first time. Why have I not been cast out yet? I doubt the fine citizens of Prodigium care to expend their resources on an exiled man they perceive as an enemy."

The celenian man nodded to the others and all four backed away, weapons shifted to their sides. The man pointed at the bed next to Tuvhe's.

"That poor sod has been unconscious, and the apothecaries doubt he's waking up. Too much blood loss. Someone needs to see him back to his nation."

Tuvhe traced a line from the man's finger to the bed of his neighbor.

"Utic?"

Utic laid unresponsive, wrapped over in multiple layers of gauze and linen. What skin remained exposed was pale and rubbery. A bloodied water lily sat pinned to the gauze that crossed his chest.

"He's still alive, though?" Tuvhe asked in confirmation.

"Aye," the man responded. "Who knows for how long. Best to get him to his family so they can at least say their goodbyes."

Tuvhe sat in silence as he stared at his fellow Tomekeeper.

We've barely started this journey, and you've already been taken from the playing field. Damn that Terrolaff.

Another spark bit at Tuvhe as he forced himself up and onto the side of the medical bed. He turned his gaze back toward the celenian man. Tuvhe had been given a mission, and the clock was already ticking.

"How soon can we go?"

Zall watched Qurena's frustration build through the wall of fire between them. She searched around the edges of the stone archway, desperate to find a crack or weakened support to break through. Zall knew that she wouldn't. There was no way into the tunnels outside of the now-barricaded entryway. Once he stepped into the darkness, he was free.

A huff escaped Qurena's lips.

"You can look all you want, bird. You're not catching me again," Zall said.

Qurena clenched her teeth.

"You're a right arse, Destus. You told me you weren't going to fight anymore. I genuinely believed you wanted to change after our talk last night."

Zall looked away.

"I didn't fight. I'm forbidden to engage in combat, at least for now."

"Sending out tornadoes of fire into the city isn't combat?"

"It's not if there's no specific target."

Qurena huffed again.

"You don't get it, do you? You just want to fight and destroy and-"

"And what, Qurena?" Zall's temper flared. He turned to his pursuer and stepped up against the wall of flames. "You expect me to let everything that's been done to me go because you told me to? You think one breakthrough in a moment of my own weakness lends itself to a life of forgiveness?"

"No, you idiot! I just hoped that you would have been able to redirect your fury into a more practical way."

"You hoped wrong," Zall said. His words burned. "I'm going back to Hilaster's Peak. I'm righting the wrongs that were done, even if it kills me."

Qurena stepped back and flapped her wings. The resulting wind barely affected the flames, fed by the fire lit in Zall's open palm. She looked at him with anger, frustration, and a tinge of sorrow.

"I promise you this, Destus. I will find you. On my own honor as a celenian."

Zall let out a single laugh.

"You're dedicated, bird. That's for sure. I look forward to our next fight. I won't hold back."

Zall stepped back into the tunnel and closed his palm, his body swallowed by the shadows as the flames extinguished.

The coldness of the travertine tile pressed through I'el's leather pants and against the bottom of her thighs as she sat on the edge of Prodigium's circular wall. She kicked her feet against the air, the warmth of the sun pressed against her back.

"Got room for one more?" Kliev's voice drifted.

I'el looked back at him and smiled.

"Of course."

Kliev stood on the wall's edge and dropped, wincing from the chill of the tile.

"Ah, that stings a bit. What are you doing all the way up here?"

I'el pointed out across the waters of the Erineal Strait.

"You see that patch of green over there? That's the Hicarian forest. Next to that is the Krijyan mountains, and further back the edge of Empyron." Her finger moved from Hicaria and back across the strait. "It took us one day by air and five by carriage to get here, and we're almost full circle. Truly, only one week ago, you jumped in front of me smelling like the Chestastis and showering me with grimphom guts." She placed her hand on her chin with a bubbly bounce. "Isn't that amazing?"

I'el looked sideways at Kliev. His attention was locked entirely on her.

"Yeah, amazing," Kliev mumbled. His ears curled forward and he scratched the back of his left. He cleared his throat. "Now that I think about it, should we be up here? Won't the winds blow us off the side?"

"No winds today," I'el answered. She let out a giggle as Kliev mimicked falling off the edge. "I promise."

Kliev adjusted his tunic and leaned back.

"Hey I'el, you said last night that it would be okay if I traveled with you back to Noli's Orchard. Is that still... on the table? You genuinely meant it?"

Of course you did. Tell him!

Noli, I can handle this. Thanks.

I'el met Kliev's unwavering gaze.

"I did, Kliev. You have a lot to figure out regarding your situation back in Krijya, plus it would be nice to have someone that can help me hunt. You're going to have to earn your keep, though. I've seen how much you eat."

The two burst into a fit of laughter that echoed down Prodigium's wall. I'el wiped a tear from her eye and looked back out at Hicaria. Her world, much like the flowers and trees that littered the forest, had grown exponentially in such a short time.

Fwen's glare bored into the back of the celenian that guarded her cell. The pungent smell of mildew refused to leave her, and daylight barely managed to creep through small slits in the dungeon's wall. She could hear the rumbling of footsteps in the floors above them.

"I need to use the bathroom."

The celenian sniffed and stayed in place. Candlelight formed yellow rings against his bald head.

"There's a bucket in there beside you."

"Yes, but you're still here in front of me," Fwen scoffed. She scooted forward on the wooden bench underneath her.

"I won't turn around, Tomekeeper. You have my word."

"Your word means nothing to me, Wingsong. I've trusted literal rats more than I've trusted your pretentious kind."

The celenian shuffled in place.

"Aw, does that bother you?" Fwen pressed. "I guess you aren't too high up the entitled list, though, since you're stuck down here in the dumps with us."

The celenian turned and approached the cell door. He peered through the bars and blew hot air from his nose.

"You'd do wise to shut your mouth, Tomekeeper. I'm the one in charge. They don't care what happens to you down here."

Fwen stood up and approached the bars.

"Ooo, a power complex. I bet the monarch loved that about you. It's probably why he put you here to begin with. Out of sight, out of mind. I'm guessing one too many drunken nights or maybe a tendency for violence."

The celenian lurched forward and swiped for Fwen's neck, a raging bull pressed against the door.

"Bad move," Fwen smirked. She grabbed the side of the guard's arm and released a tendril of black smoke that wrapped around his armor and up through his nose. The guard stepped back and swiped it away, screaming in pain. His eyes rolled up into his head and he fell forward into the cage door with a loud rattle. Fwen knelt and took the ring of cell keys from his belt. "You should watch that temper. Too much anger will be the death of you."

Netot's unsettling laughter filled her mind.

"I'm glad you liked that one," Fwen responded. She unlocked the door and pressed against the door, inching it open enough to slip her slender frame through. Her boots clacked against the floor as she walked further into the dungeon to her destination.

Fwen approached a solid metal box jutting from the back of the dungeon wall. Its dull gray color looked even darker in the limited candlelight. She walked up to the door and slid open a small hatch located near eye level. Verina was inside, tied to the box by multiple layers of chains and floating in water that reached up to her neck. A leather muzzle was placed over the bottom half of her unpainted face. It was torture in the purest sense.

Fwen unlocked the door and pulled it open. The water rushed out with a roar across the dungeon floor. She stepped into the doorway and looked at Verina. The Terrolaff's left eye was covered by a black eyepatch, and her right widened with glee at the sight of her partner.

"Let's get you out of there," Fwen grinned. "We have a lot of planning to do."

Thus began the final centennial cycle, the war that tore apart a world, and the end of all things.